For Joe, the best
of colleagues

Rob

Poverty and Charity in Early Modern Theater and Performance

Studies in Theatre History and Culture
Edited by Heather Nathans

POVERTY & CHARITY

in Early Modern Theater and Performance

Robert Henke

UNIVERSITY OF IOWA PRESS • IOWA CITY

University of Iowa Press, Iowa City 52242

www.uiowapress.org
Printed in the United States of America

Design by Omega Clay

The University of Iowa Press is a member of Green Press Initiative and is committed to preserving natural resources.

Printed on acid-free paper

Library of Congress Cataloging-in-Publication Data
Henke, Robert, 1955–
Poverty and charity in early modern theater and performance / Robert Henke.
pages cm. — (Studies in theatre history and culture)
Includes bibliographical references and index.
ISBN 978-1-60938-361-9 (pbk), ISBN 978-1-60938-362-6 (ebk)
1. European drama—Renaissance, 1450–1600—History and criticism. 2. European drama—17th century—History and criticism. 3. Theater—Europe—History. 4. Poverty in literature. 5. Charity in literature. I. Title.

PN1791.H46 2015
809.2'0094—dc23 2015005554

To our wonderful twin girls, Gwyneth and Marina

"There was a star danced, and under that you were born."

Passano inanci, e adietro, e non mi vede . . .
Pero che povertà mi fa invisibile.

They pass before me and behind me and do not see me . . .
Because poverty makes me invisible.

Giovanni di Giorgio il Cieco, 1557

Gi è uomeni de carne, com a' seóm nu. . . . E sí fa pan com a' fazóm, e sí magna com a' fazóm nu.

They are men of flesh and blood like us . . . . And they make bread like we do, and they eat like we do too.

Ruzante, *Il parlamento*, 1529

Poor naked wretches, wheresoe'er you are,
That bide the pelting of this pitiless storm,
How shall your houseless heads and unfed sides,
Your looped and window'd raggedness, defend you
From seasons such as these? O, I have ta'en
Too little care of this! Take physic, pomp,
Expose thyself to feel what wretches feel,
That thou mayst shake the superflux to them

King Lear, c.1605

Contents

Acknowledgments

For sustained intellectual and collegial support over the entire course of this project, I heartily thank Theater Without Borders, an international research collective devoted to collaborative work on early modern theater from transnational points of view. Members of TWB heard drafts of several chapters in this chapter, and offered challenging, spirited, and helpful comments. I wish to thank particularly Susanne Wofford, Eric Nicholson, Richard Andrews, Jacques Lezra, David Schalkwyk, Pamela Allen Brown, Michael Armstrong-Roche, Eric Nicholson, Natasha Korda, Melissa Walter, Peg Katritzky, Christian Billing, Clare McManus, Pavel Drábek, Shormishtha Panja, Natasha Korda, Jane Tylus, and others who heard my papers at our annual gatherings.

I came across the work of Rosa Salzberg on Italian street singers at just the right time to be able to incorporate it into my own chapter on piazza pamphlets. Although I have never met Tom Nichols, his book *The Art of Poverty* was invaluable in helping me choose visual images regarding early modern poverty that I have included here. Erica Conti helped me with some of the Italian translations, and Ervin Malakaj assisted me with some German passages.

For permissions and photographs of images in this book, I wish to thank Kevin Bailess at the British Library; Chris Sutherns at the British Museum; Ursula Schultheiss-Barth at the Hochschul-und Landesbibliothek, Fulda; and Vincent Reniel at the Bibliothèque Nationale de France. I stand particularly indebted to Rembrandt Duits, Paul Taylor, Berthold Kress, and François Quiviger at the Warburg Institute and to the collegial and collaborative spirit of the Warburg Institute in general. Their Iconographical Database was particularly useful to me and is to be recommended to all early modern scholars.

Thank you to the research librarians at the Biblioteca Nazionale Marciana di Venezia, the Biblioteca Apostolica Vaticana, the British Library, the Biblioteca Universitaria Alessandrina di Roma, the Biblioteca Universitaria di Bologna, the Biblioteca Nazionale Centrale di Firenze, the Biblioteca Nazionale Centrale di Roma, and those at the library of my host institution, Washington University.

A year-long fellowship from the National Endowment for the Humanities allowed me to begin this project, and several summer Faculty Research Grants from Washington University helped move it along.

Parts of this book have appeared as articles or essays in the following journals and essay collections: "Comparing Poverty: Fictions of a 'Poor Theater' in Ruzante and Shakespeare," *Comparative Drama* 41 (2007): 193–217; "Representations of Poverty in the Commedia dell'Arte," *Theatre Survey* 48:2 (2007): 229–46, Copyright © 2007 The American Society for Theatre Research, Inc. Reprinted by permission; "Sincerity, Fraud, and Audience Reception in the Performance of Early Modern Poverty," *Renaissance Drama* 37 (2009): 157–76; "Ruzante and Shakespeare: A Comparative Case-Study," in *Shakespeare and Renaissance Literary Theories: Anglo-Italian Transactions*, ed. Michele Marrapodi (Aldershot, UK: Ashgate Press, 2011), 153–73; and "Poor," in *21st Century Approaches to Early Modern Theatricality*, ed. Henry Turner (Oxford: Oxford University Press, 2013), 460–77. I am grateful to these publications for permission to reuse and rework the material.

In submitting, revising, and publishing earlier versions of chapters, I had the good fortune to work with several extremely hands-on editors, who gave me thought-provoking and generative questions: Martin Puchner for *Theatre Survey*, William West for *Renaissance Drama*, and Henry S. Turner for his edited collection *Early Modern Theatricality*.

At the University of Iowa Press, thanks to Holly Carver for her initial support for the project, to Catherine Cocks for her quick and insightful replies to my numerous email queries, to Christine Gever for her expert and meticulous copyediting, and to Susan Hill Newton for her overall guidance in the book's production.

As a distinctly non-academic debt, I'd like to thank the numerous individuals I met and spoke with over the years as a volunteer at the Catholic Worker community in St. Louis, a hospitality house for the homeless. I have learned much from their stories, as well as from Teka Childress, Ellen Rehg, and others at Karen House who have spent vastly more time with the poor than I have.

My strongest single intellectual debt is to Tom Postlewait, who encouraged me to submit this study to his prestigious series years ago when he heard a very early version of a chapter at an IFTR (International Federation for Theatre Research) conference. Those in this series who have had the good fortune to work with Tom know what a wonderful editor he is—the best. It is difficult to imagine another academic editor who has given more generously of his time, his sharp critical thinking, and his thoughtful and detailed comments. It is a deep honor for me to be Tom's last book in his series; I hope the book is worthy of him and the dedicated, generous help he gave me.

My wonderful family has sustained me in countless ways. Our three children, Nick, Marina, and Gwyneth, are now a good bit older than when I began this book, and it is astonishing to me to see the ways in which they have grown and flourished. They have encouraged me throughout the writing as they have become more and more aware of what the book is about and have begun to make the world a better place in their own significant ways.

My dear wife Suzanne has been absolutely wonderful throughout this project. She has been unflaggingly supportive at every stage and has continually inspired me to think about the purpose of it all: how a book about early modern poverty and charity might connect to the present day. With her sharp critical mind, she has given me incisive, helpful, and sensible comments on several chapters. She is goodness itself, without the fanfare.

Introduction

Shakespeare's *As You Like It* (c.1599) and *King Lear* (c.1605–6) each stage an aristocratic young man forced out into the open world by a cruel and jealous brother. Although Shakespeare's aristocratic characters often use the word "beggar" metaphorically, whether in self-deprecation or as taunt, in these two instances Shakespeare "unmetaphors" the conceit. In each play, the dispossessed brother ends up participating to some extent in the actual life of a beggar.

Prevented only by Adam from being burned alive (2.2.19–24)[1] Orlando quickly sees that he has been forced into the pinched alternatives of the dispossessed: either to beg or to steal. As he protests to his servant, "What, wouldst thou have me go and beg my food? / Or with a base and boist'rous sword enforce / A thievish living on the common road" (2.3.31–33). Adam's generous offer to share his life savings with his master only temporarily stays this stark choice, and when we meet them next they are homeless, starving, and desperate. Orlando bursts into Duke Senior's pastoral banquet not as a meek, suppliant beggar, but with, in fact, a "base and boisterous sword," and violently demands food. Duke Senior's surprisingly civil and gentle response, incongruously comic in its affable sociability, prompts a speech by Orlando that conjures up a communal world of reciprocal charity:

> If ever you have look'd on better days,
> If ever been where bells have knoll'd to church,
> If ever sate at any good man's feast,
> If ever from your eyelids wip'd a tear,
> And know what 'tis to pity, and be pitied—
> Let gentleness my strong enforcement be,
> In the which hope, I blush, and hide my sword.
> (2.7.113–19)

Orlando invokes Duke Senior's capacity for imaginative empathy: the disposition to dispense charity because at some point in one's life one has been the object of pity oneself. In a society where up to 60 percent of the population might suffer from poverty and require assistance at least once in their lives, such capacity to put oneself in the position of others—a capacity frequently attributed to theater itself—was often well grounded in previous experience. Knowing well the "drops that sacred pity has engend'red" (2.7.123), Duke Senior "liturgically"[2] returns Orlando's lines back to him and invites the starving young man to what is, in effect, a "good man's feast." It is a perfect match between entreaty and response, with the "beggar" Orlando serving up charitable text for the "almsgiver" Duke Senior. In inviting Orlando and Adam to table, albeit in a rough pastoral mode, Duke Senior practices the injunction, heard from both the pulpit and the pamphlet in Elizabethan England and particularly directed to great lords, to feed the hungry in times of duress.

Orlando's hunger, of course, is quickly relieved in the largess of Duke Senior's pastoral feast, which soon frees him to be a suppliant for love, not bread. But serious issues of poverty and hunger—and I would add charity—pervade this moment and course through the entire play, not as simple reflections of social reality but through the imaginative and transformative lens of theatrical fiction and theatricality. Within the fiction of the play, Orlando must imagine what it might be like to be a beggar or a thief, and the internal and external audiences of the play must imagine how one might respond to poverty.

As "Poor Tom," *King Lear*'s Edgar takes on many attributes and conditions of an actual beggar. Unlike Adam, he plays a theatrical role, but one that prompts responses of charity and empathy in others as surely as Orlando did to Duke Senior, extending the traditionally charitable, neomedieval gesture of *As You Like It* into a radical call for economic redistribution. From the blinded Gloucester, not recognizing his son, comes neither disgust nor condemnation at the sight of poverty but the powerful reflection that "distribution should undo excess / And each man have enough" (4.1.70–71). King Lear's famous "Poor naked wretches" speech, similarly arguing for both compassion for the poor and economic redistribution, occurs just before the discovery of Poor Tom and anticipates his emergence from the hovel. If "Poor Tom" is a fraud, the responses he elicits are surprisingly generous and favorable, and generally not felt by audiences merely to reflect mistaken credulity on the part of the Duke and the King. Gloucester and Lear themselves have been dispossessed, forced to "feel what wretches feel" and to learn that they should have "ta'en more care" of poverty and economic inequality.

In the cases of *As You Like It* and *King Lear,* Shakespeare draws lines of connection, imagined at least in the hypothetical world of dramatic fiction, between those at the very highest level of society and those at the lowest. If the son of a peer might be figured as touching the life of a beggar, the latter is not imagined in these two plays as a notorious and dangerous rogue, pariah, or criminal. Instead, the aristocrat-turned-beggar constitutes an object of spiritually beneficial pity in *As You Like It* and becomes a prompt for compassion and economic justice in *King Lear.*

This relatively sympathetic vision of the poor, reflecting a world of reciprocal exchange between receiver and giver, sharply contrasts with the views on beggars typically expressed in two kinds of English documents prominent at the time of these plays: official state edicts such as the important 1598 *For the Relief of the Poor*[3] and the literature of roguery and vagabondage that reached its English apogee in Thomas Harman's 1566 *Caveat for Common Cursetors.* Following a series of disastrous harvest failures in the mid-1590s, the 1598 act marked a decisive shift toward a system of poor relief based on involuntary poor taxes and "discriminate" giving to only those judged worthy of relief. According to the official policy, charity should no longer be the province of individual, voluntary giving but should fall under the jurisdiction of church wardens and other parish overseers of the poor, with each parishioner paying a required poor tax. The 1598 act further stiffened penalties against unlicensed beggars and heightened the public scrutiny of so-called sturdy beggars presumably able to work but instead allegedly given to dissimulating destitution and fleecing the naïve bystander.

The act, which was renewed and amplified in 1601, reinforced the negative perception of the poor colorfully elaborated in the texts of Harman and others. In these rogue or beggar catalogues, and other popular discourses on the poor, as William C. Carroll has shown, beggars became the objects of extraordinary and often contradictory projections: they were supposed to be lazy, dangerously industrious, seditious, sexually insatiable, enemies of private property, frauds, cheats, and thieves.[4] Most especially, they were thought to be consummate actors, capable of feigning blindness, lameness, madness, and a host of other maladies and fictions. Between the poor laws and the colorful rogues' catalogues, beggars acquired a symbolic prominence that reflected what was probably an increased physical profile as well, as a demonstrable rise in poverty made the already-public act of begging even more conspicuous in the "theater" of the city.

Although a stereotypically negative image of the poor and a rationalist and collectively administered approach toward charitable relief do appear to acquire new prominence in England around 1600, the two examples of charity that we have seen in *As You Like It* and *King Lear* suggest that negative images and disciplinary practices hardly tell the entire story. Especially in times of crisis, many preachers, theologians, and other public figures still made a case for voluntary, "indiscriminate giving" that went well beyond what the state mandated.[5] Although with historical hindsight the transition from traditional, charitable exchange to state-run poor relief seems inevitable, the issue was hotly debated and far from a foregone conclusion during the late 1590s. And even after even stricter policies than those of 1598 were passed in England, actual responses to the poor continued to be multiple, complex, and variable. What people actually believed and did was a hodgepodge, not amounting to consistent ideology or practice. This heterogeneity of response, moreover, matches the different situations, attitudes, and characters of the poor themselves, which were far more diverse than the monolithic and almost exclusively negative beggar stereotypes encoded in the official documents and the beggar books. There could be an enormous gap between official policy and actual practice. Not all English responded to the poor as did the righteous, pitiless Thomas Harman. Those who had recently dispensed pity might soon be pity's object: one year's laborer could be next year's beggar, and even a prosperous merchant could quickly experience the disastrous vagaries of venture capital. A given individual could spurn a beggar one day and dispense charity the day afterwards.

The two English plays that we have observed so far suggest that theatergoing might be a particularly propitious way to both conceive and feel the complexity of early modern poverty. Early modern poverty was complex and elusive because of the sheer variety of the poor themselves, the wide range of cognitive and emotional responses to the poor (including positive as well as negative responses), and the considerable gaps between official policy and what actually happened on the ground. Theatrical art, which in its rich temporal sedimentations frequently draws on the *longue dureé* of cultural practices and attitudes, could in the sixteenth and seventeenth centuries set images of medieval, traditional charity next to ideas of emerging disciplinary poor relief, and for audiences of heterogeneous dispositions and beliefs. Even in the course of one play sitting, and even for a single spectator, theater could appeal to different instincts and attitudes, affording him or her the experience to imagine different situations and circumstances. Early modern "theatricality," in other words, could do much more in regard to poverty than to dismiss beggars as fraudulent actors in the manner of Harman's *Caveat* and other beggar books: it could shed imaginative insight into different economic and existential conditions, just as the theatrical spectacle of "Poor Tom" causes Lear to see the world differently.

But in order to understand how the theatrical imagination could cast different light on the early modern wretched of the earth, it is crucial to approach the issue through a transnational, European perspective, which I intend to do in this book. Notwithstanding the insular approach of many critics today writing about Shakespeare and early modern English drama, plays like *As You Like It* and *King Lear* resonate deeply with continental intertexts. In the sixteenth as in the twenty-first century, poverty knew no borders, and as professional theater arose more or less contemporaneously across Europe, every geo-linguistic theater took up the issue in comparable ways, interesting for both similarities and differences. To the measure that a theater or performance tradition was attuned to the economically perilous life of the professional actor, it tended to address poverty, hunger, and charity to a greater extent. Choosing three actor-based theater/performance traditions in addition to Shakespeare, this study will examine variants of a single European phenomenon, showing more thoroughly than a monolingual study could how early modern theater represented variation in types of the poor, differing responses to poverty, and slippages between policy and practice. In so doing, it will attempt to demonstrate how early modern theater provided—and can still provide—complex structures of thought and feeling regarding poverty, in ways that can still illuminate and even empower in the twenty-first century, a time unfortunately marked by ever-increasing inequalities between rich and poor.

As town-based historians have, in the last twenty or thirty years, nuanced our picture of the early modern poor and poor relief by demonstrating the varieties of supplication and the wide range of responses to it,[6] we need to take a fresh look at poverty in early modern theater and performance, concentrating somewhat less on the figure of the colorful and notorious English rogue/beggar and the disciplinary efforts to control him (often viewed through a Foucauldian lens), and more on the question of charity and the contested but variable responses to the poor all across Europe. A transnational study of the problem, considering mainly Italian and English but also German, French, and Latin texts and performance practices, should provide a fuller picture of the issue than one cordoned off by the Channel.

After this introductory chapter, Chapter 1 will examine historical antecedents and contexts, demonstrating the range and complexity of responses to the poor in Italy and England, as well as across Europe. Because sixteenth- and early seventeenth-century preachers and writers in times of crisis often revived patristic and medieval discourses on poverty such as those of St. John Chrysostom and Thomas Aquinas, some attention is paid to early attitudes toward the poor. Particular attention is given to poverty and responses to poverty, such as the poor laws that suddenly emerged throughout Europe beginning in the 1520s, as a transnational phenomenon. In the cases of Italy and England, I examine the persistence of voluntarist, individual giving (such as ran counter to the poor laws) and the development of new engines of charity such as the confraternity.

If Edgar's "Poor Tom" both borrows from and transforms Harman's fraudulent "Abraham Man" and other theatrical frauds excoriated in the *Caveat* and similar English texts, those texts must be seen in the light of a rich, pan-European continental tradition that goes back to German texts of the fourteenth century: the topic of Chapter 2. The continental (especially German and Italian/Latin) beggar book varies considerably from the English texts in the foregrounding of specifically religious fraud on the part of itinerant beggars. Texts such as the early sixteenth-century German *Liber vagatorum* illuminate crucial elements of Shakespeare's "Poor Tom," who is imbued with forms of religious aura in which "fraudulence" or "sincerity" is in the eye of the beholder. Shakespeare seems attuned to the possibility that a thoroughgoing skepticism of the bystander, reader, or playgoer in regard to the itinerant holy man might also acknowledge the possibility that he was *not* altogether fraudulent (a kind of skepticism about dogmatic skepticism). The likelihood of a direct German-to-English transmission of these texts renders them all the more important for understanding Shakespeare.

In the early sixteenth century, just after the Gutenberg revolution, a rich body of Italian piazza pamphlets emerged that frequently addressed poverty, hunger, and economic inequality: the subject of Chapter 3. Late fifteenth- and sixteenth-century Italian piazza singers, who frequently wrote, published, performed, and sold their cheap publications, provide one of the few examples in early modern print of the poor actually speaking for themselves, as many of the *canterini* lived in poverty themselves. The most famous of these singers, Giulio Cesare Croce, had an aristocratic patron but repeatedly suffered from want; the voices of the most obscure of these performers, some of whom were actually blind, reach across the centuries with lines like "Poverty makes me invisible" (Povertà mi fa invisibile).[7] Print, of course, played a crucial role in the representation of the poor. Although print certainly represented negative typologies of the dispossessed, in the very early, pre-Tridentine era a more variegated picture emerges. This more sympathetic presentation of the poor was performed by the *canterini* in the piazza even as it was read by those who bought their cheap pamphlets.

Chapter 4 turns to another phenomenon of the early sixteenth century. Angelo Beolco, known as Ruzante, may have been the greatest poet of hunger ever to write for the stage. Ruzante, worthy of Plautus, Shakespeare, and Molière in the pantheon of great actor-writers, places the performative virtuosity of the solo and duo stand-up act at the center of his plays. The quintessential Ruzantean performer is often destitute and impoverished: the desperate but absurdly valiant inventions of the Ruzantean protagonist constitute "fictions of the poor" that are not simply lies to be exposed by the knife of Harman's cruel analytic, but kinds of cultural productions in their own right, comparable to Falstaff's self-generating "buckram men" as he spins his highwayman's tale. Although Shakespeare would probably not have known about Ruzante, his Paduan predecessor parallels his life and work in striking ways, particularly in regard to a representation of poverty and charity that includes a deep knowledge of the connections between urban and rural poverty. The

Stratfordian and Paduan playwrights, both closely tied in their actual lives to the land, are unusual among early modern playwrights in that they seem to have some sense of how farmers and peasants and shepherds might actually have lived, and how rural and urban poverty were inextricably linked.

With its fundamental opposition between the hungry Bergamask *zanni* and the prosperous but stingy Venetian Pantalone, the commedia dell'arte (the subject of Chapter 5) stages poverty and hunger front and center, trading on the conceit—and frequent reality—of the actor himself as hungry, hardly distinguishable from a beggar. Shakespeare and contemporary English playwrights do not privilege the master-servant relationship to the degree found in the commedia dell'arte and scripted early modern Italian theater. Still, seeing the importance of hunger and the agon of plenty and scarcity in the Italian professional theater can draw out Shakespearean leitmotifs that may be somewhat buried and marginalized, such as the servant Launcelot Gobbo's complaints about his Venetian master's stinginess (*Merchant of Venice* 2.2.106–7). A thorough study of poverty and charity in the first, Italian phase of the commedia dell'arte will turn, at the end of the chapter, to France and the Comédie-Italienne, examining the detailed and poetically evocative scenarios of Molière's contemporary Domenico Biancolelli. As the second great Harlequin/Arlecchino (a hybrid, Gallic-Italian *maschera*), Biancolelli carries on the "playing with poverty" earlier made famous by the Mantuan actor Tristano Martinelli, who invented the famous role in Paris.

The wider, transnational reach of continental writing and performance regarding the poor should frame Shakespeare's treatment of poverty and charity—examined in Chapter 6—in a new key. Analyses of key moments in *Henry VI, Part 2*, *The Taming of the Shrew*, *Coriolanus*, *The Winter's Tale*, and *As You Like It*, among others, demonstrate the wide range, in Shakespeare's work, of types of poverty and kinds of responses to it.

Each of the five case studies examined here (two playwrights, one literary form, one performance practice, and one type of theater) displays complex and heterogeneous accounts of the poor, going well beyond the neatly censorial view but not limited to uncritical sympathy as well. The beggar catalogues, to be sure, cannot be regarded as sympathetic to the poor—they in fact systematically set out to unmask the deceptions of dissembling beggars—but they display some internal inconsistency in this regard and complexly illuminate the unavoidably performative nature of early modern begging. The Italian piazza singers, at least in several important cases, represent the voices of the poor themselves. Although Ruzante could render the destitute *villano* the object of mockery and assisted his patron, Alvise Cornaro, in executing policies that were often not favorable to the poor, he also had deep rural roots and witnessed the poverty of Paduan peasants at close hand. During the great Venetian famine of 1527–29, he wrote a series of plays exhibiting both remarkable sympathy for the poor and the author's characteristic irony and dark humor. The commedia dell'arte drew from a mythopoetic literary-theatrical tradition based on the ur-exile of the dispossessed Bergamask peasant to Venice, where he finds his master Pantalone attending him, just as Marx declares that the grimly "freed" medieval serf "found his master waiting for him" in the city.[8] The figure of the starving *zanni* became programmed into the DNA of the commedia actors, who, although mostly observant and orthodox Counter-Reformation subjects, could certainly be sensitive (as indeed many Counter-Reformation authorities also were) to the church's traditional and radical teachings on greed, usury, poverty, and redistribution. More so than his fellow London playwrights, Shakespeare resembles Ruzante in having deep roots in the countryside, which appears to translate into some understanding of rural poverty. But also like Ruzante, Shakespeare's own business practices do not suggest simple support for the underdog, and his multivoiced texts provide all manner of perspectives on the issue. In all these cases, representations of the poor are complex and various—neither simply censorial, nor straightforwardly sympathetic and positive—and only a transnational perspective shows the whole picture.

Early modern theater and performance repeatedly addressed poverty, hunger, and charity because there were particularly resilient connections between the medium and the social problem. There may even be some historical connection between theater and poverty: the sharp population increases in many European cities from about 1450 on were both a symptom of early modern poverty, as people from economically distressed rural areas flocked to the city, and an aggravating factor, because cities generally were not able to handle the new influx. But as Siro Ferrone has argued, it was exactly the widespread immigration into cities and the increased urban population that operated as a necessary condition for the rise of early modern professional theater in Italy, England, Spain, and France, providing a critical circulating mass of audiences, money, actors, and commerce.[9]

Purpose-specific theater buildings and outdoor public performance sites were often located in urban areas frequented by the poor and by those, such as thieves and prostitutes, whose lives and livelihoods were conditioned by poverty. Northern Italian piazzas such as the Piazza San Marco in Venice staged beggars, thieves, prostitutes, charlatans, acrobats, sleight-of-hand performers, wandering musicians, and itinerant actors culturally adjacent to the organized commedia dell'arte actors. Although the famous commedia dell'arte troupes played the halls of courts and palaces, they also performed in rooms such as the so-called Baldracca theater in Florence, which gave onto a street full of brothels and taverns.[10] The Red Bull and Fortune theaters were built in the Clerkenwell district of northwest London, also teeming with prostitution and poverty, and in Southwark, the site of the Globe, the Rose, and the Swan, there were several apprentice riots over the price of food during the 1590s,[11] one of them explicitly associated by the authorities with theatrical activity.[12]

But there were also pervasive ties between early modern theater and the responsive dimension of poverty: charity. (Unlike Harman, the early modern public did not consider all poor people to be rogues, and their presence elicited debates on charity and not merely discipline.) The Spanish *cofradías,* which enabled the birth of professional theater in Madrid by leasing playing spaces to actors, required that a substantial percentage of the companies' profits, which they explicitly termed "alms," be handed over to them for their charitable work.[13] The "rights of the poor" levy on professional actors performing at the Hôtel de Bourgogne, decreed by the Parlement of Paris, required that the "surplus of pennies" gained by the actors be directed to the poor.[14] And the first extant *Arte* actors' contract, drawn up among eight actors from the Veneto region in 1545, stipulates that in the case of an actor unexpectedly leaving the company, he be obliged to pay a penalty of one hundred lire, a third of which was to go to the poor.[15]

A particular kinship obtained between the actor and the beggar. Early modern actors, many of whom led an itinerant existence, were persistently associated with poverty and begging. Paula Pugliatti, in *Beggary and Theatre in Early Modern England,* has surveyed the originally medieval designation, in the English poor laws, of "players" as beggars and vagrants subject to prosecution.[16] The 1572 act *For the Punishments of Vagabonds and for Relief of the Poor and Impotent,* the culmination of the disciplinary discourse analyzed by Pugliatti, branded actors and performers not connected with a livery company as itinerant vagabonds, subject to punishment. Although commedia luminaries such as Isabella Andreini and Pier Maria Cecchini continually strove to differentiate the disciplined actor from the degraded piazza *buffone* singing for his supper, the itinerant commedia actor could be only an injured mule away from being taken for a vagabond. In *Le fatiche comiche* (1623), the *Arte* actor Domenico Bruni in the voice of a fictional persona describes the discomforts and indignities of life on the road, lamenting that no Florentine inn would accept him because he "looked too much like a beggar."[17] Furthermore, Italian, English, and other European actors often continued to be associated with beggars and poverty well beyond the point that their social status justified it, either despite their best efforts or, in some cases, by deliberately staging or "troping" poverty as a theatrical gag or poetic conceit.

If the actor was perceived to be a beggar, the beggar was thought to be an actor. Both the official, disciplinary edicts and the rogue books and beggar catalogues cast the beggar as a consummate performer, capable of assuming almost any role imaginable. Because of the consolidation of the poor laws and the emergence of the beggar in print literature, the view of the beggar as fraudulent became dominant in the late fifteenth and sixteenth centuries as it had not been before. New border controls and identity surveillance might well have forced many itinerant indigents to fabricate identities, creating homologies between the literary fictions flourishing in print and the fictions of everyday life.

The beggar might also be considered an actor because the scene of supplication shares salient elements of the actor-audience relationship. As the grand medieval institutions of charity, run out of monasteries, hospitals, and churches, gradually eroded in the fifteenth century, the beggar was increasingly on his or her own, needing to present the case for alms forcefully to an audience. The lines between showing one's indigence to the bystander, exaggerating one's destitution, and telling lies about one's condition could become very thin, and it might even become difficult for the beggar himself to tell the difference. In the third book of the anonymous picaresque novel *Lazarillo de Tormes,* after giving up all hope that his current master, the squire, will provide him food and livelihood, Lazarillo describes his begging in the following way:

> Desque vi ser las dos y no venía y la hambre me aquejaba, cierro mi puerta y pongo la llave do mandó y tórnome a mi menester. Con baja y enferma voz y inclinadas mis manos en los senos, puesto Dios ante mis ojos y la lengua en su nombre, comienzo a pedir pan por las puertas y casas más grandes que me parecía. Mas como yo este oficio le hobiese mamado en la leche (quiero decir que con el gran maestro el ciego lo aprendí).

> When I saw that it was two o'clock and he still hadn't come back, and I was going through the tortures of hunger, I shut the door and put the key where he'd told me to and went back to plying my old trade. In a low, sickly voice, with my hands drooping over my breast with God in front of my eyes and His Name on my tongue, I set about begging bread at the doorways of whichever big houses looked most promising. It was a calling which I'd sucked in with my mother's milk; what I mean is, I'd learned it in my youth from a great master, the blind man.[18]

Certainly Lazarillo plies his "old trade" of begging, learned as an "apprentice" from previous masters, with craft and skill. But because he "performs" in the throes of crippling hunger, judging his presentation to be mere fraudulence seems to be inaccurate as well as ungenerous. He exaggerates, distills, and crystallizes the truth of his desperation. In the Latin sense of "performance," by which *per* can mean "through to its completion," Lazarillo performs his very real destitution by extending physical and vocal forms to an exaggerated and "completed" degree. Just as suppliants operated on a spectrum between the poles of pure genuineness and total fraudulence, bystanders assessing the beggar's petition moved between absolute credulity and pure doubt. Theater, much more than the official policies and the beggar/rogue catalogues, explored these nuanced gradations between extremes, on both sides of the "actor-audience" duo.

Theater, to be sure, does not function merely as documentation, as a simple reflecting glass for social history. Just as begging and supplication themselves involve complex (and not simply fraudulent) modes of fictionalizing, theater and performance pass the data and conditions of social poverty through fictionalized forms of distortion, exaggeration, marginalization, displacement, and condensation. Such "dream work," as it were, on the naked *materia* of hunger and inequality, will be the subject of these pages. The raw and disturbing stuff of acute need and deprivation are transformed into complex theatrical and mythopoetic forms: the tortured and grotesque lines, impressions, and cavities of a *zanni* mask deployed by the actor as a distilled map of his very body; the impossibly complex (and usually doomed) plot strategems of the *zanni* to obtain food; the displacement of human suffering onto emaciated animals; the wild, gluttonous fantasies of Cuccagna literature offering oneiric compensation for starvation. On the street, there is nothing funny about hunger; in the theater, the grotesque, desperate, distended *zanni* actor serves his empty belly up for laughter, if often of a precarious and disturbing nature that leads the audience, consciously or unconsciously, back to some recognition of socio-economic life.

1 Historical Attitudes, Policies, and Practices

Introduction

Attitudes and practices regarding the early modern poor varied significantly, depending on individual temperament, confession, institutional situation, the relationship one had to the suppliant (i.e., kinship relationship or stranger), and whether or not it was a crisis period, such as after a harvest failure. One's responses to the poor might also depend on whether one had experienced need in the past, or was anxious about the possibility of needing assistance in the future. Over half the European population were vulnerable to poverty in the case of a crisis, and some 15 percent, the so-called conjunctual poor, fell into poverty (a relative term) at least once in their lives.[1] Between 1480 and 1700, official policies, which of course had important effects on public opinion, did gradually move toward a more secular and rationalized approach to the poor. Still, every age is characterized by residual as well as nascent and dominant values. On the one hand, the idea that a sharp distinction obtained between the "legitimate" poor deserving of assistance and the "illegitimate" beggar who needed to be disciplined can already be found in medieval texts. On the other hand, the idea that one must give generously to the poor without inquiring too assiduously about their perceived legitimacy showed remarkable tenacity, surfacing, for example, in Elizabethan homilies written after the harvest failures of the 1590s. European poor relief progressed in an incremental and cumulative manner, with many older charitable practices being retained or reconfigured. Despite the sweeping pronouncements of poor laws passed in the 1520s, there was significant continuity with the past well after the measures were instituted, and there remained considerable opportunity for lay individuals either to dispense charity individually or through collectives such as confraternities. Theater, which was quite capable of articulating marginal positions and reversing hierarchies, could explore the residual and variable nature of attitudes to the poor, making a beggar as important as a king if only in the fleeting passing of the enacted scene. The relative, fluctuating, and variously defined nature of poverty[2] meant that witnessing a beggar or impoverished person onstage could easily elicit a "There but for the grace of God" response, or its contrary: the demonizing "othering" of figures too potentially close to one's own state for comfort.

Biblical, Patristic, and Medieval Views

With the advent of print in the late fifteenth century, biblical, patristic, and medieval attitudes toward poverty became more available to sixteenth-century readers than they had been earlier and are therefore especially worth reviewing in our attempt to understand early modern attitudes.

Between Jesus' utterances and the representation of a socialist community in the Acts of the Apostles, the New Testament provides clear if disturbing pronouncements on wealth and poverty—views that have hardly described official church policy since then. In the Gospel of Matthew, according to Lee Palmer Wandel, the pronouncements of Jesus changed the relationship between private property and faith by overturning the Ten Commandments' protection of private property ("Thou shalt not steal") with a doctrine not so much of redistributing wealth but of abandoning it altogether.[3] It was left to the first Christian church described in the Acts of the Apostles to provide a paradigm for communal ownership—a paradigm to which humanists such as Erasmus and More would call attention. The first hermits of the eastern Mediterranean, like their successors in the extraordinary revival of hermitism between about 1095 and 1150, radically committed to a property-less existence.[4] Just as the communitarianism of the Acts of the Apostles can be seen as a corrective to Jesus' apparent abolition of private property, Benedict's monastic order can be viewed as moderating radicals such as Simeon Stylites (390–459) by retaining and safeguarding property under the idea of common ownership.

Because they wrote significant treatises on the topic that were edited and published in the sixteenth century, the teachings on wealth and poverty of the Greek Fathers are particularly important for their residual effect in the age of Ruzante and Shakespeare. Clement of Alexandria, St. John Chrysostom, Saint Basil, Gregory of Nyssa, and Gregory Nazianzen passionately advocated for the poor, simultaneously mounting a ferocious attack on the greed and selfishness of the rich. As Michel Mollat has remarked, it was not accidental that these figures mostly lived in cities, such as Constantinople, Alexandria, and Antioch, where poverty was severe; Saint Basil is said to have founded a hospice and soup kitchen in Caesarea.[5] The Greek Fathers, drawing from the Stoic and Cynic contempt for wealth (and the impulse to live naked under the sun, like a dog) as well as scriptural tradition, argued forcefully on behalf of almsgiving and the veneration of poverty as a spiritual good, an offering to Christ himself "of whom the pauper was an image."[6] St. John Chrysostom (347–407) argued that one-tenth of the wealthy's income should be confiscated for the poor, anticipating Aquinas' argument that almsgiving effectively returned to the poor what was owed them.

The powerful homilies of Chrysostom and other Greek Fathers frequently relied on exemplary tales of charity. Hearing the story of St. Martin cutting his cape in half for a beggar, or Chysostom's famous homilies on the Dives-Lazarus story, probably influenced ordinary Christians more than official state policies.[7] The Dives-Lazarus parable ends with a topsy-turvy scene in the afterlife in which the rich man has now himself become a beggar, beseeching Lazarus via Abraham to dip his finger in water and cool the now-dispossessed rich man's burning tongue. The "reverse-beggar" theme, in which the king or rich man who has spurned beggars now turns into one himself, becomes for Chrysostom a story about the leveling theatricality of lives *sub specie terrae*: "Just as that man who acts the part of king or general on the stage often turns out to be a household servant or somebody who sells figs or grapes in the market, so also the rich man turns out to be the poorest of all."[8] Chrysostom narrates the dramatic and imaginatively suggestive encounter between the rich man, drowning in luxury and consumption, and the abject beggar Lazarus, lying prostrate at the rich man's gate and encountering no pity except from the dogs (the beggar's "Cynic" companions?) who lick his sores. By repeatedly refusing to give alms to the beggar, the rich man rejects a messenger from God, who has been sent to teach him virtue and to give him an occasion for love and redemption. For Chrysostom, who founded a series of hospitals for the poor in Constantinople, not pride but luxury is the very worst of offenses, the primal generator of sin. Not sharing one's possessions, if fortune has granted one an excess of resources, amounts to nothing less than theft.[9] The "rich and greedy" are like "robbers lying in wait on the roads, stealing from passers-by, and burying others' goods in their own houses as if in caves and holes."[10] Chrysostom produced a powerful critique of greed and acquisition that had a powerful effect on early modern readers when the texts were edited and printed in Greek, Latin, and vernacular translations.[11]

Medieval attitudes and practices regarding poverty were of course variable, diverse, and contingent upon context. The Greek patristic valuation of involuntary as well as voluntary poverty as a spiritual value, with the concomitant advocacy for a radical redistribution of wealth, hardly describes the prevailing medieval view. Only in the eleventh through the thirteenth centuries, and in fact spurred in part by the dissemination of patristic ideas,[12] did the elevation of poverty as a spiritual state begin to be articulated, first in the revival of hermitism at the end of the eleventh century and then in the new mendicant orders founded by St. Dominic and St. Francis in the early thirteenth century. In some ways, this relatively brief flowering of *povertas*, which has come to represent the popular image of medieval attitudes about poverty, is somewhat aberrant. The discriminatory distinction between the poor who were deserving of assistance and those presumed to be freeloaders, or "sturdy beggars," which actually has an ancient pedigree, can be located in the twelfth-century *Decretum Gratiani*;[13] and as early as the fourteenth century, Nuremberg required beggars to wear tokens, with special municipal functionaries assigned to count, control, and regulate beggars. Generally, medieval authorities and the general populace did not consider the social reality of actual poverty to carry spiritual value, as had the Greek Fathers.

What does, however, crucially distinguish the dominant medieval attitude from the prevailing early modern view was the idea that poverty was *acceptable* and therefore had to be met with regular assistance. This view does not necessarily presume any inherent value to poverty, but considers the poor to be part of the natural order of things. For poverty to gain spiritual value in the medieval view it had to be voluntary: a willful renunciation of wealth that follows the example of Jesus. (Gregory Nazianzen and St. John Chrysostom do not appear to make this distinction: Lazarus has not freely chosen his state, but his poverty is still deemed to have inherent spiritual value.) But once one accepts that "the poor are always with us," one must make sure that they are provided for with an adequate network of charity that is informed by habits of mind positively disposed to helping the poor. There was no serious objection, as there would be later, to people living off charity. The church devoted from a fourth to a third of its income to charitable assistance, constructing a critical mass of monasteries, hospitals, almshouses, confraternities, and parish resources for charitable assistance.[14] By and large, the medieval poor could count on regular assistance.

Unlike the teachings of the Greek Fathers, which were certainly radical in their socio-economic implication, the medieval view implied a certain social stability: the poor were supposed to accept their fate with quietude. Both the renunciation of wealth and—contrary to Jesus, the Acts of the Apostles, hermitism, and the Greek Fathers—wealth itself were sanctioned. The *Life of St. Eligius* expressed it thus: "God could have made all men rich, but He wanted there to be poor people in the world, that the rich might be able to redeem their sins."[15] And if the poor must exist, so must the rich. The beggar-almsgiver encounter therefore became a kind of gift exchange: the rich gave money, food, clothing, or shelter to the poor so that the latter would bless them and pray for their souls. What underpinned these acts of charity was the fact that medieval habits of mind did tend to judge in favor of the poor, according to the formula *in dubio pro paupere* (in doubt [believe] the poor person). The almsgiver, in the eyes of God, was rewarded for his good intentions and could still accrue spiritual benefit even if the beggar were lying. If the itinerant pilgrim, relic seller, hermit, priest, or preacher smacked of a vagabond, he might still be capable of doing your soul some good. In general, largely because the sheer numbers were smaller, itinerancy itself was not considered to be as great a danger as it would be from the fifteenth century on. And it was even possible, following the "For I was naked, and ye clothed me" passage in the Gospel according to Matthew (25:34–36), that the poor person might be Christ himself (Fig. 1). The idea of spiritual exchange, based on the principle of individual, voluntary, and non-rational, or fideistic, charity, proved remarkably tenacious, as we have seen in the opening example from *As You Like It*.

Medieval charity, buttressed by various institutional structures, was often a very public and even theatrical act. The calendrically regulated,

FIG. 1. After Georg Pencz, "Clothing the Naked," from the series *The Seven Acts of Mercy*, c.1534. Engraving. Department of Prints and Drawings, British Museum, London. Copyright The Trustees of the British Museum.

mass distributions of food performed at the Abbey of Cluny, were meant to be public and, in fact, theatrical demonstrations of charity.[16] When Saint Louis, observing the idea that it was the duty of the king to personally dispense poverty, invited the poor to his own table, it was a theatrical performance.[17] Images of kings dispensing alms to the poor (Fig. 2), or high-ranking figures inviting beggars to their table (Fig. 3), bespeak this public nature of medieval charity. But with Cluny's distributions and Saint Louis' charitable table, socially codified expectations guaranteed the efficacy and felicity of the performance, whose meaning was stable and dependable. With exceptions like radical medieval "performers" such as

St. Francis, whom Dario Fo has seen fit to bring to life, we may generalize that medieval charity was certainly theatrical, in that it constituted an important public spectacle, but less complex and interesting than what we will observe in early modern voluntaristic (i.e., not state-controlled) charity. Random early modern giving, stripped from medieval institutional moorings, became to a greater degree up for grabs, depending on variable, aleatory factors directly relating to the heart of performance: the full-bodied rhetoric of beggars working on the hearts and minds of potential almsgivers, in a scene that could be played anywhere and anytime. Certainly there could be complex medieval exchanges and simple early modern ones. But the early modern charitable encounter tended to be more dramatic, because the potential almsgiver had to examine and

FIG. 2. King dispensing alms to a poor person. From Daniel Sudermann, *Centuria similitudinum* . . . . (Strassburg, 1624). Warburg Institute Library, London. Photo: Warburg Institute.

FIG. 3. Joseph Koler, "St. Ulrich Dines with Beggars," from the series *The Life of St. Ulrich*, in the Church of St. Blasius, Kaufbeuren, Germany. Warburg Institute Iconographical Database. Photo: Berthold Kress, visiting curator of the Warburg Institute, with kind permission of the parish.

discern the truth of the suppliant. And he or she might not always conclude that the beggar was a fraud. The jettisoning of *in dubio pro paupere* problematized and extended the scene of the street in interesting ways.

Early Modern Poverty

The feudal system, by and large, provided the stability of established and dependable social roles and functions for many years.[18] Up to the fourteenth century, argues A. L. Beier, times of agricultural crisis did not exacerbate vagabondage, and peasants undergoing hardship could eke out subsistence livings on wastelands and forests or survive by the stability of the manorial house.[19] Medieval economic culture was not unaware of markets but resisted the notion of unchecked individual economic freedom. Economic activity, as Keith Wrightson has stated, was "subordinated to ethical ends."[20] But by the fourteenth century, the feudal system began to be an obstacle to the development that many desired: the seigneurial duties and taxes prevented farmers from properly investing in their land, and the regular dues that feudal landowners received from peasants did not provide an incentive for development. Market forces began to encroach upon the European countryside in systematic ways. According to Wrightson, "Lords who no longer had an interest in preserving standardized holdings for the purposes of exacting labour services and seigneurial dues no longer opposed accumulation. Land no longer burdened with servile obligations became more attractive to potential buyers."[21] Tenancies were renegotiated so that freeholders became tenants and tenants became laborers.[22] In England, between 1530 and 1570, greatly expanded economic opportunities and advancement for some unfortunately meant dispossession and poverty for those who could not afford to retain their land.[23] Once the market economy began to predominate and labor became a vendible commodity, disparities among farmers quickly grew. The practice of enclosure, which favored overall economic efficiency and growth but turned many farmers into beggars,[24] was practiced in Italy as well as England. In Germany, peasants provided a tax basis for their princes, for which they received protection, and in France peasant proprietors received some provisions from the monarchy in France. Lacking these protections, Italy and England suffered the most from enclosure and land dispossession.[25]

Dispossessed peasants across Europe paid dearly for their liberation from feudal ties;[26] they faced the grim alternatives of wage labor (subject to the uncertainties of employment and the fluctuations of the market), migration, or begging. As a "seller of himself,"[27] the "freed" serf is adjacent to the figure of the itinerant European performer, whose numbers (difficult though they may be to document) appear to have grown in the sixteenth century. Large numbers of peasants became day laborers working for wages. Agricultural day labor, however, was a crushing existence: it has been estimated that a rural worker in the south of England would have earned about 8 pence per day, or 10.4 pounds a year.[28] Whether in the countryside or in the city, wage labor was conditioned by the market. By 1524–25, in English country towns, two in five persons had become wage laborers.[29] Destitute countrymen, forced into itinerancy, were willing to work for the low wages that employers were happy to pay.[30] With the price of foodstuffs and other essentials continually rising across Europe in the sixteenth century (and inflation was not helped by the influx of gold and silver into Europe from the New World via Spain), real wages fell sharply: 40 to 50 percent lower for construction workers in 1600 as compared to 1451, for example.[31]

Many peasants dispossessed by these agricultural crises and unable to survive as day laborers or with meager cottage industries emigrated to the city to search for employment, but both en route to and once installed in the city they were frequently constrained to beg. Migrants streamed into east London, where suburban developments were quickly erected to try to accommodate them but generated dense pockets of squalor.[32] Orders against the construction of new buildings attempted to stem the influx, and newly established workhouses aimed to control those who were already there, but to little effect; the concentration of impoverished people provided ideal conditions for the spread of the plague in London, where there were outbreaks in 1563, 1593, 1603, and 1625.[33] Similar conditions caused by a massive demographic influx into Venice led to the rise of infectious diseases there, of which typhus was the most frequent; this led to the creation of the Venetian Provveditori alla Sanità in 1485, which closely monitored vagabondage and begging as perceived abettors of infectious disease. In 1494, the Sanità of Milan recorded that many "beggars from the mountains and the valleys" were coming into the city and that "from living and sleeping poorly the danger has arisen that plague infection might break out."[34] Urban living conditions in Italian cities, as recorded in the poems of Giulio Cesare Croce and other popular Italian "poets of poverty," could be dismal indeed, with people living in dark, dank basements and sleeping on putrid beds.

The Italian wars worsened already bad agricultural conditions, spawning numerous discharged or fugitive veterans who had trouble finding work and might roam the countryside and swarm into cities as beggars and vagabonds. Since, according to many of the poor laws, a discharged soldier soliciting alms might constitute a legitimate object of charity, it was a tempting disguise to assume, or at least it was charged with being so in beggar books and official edicts, which repeatedly warned the innocent of this potential subterfuge. The Tudor regimes summarily dismissed soldiers and seaman, who were then prosecuted as vagabonds unless licensed by two justices of the peace for begging.[35]

As an important symptom of poverty, prostitution would have been of particular interest to early modern playwrights, if for no other reason than the proximity of many theaters to brothels. In addition to the Baldracca theater in Florence mentioned above, the theater neighborhoods of London were dense sites of both poverty and low-end prostitution: Clerkenwell, site of the Red Bull and Shakespeare's residence for time; Shoreditch, where the first amphitheaters were built; and Bankside itself.[36] Bankside included well-known brothels such as the Unicorn, whose lease Philip Henslowe acquired in 1597, and spawned a large number of alleys, in the Bear Gardens area and elsewhere, where the more mobile prostitutes worked their trade in rooms let by alehouse keepers and the like.[37] In Italy, along with the famous high-end courtesans in Venice and Rome, were the more numerous street workers forced into the trade by economic duress, sometimes even encouraged by desperate parents who saw in their the teenage girls' sexual maturation a cure for their financial troubles."[38] Nicholas Terpstra describes how homes such as the Florentine Casa di Pietà were founded to help orphaned or poor teenage girls escape the brothel houses, some of which were located near one of the most important sites of commedia dell'arte performance.[39] If, as Terpstra argues, it was often taken for granted that female servants were the sexual property of their masters, then Pantalone's sexual predation of the servant Franceschina carries particular social resonance.[40]

Early Modern Policies and Attitudes

There is no question but that the demonstrable spike in poverty, and particularly the pressures that it exerted in cities such as Venice and London, caused fundamental changes in attitude that also affected policies and practice. By the late fifteenth century, poverty had become a mass phenomenon in Europe, as it never had been in the medieval period. The vagabond beggars streaming into European cities in such large numbers were of grave concern to municipal health officials, owing to the not unwarranted fear that they could be carrying infectious diseases. The new multitudes of masterless men were also thought to be a threat to private property, and of course many of them did revert to petty crime. Begging was an extremely prominent and conspicuous activity—it had to be in order to be successful—and beggars cannily worked urban traffic and crossroads, positioning themselves in liminal sites such as outside the city gates and at the thresholds of churches.

As Geremek and others have detailed, politics, ideology, doctrine, and municipal alarm all seem to have come to a head at about the same time, resulting in the establishment of new poor laws across Europe within a span of twenty years, with clear evidence that municipal officials were aware of preceding laws and experiments. Nuremberg in 1522, Strasbourg in 1523, the Belgian towns of Mons and Ypres in 1525, Venice in 1529, the Flemish town of Lille in 1527, an edict issued by the Emperor Charles V in 1531, Lyon between 1531 and 1535, London in 1531, and Paris and Madrid in the 1540s all instituted new laws that took strikingly similar forms. Individualized begging was prohibited or severely limited, with strict distinctions enforced between the "impotent" and deserving poor and the "sturdy beggars" deemed able to work and liable for punishment and incarceration if caught illegally begging. Voluntary, individual almsgiving was prohibited, at least on paper, in favor of poor taxes, usually collected by parishes. Generally municipal, secular authority tended to appropriate functions and duties previously assigned to the church, although in practice the institutions administering poor relief often mixed lay and ecclesiastical governance. In theory, charitable functions were centralized and bureaucratized.

Although much has been made of the "secularization" of poor relief in these reforms, a detailed look at the Venice law demonstrates the melding of the sacred and the secular. On April 3, 1529, in the midst of a terrible famine, the Venetian Senate passed its scheme for poor relief, albeit with significant dissension: 116 for the decree, 34 against, and some 49 undecided.[41] Certainly the plan takes a very strong stance against public, "professional" begging, which is deemed a "wicked custom and an evil way of life." It is especially important that beggars who are not from Venice be sent back to their homes, subject to local procedures for poor relief. The mobility of the poor is also constrained by assigning each poor person to a particular parish and stipulating that they not move from parish to parish.

But far from aiming to eradicate charity, the plan attempts to promote it—"the most important form of good work"—and in the name of spiritual values. Those deemed worthy of alms are not the mere unfortunate beneficiaries of aid; they are the "poor in Christ." The scheme requires ongoing coordination between secular and sacred authorities, between the Provveditori alla Sanità and parish priests and deputies. The state-originated plan is to be promoted weekly during parish homilies; on festival days priests are to preach the importance of giving alms to the poor from the pulpit. For those deemed to be the legitimate recipients of charity, such as women and children who cannot completely support themselves with a craft, the Provveditori alla Sanità is to charge each parish priest to "go throughout his district seeking alms from the well-to-do (*potenti*)." The alliance between sacred and secular in arranging for the poor extends throughout the city: craft guilds are to help provide employment at reduced wage for sturdy beggars who cannot be employed by the sea vessels and galleys. The confraternities of Corpus Domini are to work in a stop-gap, emergency manner "commending the poor and exhorting all men to give" until the parish priests and deputies, in many ways the motors of the system, establish the structure. The parishes even operate partially like craft guilds themselves, offering "materials" for women and widows to "exercise whatever skills they possess."

No single solution comprises the scheme, which is really a diverse assortment of means, strategies, and players. The poor are certainly categorized, labeled, and disciplined. The "foreign" beggars are to be sent back to their territories with letters exhorting their "governors" to care for them; the homeless poor who cannot work are to be distributed among hospitals; the feeble (*impotenti*) who do have homes are not to beg but are to go to the parish priests for support (work or alms); the "robust and hardy" beggars who "could well live by their own efforts" are to work on vessels and galleys for half pay, or be employed by the "brotherhoods of all the craft" for reduced wages; widows and other women with children who have some skills are given "materials" to help them in their crafts by the parish priests, or alms if necessary; "poor and needy maidens of good and honorable life" can be taken into convents. Categorization functions less like Foucauldian discipline than as a variegated, tailored approach.

The new poor laws originated in German towns that would prove hospitable to Protestantism, and their centralization, rationalization, and proscription of individual begging and voluntary, individual charity can certainly be seen to run counter to medieval Catholic teaching. Insofar as the itinerant mendicant orders were aligned among the illegitimate beggars, they could serve as part and parcel of Luther's anti-mendicant campaign, as could Lucas van Leyden's image of a beggar child wearing a monk's cowl (Fig. 4, lower left). Still, the cities enacting the laws clearly cut across confessional lines. Catholic and Protestant regions alike stressed the importance, given the sharply risen numbers and the need to allocate scarce charitable resources to the proper place, of distinguishing between those deserving and those undeserving of poor relief—although in practice Catholics tended to put somewhat less pressure on the "examination" of the poor.[42] Most historians, including Geremek, argue that the 1520s laws, despite their German origins, primarily issued not from theological principles but from practical, municipal concerns. If there was any ideological tissue undergirding these practical city laws, it was the transconfessional and transnational discourse of Renaissance humanism, conveyed by Erasmus himself and especially his student Juan Luis Vives, the author of the internationally influential *De subventione pauperum* of 1526. Reversing the patristic and Franciscan veneration of Christ's suffering body and responding to the spectacle of the omnipresent beggar with antipathy, humanism invoked the "dignity of man" and argued that the poor need *not* always be with us—that poverty was unacceptable and could be eliminated.

There were, however, differences, if only ones of emphasis and tendency, such as the Protestants' greater stress on examination. Although Catholic cities may also have instituted prohibitions on begging and individual almsgiving, their laws tended to be more ambiguous and their

FIG. 4. Lucas van Leyden, "Uilenspiegel: The Beggar Family," 1520. Etching. Rijksmuseum (Rijksprentenkabinet), Amsterdam. Photo: Warburg Institute.

practices less consistent with policy. For Catholics, the notion that begging constituted a sacred activity and provided opportunities for spiritual improvement to the almsgiver proved extremely tenacious. In practice, and actually among Catholics and Protestants alike, charity was often dispensed regardless of the perceived legitimacy of the petitioner. The poet and Protestant divine John Donne advocated giving the poor the benefit of the doubt, asking, "How shall you know whether he that askes for alms be truly poor or not?"[43] As in the theater, the emotional responses and disposition of the giver—an inner feeling of compassion—were crucial to the exchange. In order to stir the giver's inner feelings, the poor had to be publicly visible, not enclosed in the new hospitals such as Bridewell and Bethlehem. Additionally, the giving had to be voluntary, not enforced by the government-instituted poor taxes—the heart of the new system in England and elsewhere.[44]

Varieties of Charity in Early Modern Italy

As the studies of Brian Pullan on Venice, Nicholas Eckstein on Florence, and David D'Andrea on Treviso have demonstrated, the official poor laws (most of which were not as many-sided as the 1529 Venetian edict) misrepresent the complete story of Italian charity.[45] For one thing, the laws, especially those prohibiting individual begging and voluntary almsgiving, were often either openly resisted or clandestinely ignored. The new, state-run charitable relief hardly describes the totality of charitable intervention, which in practice amounted to a hodgepodge of different kinds of activities: secular and religious, state and private, collective and individual. Nothing in the new poor laws prevented individuals, especially the wealthy, from significant interventions of charity. Girolamo Miani (1486–1537) was a Venetian patrician fighting against the League of Cambrai who, after being defeated and imprisoned, underwent a spiritual conversion and consecrated himself to a life of charity. He established a new charitable organization, and gave to hospitals, the Monte di Pietà, and other groups.[46] The Florentine patrician Ludovico Capponi, who died in 1554, was said to have given numerous alms to pious entities, leaving money in his will for dowries to marry twenty poor girls, and generally leading a life of great compassion for the poor.[47]

Individuals could also make significant contributions by joining one of the many Italian confraternities devoted to charitable work. Some of these venerable institutions had existed since the medieval period, and some were founded in the sixteenth century well after the institution of the poor laws. D'Andrea describes the confraternity Santa Maria dei Battuti of Treviso, originally founded in the late thirteenth century. Santa Maria received large bequests from individuals dedicated to the support of dowries for the poor, the comfort of prisoners, and clothing for the indigent. The confraternity was engaged in many civic acts of charity, including distributing food and clothing to the so-called shamefaced poor, or *poveri vergognosi* (formerly well-to-do people who had fallen on hard times), and helping orphans and abandoned children. Discussing the vigorous activities of Florentine charities in the early sixteenth century, Nicholas Eckstein argues that "[t]he large numbers of Florentines who belonged to confraternities believed that earnest recognition of the plight of the poor, and the concomitant material assistance that flowed from their concern—not perfunctory, symbolic charity—were the ways to achieve the sacralisation of quotidian relationships upon which the fate of literally everyone ultimately depended."[48] Early modern confraternities fulfilled many of the same charitable functions as had monasteries and helped sustain the medieval idea that charity could confer spiritual benefits.

For many who belonged to Italian confraternities, charity was a civic action—something a good citizen did for the public weal (Fig. 5). This did not, however, necessarily relegate these good works to the realm of the "secular," as the 1529 Venetian poor-relief scheme makes abundantly clear. Many charitable organizations recently analyzed by town-based historians similarly challenge the classic Weberian binaries between "sacred" and "secular," "brotherly love" and economic reality, charismatic/irrational and rational. Early modern charity could be rational, efficient, and citizen-inspired—and still be conceived as a deeply spiritual pursuit. Often, as in the case of the principal charitable institutions of Treviso, the very governance of the body was a mixture of lay and religious. Even a completely lay-governed institution operating by the principles of efficiency and rationality could consider its mission one of religious piety.[49] It is also true that the Italian Counter-Reformation, whose official beginning at the Council of Trent coincides very closely with the emergence of

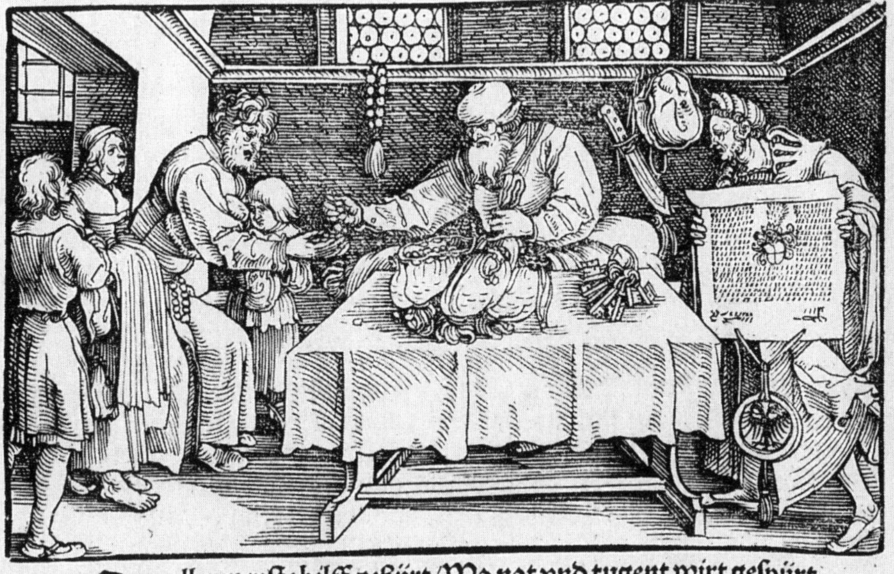

FIG. 5. "Civic Charity." Woodcut illustration from Cicero, *Officia* (Augsburg, 1531). Hochschul- und Landesbibliothek, Fulda, Germany.

the commedia dell'arte in the mid-sixteenth century, gave new impulse to charitable work, which was conceived as an effective means of conversion and of providing the poor with a Christian education. The charitable Hospital of Santi Giovanni e Paolo established in Venice, and houses for "convertite" or repentant prostitutes such as the Casa delle Convertite in Florence, founded in the early fourteenth provide examples of charity with an evangelical agenda.[50]

"Indiscriminate" Charity in Early Modern England

What most complicates the linear secularization and rationalization thesis in Italy, as we have seen, is the multiplicity of agents and institutions dedicated to charity and the perseverance of older charitable institutions such as the confraternity. With the dissolution of monasteries and other institutions dedicated to poor relief, and with the system of parish churches much more capable of exerting a unified national response than in Italy, England presents a different paradigm, but still one that defies a simple linear narrative. In regard to the official statutes, compulsory taxes and discrimination eventually won the day, beginning with the important 1598 *For the Relief of the Poor*. But as Steve Hindle argues in his discussion of the circumstances leading up to the 1598 statute, "in practice the notion of undifferentiated charity only very gradually gave way to the principle of discretionary relief."[51] According to Hindle, it could have turned out differently. Voluntary, undifferentiated giving, often framed by sharp critiques of wastefulness and excess worthy of Chrysostom's diatribes, exerted a strong pull among many English church leaders and writers well after the official poor laws turned in the other direction, and giving of this kind was executed surprisingly often by the faithful. Acknowledging this strain provides a salutary corrective to a distorted, teleological view of English poor relief, revealing heterogeneous, variable practices.

The English poor laws, while over the *longue durée* demonstrating an increase in rationalization and secularization, proceeded by fits and starts. Repeated draconian attempts to crack down on poverty in fact encountered significant resistance and renewed calls for the preservation of individual, voluntarist charity. After several crucial interventions regarding vagabond control by Thomas Wolsey after the May Day riots of 1517, England instituted a poor law in 1531 that incorporated and solidified previous English acts, following the main contours of the recently passed continental reforms. After the 1531 *Concerning Punishment of Beggars and Vagabonds* added the licensing of approved beggars, the statute of 1536 in its original form attempted to go much further, providing for regular, enforced alms collections that would, in theory, eliminate both begging and indiscriminate almsgiving. As Paul Slack demonstrates, however, the 1536 act was severely compromised by a series of provisos that effectively restored traditional charity with respect to both giver and receiver: monasteries, hospitals, and the nobility (and their servants) were allowed to give in the old way, and individual donations to prisoners, friars, shipwrecked sailors, and the catch-all "lame, blind, or sick, aged, or impotent people" were likewise allowed. Furthermore, by stipulating that people could not be forced to contribute to poor relief, the House of Lords kept alive a key element of Catholic charity: voluntarism. The major developments in the 1540s and 1550s consisted of the establishment of some five hospitals—St. Bartholomew's, St. Thomas', Christ's, Bridewell, and Bethlehem or "Bedlam" (the supposed provenance of Shakespeare's "Poor Tom")—which were largely funded by wealthy private individuals, who would play an increasingly important story in the history of English charity. The infected (St. Bartolomew's), the young (Christ's), the criminally vagrant (Bridewell), and the mad (Bedlam) were counted, enclosed, confined, regulated, disciplined, and above all kept from the public scene of charity. In general, Catholics were lukewarm about these houses of confinement, and as Slack has noted, during the Marian period the Queen herself patronized Henry VII's Savoy Hospital, which did not enclose the poor but gave relief to anyone from the street who approached its entrance.[52]

No momentous changes occurred during the Marian period or during Elizabeth's early reign, until the 1569 Rising of the North forced the government to take serious measures, resulting in the pivotal 1572 act. The first part of the act consisted of harsh and controversial penal measures against vagabonds (now including minstrels, jugglers, tinkers, peddlers, and actors unpatronized by noblemen), who were to be bored through the ear for a first offence and hung as felons for a second. Crucially, a comprehensive and compulsory poor rate was established for relief, theoretically eliminating the need for individualized begging and almsgiving. The poor were scrutinized more closely than ever before, since the funds generated by the poor tax were only to go to the impotent.

But these harsher policies elicited controversy as soon as they were announced, and during times of dearth they were enacted only very selectively. There were particular problems in getting the magistrates and other legal authorities presumably responsible for taxing and assessing individuals for a poor fund to coordinate with parish officials.[53] What rose to the surface, during the famines of 1586–87 and 1595–96, were vigorous calls from the Privy Council and from church leaders for substantial—and voluntary—almsgiving accompanied by fasting, repentance, and exhortation to avoid "too lavishe excessive and riotous spending."[54] To be sure, authorities made such declarations not to foment revolution but to stem it, in the light of disorders such as the 1596 grain riots in

Canterbury and the popular uprising in Oxfordshire in November 1596. Unsurprisingly, the earnest injunctions of texts such as *Three Sermons, or Homilies to Move Compassion Toward the Poor and Needy* (1595–96)—advocating fasting, repentance, and almsgiving among the middling sort as well as the wealthy—were not perfectly executed among the faithful; but there is evidence, as Hindle adduces for Buckinghamshire, that in some cases they often actually were observed. Parish churches called for special days of fasting, sermons, instruction, and personal contribution, followed by collections. In reference to the county of Buckinghamshire, Hindle argues that in practice "compulsory relief was almost unknown in the country before the harvest failures of the 1590s" and that the attraction of what he calls "general hospitality" was so strong that the poor laws could have moved in that direction.[55] "Collective charity was embodied less in the rate book than in the common collection, less in parish pensions than in the Easter dole, less in discretionary relief than in general hospitality."[56] In his monograph *On the Parish? The Micro-Politics of Poor Relief in Rural England,* Hindle turns attention away from public policies on poor relief and toward the many networks of informal support for the poor, especially the "conjunctual poor" (usually estimated at about 20 percent in England), who were not on regular parish pensions but suffered acute need after harvest failures and other crises. For many people in need, argues Hindle, the official parish provision collected from compulsory taxes was a last resort, and there were many relief strategies that preceded it, including in-kind charity in the form of clothing, food, shelter, and other needs. The entire picture drawn by Hindle, especially as he examines the crisis of 1594–97 and the period immediately following (when *As You Like It* was written), was one of widespread (and widely discussed) and variegated charity.

Coming to many of the same conclusions as Hindle, Ilana Krausman Ben-Amos argues against the traditional historical view of, effectively, a zero-sum match between compulsory, tax-based giving and volunteer charity.[57] Nor, according to Ben-Amos, did the growth of the market economy necessarily work to diminish the older system of gift giving and reciprocal exchange on which much local poor relief was based. Like Hindle, in his discussion of the micro-politics of poor relief that functioned under the radar of the official policies, Ben-Amos provides a rich picture of the mixed economy of caring for the needy, involving a combination of compulsory and voluntary giving. The two major collective agents of informal, voluntarist giving, especially important in times of crisis, were the parish and the craft guild—the latter continually giving aid to its members in time of need. Ben-Amos also considers testamentary bequests and private donations, which actually increased from 1550 to 1600—arguably as a response to the closing of the monasteries.[58] From 1550 to the end of the century, 133 new almshouses were established. And there is every indication that, especially in times of crisis and with some of the old charitable networks drying up, informal networks of charity at its most local levels, within the neighborhood and within the family, became both more necessary and more frequently invoked. Lear's anguished cry "I gave you all" (2.4.249) to his daughters Goneril and Regan, who would not reciprocate the lifelong gifts of parent to child by giving their father shelter, suggests that the play's large discourses about poverty, charity, and economic redistribution emerge from the breakdown of charity in its most intimate form: filial support for parents in old age.[59] Various acts of English early modern charity were both justified and, in many cases, prompted by new Protestant discourses of giving, which invoked a wide range of arguments on behalf of charity: good works were a manifestation of faith and love, a sign of grace, an education or training in Christianity, an opportunity for repentance and spiritual renewal, a proactive preventive against committing sin, and more.[60]

By the sixteenth century, in Italy and England and across Europe, the poor were certainly still "with us," but poverty and charity emerged as provocative and controversial problems and questions to a degree not seen before. Considerable time and effort were directed to new ways of addressing the ever-increasing flows of beggars through European streets and roads, but no single answer or type of answer prevailed, even in individual cities. A general trend toward increased secularization and rationalization, moving by fits and starts, did not erase the memory of older ways of thinking about and treating the poor, whether they were traditional, medieval ideas of exchange between rich and poor or more radical, neo-patristic notions of redress and economic redistribution.

2 From Augsburg to Edgar

Poor Tom and the Continental Beggar Catalogues

King Lear, Harman, and the Continental Texts

Framed by his brother Edmund as an aspiring patricide, Edgar in Shakespeare's *King Lear* suddenly finds himself a fugitive, a wanted man with only a moment to reinvent himself, following Gloucester's orders to bar all seaports and town gates (2.1.80). Before our eyes, he takes on a disguise that he believes will save his life:

> I heard myself proclaim'd,
> And by the happy hollow of a tree
> Escaped the hunt. No port is free, no place
> That guard and most unusual vigilance
> Does not attend my taking. While I may scape
> I will preserve myself, and am bethought
> To take the basest and most poorest shape
> That ever penury, in contempt of man
> Brought near to beast. My face I'll grime with filth,
> Blanket my loins, elf all my hair in knots
> And with presented nakedness outface
> The winds and persecutions of the sky.
> The country gives me proof and precedent
> Of Bedlam beggars, who, with roaring voices
> Strike in their numb'd and mortified arms
> Pins, wooden pricks nails, sprigs of rosemary;
> And with this horrible object from low farms,
> Poor pelting villages, sheep-cotes and mills,
> Sometime with lunatic bans, sometime with prayers,
> Enforce their charity. Poor Turlygod! poor Tom!
> That's something yet: Edgar I nothing am.
> (2.3.1–21)

Edgar resolves to perform for his life, and the performance becomes all the more telling because his "fictional" role of mad, vagabond beggar draws significantly from the actual position in which he suddenly finds himself: homeless, exiled, persecuted, under surveillance, and living at the mercy of charity. The role of Poor Tom is short on the kind of ruse and guile common to the English rogue books and long on sheer, naked (almost literally so) performance: one vulnerable person beseeching another with the simple but total art of the body and its theatrical projections and prostheses, which include make-up (griming his face with mud), costume (the semi-nakedness of a loin cloth), voice ("roaring voices," "lunatic bans," "prayers"), and gesture ("strike in their numbed and mortified bare arms"). Creating a radically "poor theater" out of practically nothing, Edgar shifts with nothing more and nothing less than what lies at hand. The self-mutilation that Edgar either announces he will perform or enacts directly before us during the speech, when coupled with his later chaotic but coherent narrative of sin, devil possession, and penance, can be productively understood in the contexts of various fourteenth- to sixteenth-century continental texts presenting the beggar as a performer—and one especially gifted at employing religious guises and discourses. Three salient aspects of Poor Tom's acting should be emphasized: (1) the elementally corporeal, bare nature of his performance—a minimalist virtuosity and asceticism worthy of Jerzy Grotowski's "holy" actor; (2) the rhetorical nature of a performance designed to "enforce charity"—one that operates by marshalling the full range of vocal and bodily rhetorical resources toward the end of persuading for charity; (3) the pervasively religious aura of the figure and the performance—an unsettling mixture of devil haunting, penitence, curse ("lunatic bans"), and blessing ("prayers").

Critics have long pointed to two English rogue books, John Awdeley's 1561 *A Fraternity of Vagabonds* and Thomas Harman's 1566 *A Caveat for Common Cursetors,* as possible sources for Edgar's particular type, the "Abraham Man," who has left or escaped from "Bedlam" hospital, London's hospital for the mentally ill. Calling himself "Poor Tom," according to Awdeley's extremely brief account, the Abraham Man "feigneth himself mad" and "walketh bare-armed, and bare-legged,"[1] or as Edgar puts it, with "presented nakedness" and a mere blanket cast over his loins. For Harman, the swindler's repertoire consists of an oral-formulaic collection of terrible tales about how he has been beaten in Bedlam or some prison, just as Poor Tom obscurely alludes to having been "whipt from tithing to tithing, and stock-punish'd and imprison'd" (*King Lear* 3.4.134–35).[2] Harman's Abraham Man, like Poor Tom, who haunts "low farms, poor pelting villages, sheepcotes and mills," is a specifically rural character, whose own dispossession reflects the very poverty of the "pelting" countryside in this period of agricultural calamity. (And in contrast to almost all other early modern English dramatists, whose background was predominantly urban, the Stratford-raised Shakespeare might have actually seen some of these rural types.) Just as Edgar, being a "horrible object," resolves to "enforce . . . charity," Harman's Abraham Man intrudes upon farmers' houses and demands charity from its terrified inhabitants with "fierce countenance."[3]

But despite these salient points of contact with Shakespeare's Poor Tom, the English texts somewhat miss the mark in their emphasis on the Abraham Man's ruse and craft: a quality shared by almost all of the English frauds. So Harman deems a certain Stradling (his exhibit A for the Abraham Man) to be "the craftiest and most dissembling knave," who is capable "with his tone and usage to deceive and abuse the wisest man that is."[4] In claiming that the Abraham Man can "pick and steal, as the upright man or Rogue," Harman tends to collapse his designated subject into the general, overriding archetype of the dissembling rogue. Harman's rogues are almost infinitely resourceful (except when they are being unmasked by the author himself or another authority), but in body, voice, gait, gesture, make-up, and costume they are less performatively virtuosic than the continental beggars of the catalogues. Stephen Greenblatt relates Poor Tom's verve to the performative bravado of contemporary exorcists, as anatomized by Samuel Harsnett in his 1603 *A Declaration of Egregious Popish Impostures*: a long-acknowledged source for the names of the devils Edgar claims to be possessing him.[5] Both kinds of texts aim to debunk fraud: Harman's rogues bamboozle their victims regardless of religious confession (and with almost no reference to religious aura or rhetoric); Harsnett sharply divides the world between credulous Catholics, naïve enough to be taken in by the hocus-pocus incantations of the exorcist and the grotesque gyrations of the possessed, and wily Protestants shrewd enough to see through the exorcist's cheap tricks. But both the Harman and Harsnett texts pose the question of belief or disbelief more starkly, I would propose, than is appropriate for Poor Tom, who conjures up an intermediate field of performance and reception between belief and doubt, in which the truly skeptical position might be to acknowledge that the ostensible charlatan could also possibly be telling the truth.

The English rogue books, in fact, appear to derive from the southern German tradition. Sebastian Brant's 1494 *Das Narrenschiff*, published in the same city as the *Basler Betrügnisse* (Basel) and translated into English by Alexander Barclay in 1509, describes in chapter 63 manifold types of beggars surely taken from other German texts but cast in an even harsher and more censorial tone: false miracle mongers, relic sellers, cripples, epileptics, and others. Bronislaw Geremek argues that Robert Copland's *Highway to the Spital-House* (1536?), which describes both "deserving" and "undeserving" types of the poor lodging in a hospice, was directly influenced by Barclay's translation of Brant's text.[6] It may have been the case that the English writers took the idea of beggar types from *Das Narrenschiff* or (for those who could read German) from one of the myriad and frequently reprinted versions of the 1509–10 *Liber vagatorum* or other German texts. They may well have fused the idea of the beggar with the notion of the vagabond-rogue that they could have absorbed from *Till Eulenspiegel*, translated into English in 1548, or from translated Spanish picaresque novels later in the sixteenth century. The rogue tended to eclipse the beggar.

These and other German texts, as well as a 1484–86 Latin manuscript from Italy, in fact capture the particular melding of religious enchantment and disenchantment operative in Poor Tom better than the almost completely non-religious and altogether debunking English texts. If Shakespeare, according to Deborah Shuger,[7] may draw on neo-medieval notions of economic redistribution for King Lear's "Poor naked wretches" speech, the idea of the beggar informing Poor Tom may be more cognate with late medieval continental discourse than it is with the aggressive Protestant texts of Harman and others.

To be sure, these late medieval / early modern German and Latin texts scarcely aim to hallow their subjects, deemed to be frauds meriting both exposure and punishment. But they emerge from continental geographical and temporal contexts in which the public might just as easily believe as disbelieve the itinerant beggar posing as (or actually being) a hermit, priest, friar, relic seller, indulgence monger, baptized Jew, survivor of religious persecution, or tormented soul practicing penance and seeking redemption. There is a fascination, unlike anything evoked by the English beggar catalogues, with both the performative aura of the beggars and their capacity to elicit feelings ranging from credence and compassion to disbelief and disgust. Visual representations accompanying German and Italian beggars frequently belie the texts' censorial postures by representing the beggars neutrally, as does the frontispiece to the 1545 *Nuovo modo di intendere la lingua zerga* (Fig. 6).[8] The images used for the *Liber vagatorum* reflect a general southern German tendency to depict a greater ethical range (i.e., the subjects are not all undeserving frauds) in the visual field relative to the textual arena. The author of the *Liber vagatorum*, and Martin Luther in a preface written for a 1528 edition of the text, declare their own vulnerability; they have themselves been victims of these charismatic charlatans, whose performances have evidently exercised a peculiar power. If Shakespeare, in *As You Like It*, can take an easy target of Protestant skepticism such as the hermit—excoriated in Spenser's *Faerie Queene* as the cunning fraud Archimago—and render him a plausible holy man, then he might also reverse, or at least complicate, the valence of vagabond beggars who evoked the religious fears and hopes of their publics.

The *Liber vagatorum* derives from a long line of German beggar catalogues that actually have their origins not in literature but in municipal registers. They arise at precisely the same time (the fourteenth century) and place (southern Germany) where the first early modern European poor laws were devised. What unites these early German texts, their development and flowering in Italy and Germany, and the late English catalogues of Awdeley and Harman is the persistent, indeed obsessive, impulse to name, typify, and categorize beggars and vagabonds. Faced for the first time with numbers of poor so great that one could not possibly know each of their names, the problem of identification became paramount—and it was easier to think in terms of categories than individuals. If, following the new poor laws, one was compelled to send itinerant beggars out of the city back into the devastated countryside to a fate of probable starvation, it was easier if one believed these individuals were evil imposters wrongly diverting the scarce resources of charity from the deserving, and local, poor. In the face of the terrifying prospect of squadrons of beggars invading European cities, beginning in the late fifteenth

NVOVO MODO DE
INTENDERE LA LINGVA
ZERGA. Cioe Parlare FORBESCHO.
Nouellamente posto in luce per ordine
di Alfabeto. OPERA non men
Piaceuole che utilissima.

M.D.XLV.

FIG. 6. Frontispiece to *Nuovo modo de intendere la lingua zerga* (Ferrara, 1545). British Library, London. Copyright The British Library Board.

century, the beggar books satisfied a "blessed rage for order": the comfort of categorizing and rationalizing the dizzying and threatening multitude.

Such an account, admittedly psychological and speculative, is not incongruent with Geremek's more historical and discursive explanation: "This procedure is the effect of the method of medieval teaching, which relies upon the principle of classifying by means of enumeration."[9] The very method of analysis into disparate categories, with talismanic names distinguishing one indigent group from another, thus derives for Geremek from figures such as the Carolingian scholar Alcuin. As with medieval bestiaries, one comes to know the unknown through the known. Still, Geremek argues for a factual basis for the beggar catalogues, concluding that "there is no doubt that . . . [such judiciary documentation] is based on real facts."[10] For all their evident literary verve, the clerks at Augsburg and Basel must have been responding to something. The insistent and practical need to distinguish between two fundamental groups of beggars—those deserving and those undeserving of charity—could have easily been extended to an extension and multiplication of categories beyond the practical binary one.

And some "performances of everyday life" among the downtrodden can actually be located in archival records. An entry in the Venetian Provveditori alla Sanità records dated 10 April 1548 (three years after the first extant commedia dell'arte contract) reports that a certain Giacomo Antonio di Vicenza was exiled for "making himself shake, wearing a blood-stained cap on his head, although he is healthy and energetic."[11] This is very similar to the category of the "Attremanti," or "Tremblers," in the Latin beggar catalogue *Speculum cerretanorum*. In 1548, a certain Aaron Francoso di Sarzana was arrested by the Venetian Inquisition and confessed to having been baptized four times as a Christian—performing conversion for his livelihood.[12]

Many details of the beggar catalogues simply have the ring of truth. They describe wretched performers exploiting both the "aura" and the simple convenience of liminal spaces around churches, such as doors and thresholds, in ways that match archival documents. The large number of religious frauds detailed in the continental books reflects the pervasive presence in the period of itinerant religious who either were fraudulent or easily gave off the appearance of being so, thus coming under attack from reformers such as Martin Luther. These wandering holy men evoke a world, also congruent with archival documents, in which a very thin line obtained between itinerant entertainers (musician, acrobat, storyteller, actor) and vagabond beggars. What most plausibly matches the beggar catalogues and real life, however, is that the need for identity transformation and fictional role playing—what Edgar undergoes as he hears his name publicly proclaimed—appears to be all but structured into the poor laws. In Milan, as Giovanni Liva has demonstrated, special attention was devoted to identifying and persecuting "foreigners" in liminal places. Fiction, however, provided a way out for the starving beggar with his wits still about him. The controls, argues Liva, "ignored the fact that it was very easy . . . to give a false name"—whence a late seventeenth-century edict fining any foreigner who had tricked the authorities by "altering their declarations of first and last name, country, or the place from where they came."[13] Itinerant improvisation—taking on various roles and identities in order to survive to the next day, exaggerating, distilling, reversing, and transforming the raw facts—this was the stuff of existence as the disciplinary screws of the authorities tightened around the poor. It is possible that life on the street and the art of the disciplinary beggar books worked in mutually reinforcing ways. Illiterate beggars were clearly not reading the new literature, but those involved in the discourse and practice of enforcement might have been, and actual beggars could have played into the discursive categories prepared for them.

Early German Texts

In the 1342 Augsburg municipal register account of five fraudulent beggar types, four of the five trade on specifically religious motifs, all featuring virtuosic one-on-one performance technique rather than the criminal networking characteristic of the English rogue books and the Spanish picaresque novels.[14] Anticipating a category from Teseo Pini's *Speculum cerretanorum*, the *Hürlenzern* posed as Jews baptized into the Christian faith—many times over. The *Clanniern*, or false pilgrims, cleverly exploited the liminal spaces bordering churches, as did several of the types from the *Liber vagatorum*. The *Grenzier*, the only one of the five types not given an explicitly religious function, feigned sickness. The *Münser* posed as Capuchin monks, and the self-flagellating *Serpner* as penitents. In just a year, the Augsburg categories expanded to nine, broadening the range of penitential performance techniques. Included in the added categories are the *Fopperin*, "die nement sich unsinne an" (who call themselves mad).[15] Another category of pilgrims, the *Mümser*, drag chains; the agonized and repentent *Sinweger* claim to have killed father, mother, and brother; and the *Spanvelder* dress their legs in order to simulate wounds.[16]

Apart from a 1350 Breslau document that catalogues eleven types of petty criminals and a 1381 municipal register in Constance that provides the nicknames and salient characteristics of notorious brigands,[17] the next major extant German text, and probably the chief textual antecedent of the c.1509 *Liber vagatorum*, is an important fifteenth-century report from Basel. Like the Augsburg catalogues, *Die Basler Betrügnisse der Gyler* issues from municipal registers—texts with an avowedly documentary aim. According to Friedrich Kluge, three nearly identical copies of the text survive: one from a book of municipal depositions dating 1411–63 (and probably written between 1430 and 1444); the second as a text added to a judicial statute of 1457; and the third as an insertion in the Basel chronicle of Johann Knebel in 1479. The multiplicity of texts, as Geremek argues, suggests the wide interest and dissemination of this particular text and others like it.[18] As well as furnishing a likely source of the *Liber vagatorum*, the *Basler Betrügnisse* may well explain the transmission from Germany to Italy of the beggar catalogue genre. Teseo Pini, the Italian vicar and author of *Speculum cerretanorum*, served under Bishop Girolamo Santucci (1427–94), who was sent by Pope Sextus IV to Germany, where he stayed until 1478. As Piero Camporesi argues, "[i]t is very probable . . . that in one of the returning legate's chests also traveled the manuscript of *Die Basler Betrügnisse der Gyler*, which constituted the nucleus of *Liber vagatorum*: pages that were not turned in vain" by Santucci.[19]

The *Basler Betrügnisse*, consisting of twenty-six to thirty categories depending on the version, constitutes a major expansion of the genre, reprising a few of the Augsburg types but adding many more, versions of which would be recycled in the *Speculum cerretanorum* and the *Liber vagatorum*.[20] (Generally, types often resurface in these texts under altered or altogether different names.) Several categories (*Grantener, Sweiger, Valkentreige, Brasseln*) practice the kind of self-mutilation and application of grotesque substances to the body that we have already encountered, which is cognate with Poor Tom's striking his "numbed and mortified bare arms" with various sharp objects. As in all the continental texts, much attention is given to religious fraud: converted Jews (*Vermerin*, following the *Hürlenzer* of the Augsburg registers), relic sellers (*Theveser*), pilgrims (*Klamerierer*, following Augsburg), false priests (*Galatten*), and others. Anticipating a somewhat fuller development in the *Liber vagatorum*, the *Spanfelder* seem particularly apposite to Poor Tom: arriving in a town, they deposit their clothes, kneel nakedly in front of churches, and shake with cold and utter fearful cries. The *Krocheren*, who also prostrate themselves naked before churches, make manifest the penitential nature that is merely implicit in many of the other types: desiring to expiate their sins, they sit naked in front of a church and beseech those passing by to whip them. It is the *Vopper* (expanding from the *Fopperin* of the 1343 Augsburg register), however, who most strikingly evoke Poor Tom, conjuring a spectacle like nothing to be found in the English texts. The *Vopper* are divided into two types: the first go about "as if they were mad" and publicly rip apart their clothes. The second, the *Vopper die da ditzent*, cry that "sie betreffen met dem bösen geist" (they have met with evil spirits), seeking alms so that they can be delivered from the devil. The overall tone of the *Basler Betrügnisse* is relentlessly harsh and censorial, and no accompanying visual imagery softens the blow; but in its elaboration of the performative techniques and narratives of the types well beyond what is indicated in the Augsburg entries, it points the way to the *Liber vagatorum*.

Liber vagatorum

The *Liber vagatorum: Der Betler Orden* was a seminal text, published in countless editions, under three different titles, from 1509 to 1755.[21] In this German text, the beggar catalogue reaches its mature form, and it is hard to imagine cosmopolitan English writers not being aware of it. Martin Luther, who actively advocated for the reformation of poor relief along with his campaign against the mendicant orders, wrote a preface to the 1528 edition.

Of all the types described in the *Liber vagatorum*, the *Schwanfeldern* (elaborated from the *Spanfelder* of the *Basler Betrügnisse*) seem particularly apposite to Poor Tom, for their implicit "stage directions" of removing one's clothes, shaking from cold, self-mutilation with sharp plants, and supplication:

> Das sind betler wenn sie in ein stat kommen so lassen sie die klaider in den herbergen und sitzen für die kirchen bey nackend und zittern jamerlichen vor den lewten das man wenen sol sie leyden grossen frost so haben sie sich gestochen mit nesselnsamen und mit andern dingen das sie sunckel werden.

> These are beggars who, when they come into town, leave their clothes at the inn and then sit down naked in front of churches, and shake miserably in front of the people in order to make them think that they suffer from terrible cold. They prick themselves with nettles and other things to make themselves annoying.[22]

Here, and throughout the text, religious fraudulence plays center stage. The *Lossnern,* who like Poor Tom claim to have been in prison, carry their chains still with them as a continual sign of penitence governed by the vows they have made to various saints. Even more performatively virtuosic penitents are the *Klencknern,* who at church doorways or religious gatherings bemoan their past captivity at the hands of the infidels and "um deren willen sie mit grosser jamerlicher klagen der stymm bitten und haischen" (for the sake of the saints with loud, mournful cries of their voice supplicate and beg).[23] The *Vagierern,* wandering scholars who profess to know the black arts, are explicitly called "devil conjurers" (*beschwerer der tewfel*) for their ability, according to the author, to unleash devilish powers. The *Dobissern,* or false anointers, exploit the credulity of simple farmers by touching them with images of the Virgin or of saints; like the canny *Schleppern* (along with the *Kammersierern,* false priests) they profit from donations of worship materials (candles, altar cloths, etc.) that they presumably need for their unholy masses. The *Deutzern,* feigning sickness, beseech alms to go on pilgrimage on behalf of "this or that" saint. A *Veranderin,* a woman who purports to have converted from Judaism (similar to the Augsburg *Hürlenzer* and the *Basler Betrügnisse Vermerin*), will reward charity by telling credulous donors the fate of their father or mother in the afterlife.

All of the *Liber*'s mendicants, with one exception, are *Veranderen* of one sort or another: changers and shape shifters. The only unambiguously good category in the catalogue is that of the *Bregern*: "Das sind betler die kain zaichen von den heyligen oder wenig an inen haben hangen und kommen schlechtlich and einfaltigklich für die lewt gangen und haischen das almosen umb gottes und unser lieben frawen willen" (They have no or very few tokens of the saints hanging about them and proceed clumsily and simply up to people and beg alms for God's or the Holy Virgin's sake).[24] They are "one-sided" (*einfaltigklich*) and pose no threat because their appearance matches their reality. The author grudgingly concedes that in some cases aid may also be given to a second group, the *Stabeylern*: vagrants who work the country from one saint's shrine to the next. But with dozens of saint's tokens hanging from their hats and cloaks, the *Stabeylern* introduce what might be called semiotic excess: the very problem that the analytic beggar catalogues are supposed to alleviate.[25]

If the clothes of the *Stabeylern* are patched together from many different pieces, like those of the mythical Harlequin, their verbal repertoires can similarly be seen as "rhapsodic," or stitched together, in the manner of oral compositions performed by actors, singers, and storytellers. In fact, much of the *Liber vagatorum* is taken up with enumerating the typical narratives deployed in the imposters' street theater, as with the *Lossnern*, close readers of late medieval romance or contemporary captivity narratives: "[T]hese are knaves who say they have lain in prison six or seven years, and carry the chains with them wherein they lay as captives among the infidel . . . and they have forged letters, as from the princes and lords of foreign lands."[26] Typical speeches recorded in the text are presented in an oral-formulaic manner, with alternative phrases enumerated at various points of insertion.

The *Liber vagatorum* recounts one after another prodigious feat of acting: acting designed to move the hearts and minds of gullible bystanders to charity, either by pity or (more usually) terror. Masters of theatrical *technē*, these traveling actors exploit the full gamut of performance semiotics, enlisting the signs of costume, make-up extending over the entire body, gesture, stance, facial expression, gait, non-verbal voice and sound, a rich verbal repertoire of speeches and stories, and props, and even occasionally addressing the senses of touch and smell. Even more impressive than the *Dützpetterin*, beggar women who can feign both pregnancy and miscarriage, is the male variant: men who feign to be carrying a child.

The false women lepers, or *Junckfrawen*, deftly combine make-up and intense physical acting, as do the *Grantnern*, afflicted with the falling sickness of St. Vitus. Close attention is paid to the make-up, prostheses, and foul substances used by the histrionic frauds, which match the swampy ecospheres inhabited by Poor Tom ("eats cow-dung for sallets; swallows the old rat and the ditch-dog" [3.4.132–33]): the *Schweigern* besmear their arms and legs with horse dung; the *Seffern* coat themselves with a foul type of salve. If we think of the actor playing Gloucester rather than the fictional character, Shakespeare's play is again invoked by the destitute but also sanctified *Zickischen*, or blind men, who take cotton, apply a blood-like substance to it, and attach it to their eyes with a kerchief. All in all, the *Liber vagatorum*, by far the single most important early modern beggar catalogue from an international perspective, provides an exhaustive and compelling account of destitute performative techniques—certainly exaggerated, but not without a basis in reality—drawing from a radically minimalist and raw form of theater.

Speculum cerretanorum

Not much is known about the life of Teseo Pini, the author of *Speculum cerretanorum*, who appears to have been a vicar from Urbino also involved in the legal profession, both as a doctor in law and as a judge. As has been pointed out, there is a possibility that Pini had access to the *Basler Betrügnisse der Gyler* through his superior, Girolamo Santucci, who had lived in Germany during the 1470s and whose library included a manuscript treatise in Latin on *cerretani*, a generic name also used by Pini himself for vagabond charlatans and beggars.[27] To be sure, there were also important Latin and Italian texts available to Pini on the figures of the *cerretano*, *ciarlatano*, and *vagabondo*, such as the fifteenth-century humanist Flavio Biondo's *Italia illustrata* (composed 1448–53), which provides an account of the origins and practices of the *cerretani* to which Pini is clearly indebted.[28] Piero Camporesi speculates that the *Speculum*, probably written between 1484 and 1486, may not have been published because of the author's death, although it does appear to have circulated in manuscript. Ironically, it was only due to an act of blatant plagiarism in the early seventeenth century by the Roman Dominican priest Giacinto de' Nobili, who used the pen name Rafaele Frianoro, that

Pini's work ever saw the light of day.[29] Frianoro translated the text from Latin to Italian, changed the names of popes and other historical figures to fit his own time, and shifted from the first to the third person whenever Pini narrated in propria persona.

Resting squarely within the censorial bounds of the beggar book, Pini certainly continues to represent almost all vagabond beggars as fraudulent, but the discourse around poverty is somewhat more cosmopolitan and many-sided than that of the German texts, touching upon radical pagan and Christian discourses of poverty. (Santucci's library was well-stocked with ancient Greek and Roman texts.) The *Biantes*, used alternatively as a generic name for the vagabonds and for a particular sect, are said by Pini to derive their name from Bias of Priene, a sixth-century BC philosopher considered to be one of the Seven Sages and, while not explicitly a Cynic, famous for sayings such as "I carry all my things with me." Several of the categories closely match the picture of the Cynic sage, living naked under the sky like Poor Tom. So Pini's *Cocchini*:

> [D]icti sunt a quatiendo, qui per hiemem nudi vadunt, quasi sua quatientes membra, stridentes dentibus, ut maiorem vim frigoris se concepisse ostendant. Ii prae se ferunt nihil praeter egestatem nuditatemque habere.
>
> Are so called from the shaking, for those who go about naked through the winter, shaking their arms and legs, gnashing their teeth, in order to show that they suffer from the tremendous force of the cold. They claim to love nothing more than their nudity and poverty.[30]

Similarly, the *Apezentes* "dicunt se nihil praeter victum concupiscere, spernere vinum et nuditatem amare" (say that they desire nothing but minimal sustenance, spurning wine and loving nudity).[31] A striking sign that Pini extends the bare beggar catalogue into a wider discursive terrain is provided by his entry for the rebaptized Jews, or *Iucchi*, a surprisingly recurrent category that appears in the Augsburg registers, the *Basler Betrügnisse*, and the *Liber vagatorum*. Pini is the first to give these figures a social context related to the contemporary problem of poverty:

> [H]i fingunt se quondam fuisse Iudeos ditissimos fenerario quaestu, et visions vidisse terribiles, miraculaque inaudita et pene incredibilia proferunt, quibus allecti, more Apostoli, dimisisse talentum et omnia que habebant, ut Christum pauperem sequerentur paupers et perfecti.

> These pretend to have once been Jews made extremely rich by usury, but who, having seen horrible visions, and astonishing and incredible miracles that they recount, have been drawn, in the same way as the Apostles, to give up all their possessions, and perfected in poverty to follow the poverty of Christ.[32]

Within the discursive framework of late medieval anti-Semitism, these fraudulent opportunists point to a genuine critique of usury and appear to advocate radical Christian charity as an antidote.

As with the German texts, most of the imposters traffic in religious motifs, but the various religious transactions performed by the beggars is considerably more articulated in the Latin text. Several of Pini's fraudulent beggars, posing as priests, conduct the Mass itself (in exchange, of course, for palpable reward), and generally Pini's charlatans can be seen to perform the various speech acts and transactions of the Holy Office. The first specific type described by Pini, the *Biantes,* are so called for their general claim to bless (*beatitudinem promittunt* [they promise beatitude])—just as Poor Tom can dispense prayers as well as "lunatic bans." The *Affrates,* or false friars, deceitfully bedecked in priestly habit, both confess and absolve, cannily pinching the Mass offerings for their unholy uses. Selling counterfeit indulgences, the *Biantes* promise to procure spiritual benefits for one's ancestors in hell or purgatory. Several of the types offer to audiences the spiritual gift of witness: the *Acatosi* claim to have been captives of the Turks or Saracens, bearing and brandishing chains to prove it, testifying to the endurance of their faith under the harsh deprivations they experienced in prison, where they still have relatives. Several categories perform the vicarious expiation, and perhaps the homeopathic cure, of compelling physical penitence, especially the *Affarfanti*:

> Fingunt enim multa miracula dicentes se magna perpetrasse flagitia divinoque quodam nutu morbo aliquo percussos et voto obtinuisse morbi liberationem, ut peccatum suum et gratiam eis factam cunctis gentibus paenitendo nuntiarent; percutiunt enim nudum corpus suum aliquibus levibus catenis . . . aiunt oportere eos talem agendo paenitentiam totum peragrare orbem.

> They claim to have witnessed many miracles, saying that they have committed terrible sins and were stricken by a terrible infirmity from God;

> they were liberated from the infirmity by a vow they made to God that as a penance they would travel the world witnessing before all of the people to their sin and to the great mercy of God, striking their bodies with light chains of iron.[33]

In these kinds of penitential performances and generally throughout *Speculum cerretanorum,* a high degree of physical virtuosity is required: from the *Acadentes,* who simulate falling; from the *Atrementes,* or "Tremblers"; and from the Tarantulists, or *Attarantati,* who vibrate and shake their heads, tremble at the knees, sing and dance, flutter their lips, and shriek and agitate like mad people. Accomplished vocal performance seems to be a particular hallmark of Pini's charlatans: the *Asciones,* who like the *Attarantati* pretend to be mad: "[N]ihil petunt sed inarticulatas voces emittunt, nutuque quid velint indicant" (They ask for nothing but utter forth inarticulate sounds, indicating what they want simply by moving their heads).[34] The performative nature of their activity—piazza performances drawing credulous crowds—is rendered more distinctly than in the German texts. Of the *Spectini,* it is said that "homines feminaeve ad eorum contiones confluent non minori delectatione quam ad videndum spectacula cucurrissent" (both men and women flock to their assemblies with no less pleasure than if they were running to comedies).[35] The *Alacrimantes* (Weepers) and the *Acadentes* (Fallers) take care only to perform when large crowds have collected. Interestingly, many of Frianoro's minor additions have to do with filling out the performative context—his version of the *Acatosi* clear out a performative space in the piazza with the very power of their strange cries in Arabic and Hebrew. Still, as we have seen here, the Latin text of Pini that Frianoro appropriated was already rich in performative detail.

Poor Tom

Although Poor Tom does not exactly position himself in the liminal zone of a sacred space, like the *Schwanfeldern* and so many other beggar types described in the catalogues, he invokes a spiritual aura through other means. If, as Stephen Greenblatt has argued, the exorcism intertexts also informing Poor Tom point to the "sham theatricality" projected from Samuel Harsnett's debunking, disenchanting point of view, so do those of the fraudulent beggar, which describe Edgar's chief object, namely, to "enforce charity."[36] Poor Tom might be seen as performing a kind of auto-exorcism, but it is put in the service of his fictional super-objective of supplication. The devils tormenting him are tantamount to furious, soul-possessing sins—"of lust, as Obidicut . . . Mahu, of stealing; Modo, of murder" (*King Lear* 4.1.59–61)—that he must expiate, with the help of the Ten Commandments–style platitudes that he spouts ("Obey thy parents, keep thy word's justice, swear not, commit not with man's sworn spouse, set not thy sweet heart on proud array" [3.4.80–83]) and the bystander's charity. In Edgar's fiction, as with the piazza poem *Barzelletta de' falliti* examined in the following chapter, the destitute speaker has fallen into poverty as a result of unbridled womanizing, dicing, stealing, and greed—sins that expose the opulence and inequities of the wealthy. Poor Tom, according to his own crazed but actually coherent narrative, had been a court servant "proud in heart and mind" who "serv'd the lust of my mistress' heart and did the act of darkness with her. . . . Wine loved I deeply, dice dearly; and, in woman, out-paramour'd the Turk" (3.4.85, 86–88, 90–92). Poor Tom's devil discourse, rather than merely rehearsing mad snatches from Harsnett, inscribes the demons into a densely poetic, if also formulaic, narrative of the sin, moral repentance, and spiritual charity familiar from the narratives of sham beggars.

In Edgar's extended, auto–stage direction, he enumerates the forms, postures, and techniques of the actor's body as he prepares to play Poor Tom. First, he applies facial make-up, liming his face with grime. Next, he attends to costume, or rather anti-costume, taking off all his clothes but a loincloth (as the mad Lear, in his "Cynic" imitation of this "learned Theban," will try to do later: "Off, off, you lendings! Come, unbutton here" [3.4.108–9]). Then, he applies a kind of debased wig, tangling and matting his hair. A "roaring voice" will be his fallback vocal register; and then, as so many of the beggar books detail, he marks his body with signs of mutilation. Ambiguously sacred, or *sacré*, in the French sense, Poor Tom can both curse and bless: he will have prepared both curses, or "lunatic bans," and prayers, in his codified verbal repertoire.

From his first appearance outside of the hovel to the point an act later when he casts aside the role (just after his father gives a powerful speech on charity and redistribution) Edgar performs for his life. Deftly melding gesture and voice, his frozen shaking beats to the time of senseless speech: "O do de, do de, do, de" (3.4.58–59) and "Humh" (3.4.47)—both added to the Folio text as possible incorporations of the actor's improvisations. Poor Tom frequently utters the kind of fearsome, non-verbal sounds frequently described in the beggar books: "[A]low! Alow, loo, loo!" (3.4.76–77) and "suum, mun, nonny" (3.4.99). Wild, grotesque, violent motions could easily complement lines like "The foul fiend bites my back" (3.6.17), and deictically rich utterances fire the actor's gestic invention: "There could I have him now—and there—and there again—and there" (3.4.61–62). (Here again the Folio text, by adding the fourth "there," may be incorporating actors' improvisations.) Grotesque head movements might accompany Poor Tom's declaration that he will "throw his head" (3.6.64) at the imaginary dogs that Lear has conjured for the trial scene, and we can generally guess that Poor Tom has mastered the body language of the suppliant beggar, as he explicitly begs: "Do poor Tom some charity, whom the foul fiend vexes" (3.4.61–62).

What might be a quintessential instance of sham theatricality, of course, turns out to have immense power—power for many critics, viewers, and readers of the play and for the play's internal audience members. Edgar's particular rendition of a beggar, with the powerful gestic, kinetic, and vocal features described above, captures something like the athletic and ascetic actor of Jerzy Grotowski's "poor theater," with Edgar taking "poor" in an even more literal sense than the Polish director-theorist. For Grotowski, the figure of the naked, suffering, vulnerable actor, stripped of the distractions of stage lighting, props, and even costume, is fundamentally compelling in a way that returns us to the elemental power of theatricality itself. We might then consider the representation of a beggar to be the ur-role, or ground fiction, of the actor himself. The very virtuosity of the role also returns us to the radically egalitarian implications of the microcosmic early modern character system spanning from king to beggar, as reflected for example in Renaissance Tarot cards (Fig. 7). Actors can play the full gamut of human experience and reveal to us the constructed nature of societal roles, a revelation that may carry either conservative overtones, as with the stable balance of "Pobre" and "Rico" in the neo-medieval system of Calderón's *El gran teatro del mundo*, or radical implications, as in Hamlet's upsetting observation that the body of a dead beggar serves "politic worms" as well as that of a king.

King Lear in fact may be seen as an extended "poor theater," with Lear,

FIG. 7. "Misero" (The Beggar). 1530–61. Engraving by Hans Ladenspelder after the so-called Tarocchi Cards of Mantegna. Department of Prints and Engravings, British Museum, London. Copyright The Trustees of the British Museum.

the Fool, Kent, Gloucester, and perhaps even Lear's retainers taking on the marks of poverty in theatrical ways that also engage their existential conditions within the fiction of the play. Of these, only Gloucester does not enter into poverty voluntarily, but although he certainly does not choose to be blinded, he self-identifies with his new degraded role and becomes a "sight" that transforms the people who behold him pitifully walking toward Dover (4.5.9–11).[37] Kent's decision to follow his master in disguise leads him to temporary itinerancy as a "masterless man" and being put in the stocks by Cornwall, a common punishment for vagrants. Probably one is meant to see Kent, lingering onstage, in the stocks at the moment when Edgar dons his beggar disguise, and the latter as two emblematic alternatives of poverty. The fool himself follows Lear into the "theater" of poverty and becomes an eloquent, emblematic sight of deprivation—a figure of "houseless poverty" (3.4.26)—that actually prompts the "Poor naked wretches" speech (3.4.28–36).

The signs of the vagrant poor—merely theatrical dissimulation, according to Harman—and the terrible realities of the unhoused are thoroughly confounded in this play. The blind vagrant, a type from the rogue pamphlets that might be nothing more than a cheap theatrical trick, is rendered terribly real by Gloucester's pathos. We really cannot determine within the given world of the play whether the rogue literature trope that discharged soldiers are always riotous and drunk is false or true (Lear asserts that they are "men of choice and rarest parts" [1.4.263], whereas Goneril sees them as "disorder'd" and "debosh'd" [1.4.242]). The role of Tom O'Bedlam, strangely introduced by Edmund himself (1.2.135–36), becomes a truer identity for Edgar than that of a duke's son ("Edgar I nothing am").[38] The marks theatrically inscribed by Edmund upon his own body (2.1.33–34), simulating a fight between him and Edgar that never occurred, prefigure the crude bodily inscriptions, performed by Edgar upon his own body with the very instruments of the Abraham Man (2.3.13–16).

Lear's impetuous decision to "abjure all roofs" literalizes the "poverty" that, by the mental habit of antithetical opposition typical of early modern English thought, connects the king and the beggar.[39] Lear fairly prostrates himself before Regan, begging for clothing, shelter, and food. She sees Lear's posturings as "unsightly tricks" (2.4.157), a cheap theatrical ploy on the order of Thomas Harman's charlatans, just as she and Goneril view his rush into the storm. Lear is not truly homeless; if he is not killed, which is of course a real possibility within the fiction of the play, he will eventually be succored by friendly forces, as in fact he is by Cordelia and the French army. Still, like Edgar his existential condition significantly overlaps with his voluntary state, and he himself provides a transformative vision of poverty and degradation to others.

The effect of Poor Tom on the play's internal audiences, especially

King Lear and Gloucester, is both traditional and radical, in the ways that we have discussed above. Poor Tom draws much of his power, symbiotically, from his association with the dispossessed king on the heath; like Lear, he has elected to "outface / The winds and persecutions of the sky" (2.3.11–12). Lear's powerful "Poor, naked wretches" speech may be literally prompted by his sudden designation of the Fool as "houseless poverty" (3.4.26) as he sends him into the hovel. While the Fool is inside the roofless shelter, and before Poor Tom has emerged, Lear utters the speech, which conjures the state of "poor, naked wretches" like Poor Tom so aptly that it appears to function as his cue:

> Poor naked wretches, wheresoe'er you are,
> That bide the pelting of this pitiless storm,
> How shall your houseless heads and unfed sides,
> Your looped and windowed raggedness, defend you
> From seasons such as these? O, I have ta'en
> Too little care of this! Take physic, pomp,
> Expose thyself to feel what wretches feel,
> That thou mayst shake the superflux to them
> And show the heavens more just.
> (3.4.28–36)

Lear invokes the medieval idea, characteristic of texts such as the *Life of Saint Louis*, that the king is responsible for acts of mercy such as feeding and clothing the poor. The king's charitable act of redistribution—"shak[ing] the superflux" or redistributing hoarded excess to the poor—restores the proper laws of God ("and show the heavens more just"), so that the radical is revealed to be orthodox.[40]

Similarly, the blind Gloucester responds to the "sham theatricality" of Poor Tom in a surprisingly forthright manner. Edgar / Poor Tom first encounters his newly blinded father being "*poorly* led" (4.1.10, Folio version; emphasis mine),[41] in the sense of being led by someone inferior in rank and, additionally, by a poor man, as if the poor are natural companions of dispossessed kings or dukes. The Old Man, servant in the Gloucester household for some eighty years, serves much the same function as Adam in *As You Like It*: a loyal servant who represents the old values of service and charity that are so endangered by the new men and woman who have displaced Gloucester. Asking the Old Man to fetch some clothing for Poor Tom, whom he now enlists as his guide in the path toward Dover, Gloucester becomes the only one in the play actually to grant Poor Tom the "charity" that is the ostensible point of the disguise (as well as concealment)—he gives him his purse:

> Here, take this purse, thou whom the heav'ns' plagues
> Have humbled to all strokes. That I am wretched
> Makes thee the happier; heavens, deal so still!
> Let the superfluous and lust-dieted man
> That slaves your ordinance, that will not see
> Because he does not feel, feel your pow'r quickly;
> So distribution should undo excess
> And each man have enough.
> (4.1.64–71)

Whatever the arbitrariness of Edgar's disguise, it has successfully elicited not only the charitable action of almsgiving in Gloucester, but even more importantly, the capacity to feel compassion for the poor, without which one cannot see the gaping economic inequities unjustly tilting toward the wealthy. Gloucester "sees feelingly" the central socio-economic problem of early modern England, the unjust superfluity enjoyed by the few at the expense of the many, condemning he who "will not see / Because he does not feel." We may be quick to censor Edgar's later "The dark and vicious place where he thee got / Cost thee his eyes" (5.3.173–74) as another example of crude didacticism belying the play's rich complexity, but Gloucester himself, as does Poor Tom in his deranged "serving man" monologue, aligns sexual lust with insatiable material craving: "the superfluous and lust-dieted man." In other words, he implies that his own adulterous lust is part and parcel of his own "superfluous" (echoing Lear's "superflux") greed and failure to respond charitably to the poor, echoing an association operative in many English sermons from the period. According to Gloucester, the rich man subjects the biblical "ordinance" to brotherly love to his own will. From feeling, to seeing, to individual charity (giving his purse to Poor Tom), the speech culminates in a general call for economic redistribution, restoring the proper amount of resources to each member of society.

This is quite a different response from the debunking skepticism and laughter of superiority that the beggar catalogues ostensibly attempt to elicit. What the beggar books we have examined in this chapter also represent, however, is the sacred or pseudo-sacred theatricality evoked by itinerant beggars and their ersatz audiences—a performative mode powerfully evoked by Poor Tom.

3 Cheap Print and the Performance of Poverty

Introduction

Representing the views of the early modern poor themselves, who were mostly illiterate and had little access to manuscript, print, or other media, poses a challenge. If the pronounced ideological bias and social agenda of beggar books, from the *Liber vagatorum* to *A Caveat for Common Cursetors*, constitutes a fairly straightforward case of discursive distortion, we may generally ask if the real lives of the early modern poor can ever be glimpsed apart from the haze of overdetermined fear and persecution. Does popular culture exist outside the disciplinary and discursive acts that suppress it?

Carlo Ginzburg, in his celebrated study of a sixteenth-century miller constructed primarily from Inquisitorial testimony, challenges the argument, attributed to Foucault, that the exclusions and limits through which popular culture arises prevent us from knowing much besides the acts of discursive control themselves.[1] In *The Cheese and the Worms*, Ginzburg argues that the miller Menocchio's utterances under testimony, when triangulated by both the judges' questions during the trial and social and book history, can approximate a relatively autonomous popular voice. Certainly, when we address the representation of the poor in Ruzante, the commedia dell'arte, and Shakespeare, we will not be listening to their unadulterated voices—although the present study argues that these writers and actors were unusually proximate to the disenfranchised. But in the examination of popular songs, poems, and dialogues printed in cheap pamphlets and both performed and peddled by piazza performers, we may occasionally come very close to the thing itself, especially in the early, relatively uncensored days of print before Counter-Reformation controls began to be issued. As Rosa Salzberg has argued in her groundbreaking work on the subject, the highly mobile and resourceful peddler-performers, who distributed the new medium to an increasingly larger socio-economic clientele, played an enormously important role in the early days of print by mediating between elite and popular culture. Many of the peddlers were actually poor themselves, capitalizing on a new form of income that provided opportunities but was still economically perilous and increasingly subject to control and repression. And many of these low-end peddlers, adjacent to beggars and destitute performers, composed, published, and performed songs and poems that explicitly addressed their own poverty and that of their intended auditors. Like beggars, the poor performers may well have exaggerated their destitution, filtering their degradation through various distorting lenses. Still, the distortions resemble those of the character Lazarillo in his histrionic begging more closely than those projected onto beggars in the censorial beggar books. To be sure, it cannot be argued that each and every author (most of whom are anonymous) of the popular pamphlets examined in this chapter was actually poor; some of the *canterini* and *cantastorie* performing these songs, such as Vincenzo Citaredo and Giulio Cesare Croce, achieved some measure of success. But even some of the successful ones, like Croce himself, never completely escaped from poverty and could speak about it with the authenticity of lived experience.

While some of the popular texts represent poverty in a naked and direct manner, other texts favor the forms of distillation and distortion. It is difficult to deny that the visionary hyperboles of the land of Cuccagna, a favorite theme of these pamphlets, constitute a form of escapism. But according to Piero Camporesi, such "escapism" still reveals things about actual early modern hunger, degradation, and disease. Homologous, in Camporesi's account, to the hallucinogenic states generated by poppy seeds and other adulterated substances mixed into peasant bread, the Cuccagna tropes oppose a "non-Euclidean logic" of deformation, hyperbole, and monstrousness to the rationalities of official culture. Normal measures and proportions are transformed, "making everything much bigger than usual and the whole world upside down."[2] The land of Cuccagna, where one is paid for sleeping and imprisoned for working, and where one enjoys the free, unlabored bounty of the earth, nicely exemplifies the figure of *reversal*, to which we can add the tropes of exaggeration, transference, distortion, fictionalizing, and marginalization discussed throughout this study.

The Figure of the Peddler-Performer

Beginning as early as the 1470s in Venice, Florence, and other Italian cities, the opportunistic but risky new business of printing often made use of street peddlers in order to distribute, advertise, and sell printed material, especially cheap pamphlets, short books, and flyers that might appeal to the average bystander in the street or piazza. For example, the logbook of the press at the convent S. Iacopo di Ripoli in Florence—a press founded around 1476—indicates the extensive use of middlemen for advertising and selling.[3] To Fra Domenico Pistoiese, who ran the press and kept the logbook, equally as important as the booksellers and stationers, with their fixed places of business, were the mobile peddlers, figures noted in his logbook with names such as "Bernardino curmatore." The peddlers can be distinguished into four overlapping categories: (1) mountebanks, or *cerretani* and *ciurmatori*;[4] (2) piazza singers, or *canterini*, who had been active in northern Italian towns since the Trecento, performing popular versions of chivalric epics and other kinds of works; (3) friars, who mainly sold popular devotional works, but other items as well; and (4) blind men—some achieving a measure of success, such as Cieco da Forlì, but most of whom must have been rather destitute, turning to peddling as an only slightly enhanced form of begging.[5]

The peddlers and *canterini* performed and sold their works in Italian piazzas such as the Campo de' Fiori and Piazza Navona in Rome, San Martino in Florence, Porta Ravegna in Bologna, and San Marco in Venice, usually accompanying themselves on a stringed instrument mounted on top of a moveable bench or trestle stage. Often they sold other items, including the ointments, potions, and cures proffered by mountebanks. The peddler-performers performed and sold small books, fliers, and pamphlets, usually in *ottavo* formats, that might cost as little as a *quattrino*.[6] The audiences attending their performances comprised a wide social range, including artisans and wage laborers as well as those from patrician, courtly, or humanist sectors, according to Giovanni Pontano.[7] The Lateran canon Tommaso Garzoni, in his *Piazza universale*, stresses the plebeian make-up of these audiences: they are a *popolazzo* ("people," with a disparaging connotation) who allow themselves to be charmed and cheated by these performers, who draw them away from the church.[8]

Whether blind or not, many of the peddlers appear to have experienced real poverty, as Salzberg has demonstrated. Tommaso di Antonio del Grasso, one of three stationers who had petitioned the Duke of Florence for an exemption from a prohibition on peddling cheap print in 1560, made another petition in 1569, in which he described himself as "poorer than ever and nearly blind," and in fact "not just poor but wretched, old, and burdened with family."[9] Vincenzo di Pierantonio, in a supplication to the Duke of Florence in 1559, describes himself as "being very poor and burdened with children," and states that "since he could not live on his salary that his bosses gave him of five lire a week, always he was accustomed to go on holidays to sell in the piazzas and through the streets, in order to save something."[10] One of the more moving texts discussed by Salzberg is that of the blind *canterino* Giovanni di Giorgio il Cieco, in which he decries that

> La povertà malvaggia, e ria
> Qual m'ha fatto venir un'ombra scura,
> Disforme, e brutto più che la paura . . . .
> Ma come spirto ch'invisibil sia,
> Niun mi vede, niun di me più cura.
> Su 'l Rialto giorno e notte tengo il piede,
> Dove gli amici, e anchor parenti miei,
> Passano inanci, e adietro, e non mi vede /. . .
> Pero che povertà mi fa invisibile.

> Cruel and vicious poverty has made me a dark shadow, disformed, and uglier than fear. . . . Like an invisible spirit no one sees me, and no one cares about me any more. On the Rialto day and night I place myself where friends, and even relatives, pass in front and behind me, and do not see me . . . because poverty makes me invisible.[11]

But both by printing this text and by performing it with the visual enhancement of his destitute body, Giovanni actually did render poverty visible.

Texts of "Direct" Poverty

A significant number of cheap printed texts performed and sold in Italian piazzas sharply dramatize the suffering and degradation of poverty—not always in ways that were pleasing to the authorities—and they do it in arrestingly direct and plangent ways without having recourse to the tropes of distortion. In their supplicatory relationship with the intended piazza audience, several of these texts explicitly perform the speech act of begging itself.

The Urbino *canterino* Vincenzo Citaredo vehemently criticized the all-too-human cause of poverty, and sharply enough that he was charged by a church official as the author of a subversive text. Although he framed the beginning and ending of his works with gestures acknowledging post-Tridentine orthodoxy, much of the intervening matter challenged the conservative notion that poverty and famine were evils sent by God that humans had to bear patiently.[12] We can only guess why Counter-Reformation authorities consented to license Citaredo's poems. Perhaps they were somehow mollified by their quietistic frames; and judging by the very few *canterini* texts placed on the Index, they may have generally thought that these cheap publications were harmless.

In the 1588 sung poem *Speranza de' poveri*, printed in Urbino, Citaredo dutifully opens and closes with a nod to the authorities who approved its printing ("Con licenza de' Superiori"): the poor can "only hope in God" and must govern themselves with patience and prudence, contenting themselves with their lot and not falling into "despair"—or revolt.[13] But a few stanzas into the poem Citaredo challenges the doctrine that famines and plagues are heaven-sent and thus beyond human control: "Dio ci manda l'abondanza: / Ma l'huom fa la carestia" (1v; God gives us abundance / But human beings cause famine). Citaredo directs a venom worthy of Chrysostom against the wealthy. Instead of fighting the pagans, the "evil, rich Christians / Make war against the poor" (2r; . . . rei ricchi Christiani / Guerra fan co' i poverelli). Citaredo decries what he views as a campaign of rage and fury (1v; rabbia . . . furia) against the poor. The rich profit at the expense of the poor's labor (2r), intentionally aim to starve them (3r; affamare i poverelli), and treat them as if they were animals. In the voice of the poor, Citaredo cries out:

Presi siam, qual pesce a l'hamo
Noi meschini per la gola.
Tutti fan tal presa sola
Per volerci divorare. (2v)

Like a fish by a hook, we miserable ones are caught by the neck; they have taken us in their grip because they want to devour us.

Just before Citaredo's final post-Tridentine gesture, he ends the poem by warning the rich that they may suffer the "reverse-beggar" fate of the rich man in the Lazarus story: "Così tu verrai mendico / Che cerchi oro accumulare" (4r; And so you who strive to pile up gold will become beggars yourselves).

In the undated but probably late sixteenth-century *Barceleta de Messer Faustino da Terdocio, in laude de l'oro e de l'argento,*[14] the speaker represents the so-called *poveri vergognosi,* or "shame-faced poor"—those who were once wealthy or upper-class but who have now fallen into poverty: "Se te trovi in povertà / Con rovina a capo in giu / Non ti giova nobiltà" (2r; If you find yourself in poverty / Ruined from head to toe / Noble birth won't help you at all). The poem's mock praise of gold and silver thinly disguises its attack on money as destructive of social reciprocity and kinship relations: if you have money, argues the poet, you'll be fine even if your father dies! (2v). The brave new world of commerce and capitalism has extinguished compassion for the poor and the practice of almsgiving:

Se va un povero dal ricco
Sol per un bicchier de vin,
Non gli mostrarebe un cricco
Un suspiro, un bagattin[.] (2r)[15]

If a poor person visits a rich man's house just to ask for a glass of wine, he won't even greet him or give him a sigh, or a scrap.

Through negatives, the poem calls for the wealthy to renew the practice of giving extra food from their tables to the poor, just as Orlando's lament for the passing of charity at "good men's feasts" (*As You Like It* 2.7.115) advocates that the wealthy fulfill their responsibility to help the poor. At the end of the poem, by comparing his emaciated body to that of John the Baptist, the speaker recasts the involuntary fall into poverty of the *poveri vergognosi* as the voluntary, spiritual poverty of the New Testament.

The *Barzelletta de' falliti* (Song of the Ruined),[16] which contains particularly gritty and striking poetic images, also dramatizes an unfortunate beggar fallen from his aristocratic caste, but moralizes his descent by criticizing the excessive consumption and sinful appetites of the wealthy. The speaker, who ends each refrain with the supplicatory "Miser me ch'io son fallito" (Have pity on me for I am ruined), addresses a socially diverse audience that includes peasants, artisans, and citizens. The abject beggar bemoans the loss of all the luxuries and privileges that he inherited by his noble birth—servants, horses, expensive clothes, delicate foods, and more—and decries his present destitute state, in which he doesn't even own a shirt, is assailed by lice and mange, and has taken to eating candles (2v). The moralizing of his fall into penury differs significantly from conventional early modern anti-poor discourse (the poor are lazy, opportunistic, etc.), because his poverty-inducing sins are precisely those of the greedy, uncharitable, wasteful wealthy. In fact, they strikingly anticipate the fictive character evoked by Shakespeare's Edgar in the guise of Poor Tom, who standing shirtless on the heath recalls his sensual past as a privileged court attendant: "Wine lov'd I deeply, dice dearly; and, in woman out-paramour'd the Turk" (*King Lear* 3.4.90–92). The *Barzelletta* speaker declares:

> Io non ero mai satollo
> di tener le braccia al collo
> delle donne poco honeste
> quali mi facean feste
> per cavarmi li quattrini
> lor mi davan i bacini
> col bocchino saporito. (1v)

> I never had enough of putting my arms around the necks of loose women who made fusses over me to squeeze out a few pennies, giving me kisses with their delicious little mouths.

Here, the graphic expression and performance of vice might be said to compromise the intended moral message, entertaining the piazza crowd with salacious accounts of encounters with prostitutes. Still, the message is clear enough: he has gambled away his fortune and been forced to sell off his beautiful clothes, his other possessions, and his farmland, vineyards, and fields (2r). So enthralled is he by cards and dice that

> [e] mi harei piu presto all'hora
> stragiocato in mia mal'hora
> cento scudi in quel confino
> che donar' à un poverino
> un danar, o un panattello
> ma cacciavolo al bordello
> ò facevo l'assordito[.] (2r)

> [t]hen, in that cursed time, I would have sooner squandered one hundred scudi in gambling houses than given to a poor person some money or some bread, but instead I cursed him or was deaf to his cries.

The *Barzelletta de' falliti* thus enacts the "reverse beggar" theme in the very persona of its *povero vergognoso* speaker, who in the abject, beggarly state to which his dissipation has reduced him experiences the very cruelty and neglect that he had visited on others before his fall (Fig. 8).

Comparable to Ruzante in literary and social magnitude is the Bolognese *cantastorie* Giulio Cesare Croce, who transformed the oral tradition of piazza and pamphlet performance into a more literary form, albeit one of pronounced residual orality. The three works of Croce examined here take a direct and explicit approach toward poverty, although he also wrote poems on Cuccagna and other topics that employ the tropes of distortion.

Croce appears to have experienced poverty more directly and personally than Ruzante (who had unbroken support from his patron, Alvise Cornaro) and sang about it in his piazza *canzoni* with a directness and simplicity that suggest that the real audience of his poems were the poor themselves, rather than the series of noble patrons to whom his poems were dedicated.[17] With less stable patronage, Croce stopped short of questioning the prevailing economic system too explicitly, and framed his works with the same post-Tridentine platitudes that we found in Citaredo. At the same time, the fact that he was never able to secure a permanent patron left him with marginal status—the feeling that he could never completely shake his rustic roots and lack of a proper literary foundation. All the much more, then, could a poet of self-declared *basso ingenio* (base wit) identify with the dispossessed.

FIG.8. Woodcut illustration of a *povero vergognoso*, from Cesare Vecellio, *Habiti antichi et moderni* (Venice, 1590). Copyright The British Library Board.

Croce was born into a poor family in 1550 in a small town twenty kilometers outside of Bologna. His father, who was a blacksmith, died when Giulio was seven years old, after which he was apprenticed to his uncle, also a blacksmith. In his autobiographical poem, Croce complains of "i gravi affanni" (l. 46; heavy troubles), "le orribili carestie" (l. 47; horrible famines), and "la fame al labro" (l. 50; hunger on his lips).[18] While, as a boy, he was working with his uncle for a wealthy Bolognese family, his talent for singing and improvising was noticed, and he was called on to perform—whence his beginning as a singer-poet. But throughout his life, sustained periods of poverty vexed the brief moments of prosperity, and Croce was frequently forced back to his native trade.

Two *canzoni* written by Croce during the difficult decade of the 1590s provide striking images of material poverty experienced personally and viscerally: the *Lamento della povertà per l'estremo freddo* (The Lament of Poverty on Account of the Extreme Cold) and the *Lamento de' poveretti i quali stanno a piggione* (Lament of the Poor Who Have to Pay Rent).[19] As with the Ruzante famine plays to be examined in the following chapter, the first piece emerged out of a specific historical calamity: the extreme cold experienced in northern Italy during the winter of 1586–87. The terrible cold thwarts the material processes of both writing and performing: the very pen he uses to write the poem constantly freezes up, and the performance has to be shortened. As he declares at the end of the poem, he must leave "perché 'l freddo mò comanda / ch'a scaldar mi vada presto" (ll. 169–70; because the cold now forces me to go away and warm myself up).[20] In this terrible period, which has now lasted five months in what Camporesi calls the "eternal present" of time experienced by the poor, the common people are freezing in their beds and, like animals, dying in their "caves" (*tane*). They continually suffer from snow, rain, and ice and are beginning to despair of ever seeing the sun again, which is anxiously beseeched as the great god Apollo, who would burn away the unrelenting dampness of the fetid earth (ll. 145–52). Wood for heating has become increasingly scarce and expensive, with the greedy wood sellers making a killing, and the poor have been forced to burn boxes, baskets, and bedsteads (ll. 55–58), probably worsening the unsanitary, contaminating conditions of their bedding—often "scattered straw" and "palliasses that are filthy and fetid."[21] Although the poem itself strives to create a community of suffering between the performer and his piazza audience (perhaps standing in the cold), class solidarity appears to be lacking in the crisis: one person steals another's coat; one takes from another's food basket; there are fistfights and angry threats (ll. 109–12). Women run to pawnshops with their pathetic pledges (ll. 59–62), and shoeless children beg under the grand porticos of Bologna (ll. 68–71). As with Citaredo, the poem ends on a relatively positive note, holding out hope for better days in the future; but the frame of fideism does not silence the harsh plaints preceding it.

The *Lamento de' poveretti i quali stanno a piggione* decries the terrible conditions experienced by impoverished urban renters in Bologna and other Italian cities, tellingly rhyming *affitti* (rents) with *afflitti* (afflictions) (ll. 40–41). As the landlords come to collect their continually rising rents, the poor, who have been selling or pawning their sheets, capes, and even wedding rings in order to survive, fear eviction and the heavy hand of the *balia* (authorities). The *poveri meschini* (poor wretches) lack clothing, proper heating, and food and are exposed to "the grim conditions of people existing in damp or flooded basements, with putrid mattresses and sordid straw."[22] Those living at the mercy of landlords are practically itinerants: "che mai stiamo fermi in un loco / per n'aver abitazione" (ll. 115–16; for we are never fixed in one place where we can live). Just as the Fool in *King Lear* contrasts Lear—and perhaps humankind in general—unfavorably with the snail who carries its house on its head (1.5.27–31), Croce considers snails and turtles better off than the men and women suffering from poverty: "Le lumache e le gallane / che sono bestie così strane, / han le case d'alloggiare, / e le posson via portare" (ll. 118–21; Snails and turtles, which are strange creatures, have their own lodgings, which they can carry with them). The speaker knows whereof he speaks: he too is constrained to pay rent and lives in a dark, low, and dingy room, "tutto pien d'umiditate" (completely full of humidity), with holes in the walls through which the cold air enters.

As with the *Lamento della povertà per l'estremo freddo*, the *Banchetto de' malcibati* (Banquet of the Poorly Fed) was triggered by a specific historical event—in this case, one of those periodic years of harvest failure that must have led many to question whether the new poor measures would be adequate. The full title of the poem links it with the remembered, traumatic past of Bolognese citizens: *Banchetto de' malcibati. Comedia dell'Academico Frusto, recitata da gli Affamati nella città calamitosa, alli 15 del mese dell'estrema miseria, l'anno dell'aspra, e insoportabile necessità* (The Banquet of the Poorly Fed. A Comedy by the Frustrated Academic, Performed by Famished People in the Devastated City. On the Fifteenth of the Month of Extreme Misery, in the Year of the Bitter, and Unsupportable Necessity).[23] The *Banchetto* serves up a short allegorical play, featuring destitute, impoverished characters such as Messer Pocoraccolta (Mister Small Harvest), Madonna Tristastagione (Lady Bad Season), Madonna Carestia (Lady Famine), Messer Bisogno (Mister Need), and Madonna Povertà (Lady Poverty). Consisting of many extended, tour-de-force speeches, the *Comedia* could well have been performed by a single *cantastorie*, such as Croce himself. It stages a version of the popular *maridazzo* form: a wedding feast featuring lower-class figures who often break into conflict. Effectively an anti-banquet, the poem's chief conceit is the burlesque reversal of the normal tropes of abundance and gluttony found in the Cuccagna literature.

Messer Appetito (Mister Appetite), who is the son of Madonna Fame (Lady Hunger) and Messer Disagio (Mister Discomfort), speaks the prologue, convening in the piazza (or the imagined circle of the reader) an audience as dispossessed as the speaker:

> Affamati e distrutti circonstanti
> Che fate qui d'intorno ampia corona,
> Scrocchi, pitocchi, poveri e cercanti,
> Lo son, come vedete, qua in persona,
> A la presenza vostra comparito[.]

> You famished and ruined bystanders who make a large circle here around me, you scroungers, parasites, poor, and itinerant, I have appeared, as you can see, here in person, in your presence.

Banished from the audience are those with fine clothes and a full purse. For those who have been ruined by this year's famine and have aching stomachs, Messer Appetito announces that a banquet will be held at Messer Pocoraccolta's expense. The concept of "poor theater" takes on a new, material meaning, for whatever benches they might have used for spectators have either been burned to provide heat or sold to buy food or pay off debts. After the prologue, the matchmaker Messer Disagio arrives at Messer Pocoraccolto's house to say that he has found a match for the latter's daughter, Madonna Carestia. It is none other than Messer

Sterile, a "huom sodo" (solid man) who brings to the match such assets as "Villa Stentarina" (The Villa of Difficulty), "Castel Languente" (The Castle of Languishing), and the hill of "Mal Contenti" (Malcontent). When Madonna Carestia appears before her father and the matchmaker, the latter extols the virtues of Messer Sterile: she'll never have to lock her door if she marries him, because he doesn't possess anything. The short play continues in this vein: the dowry offered by Messer Pocoraccolta for his daughter is a series (extended by means of the tour-de-force improvisations of the poet) of diseases and deprivations. Although in this Croce poem we have drifted away from the direct plaint of poverty to a poetics of distortion, the poem's critical point of view is nonetheless clear enough.

Peasants and Poverty: *Villani* Poems

In his pamphlets, the artisan Croce attends more often to urban than to rural poverty: his concerns are with urban rents, rapacious landlords, and dank, crowded, and unsanitary urban living quarters.[24] Many pamphlets concerning the *villano*, or peasant, figure were likewise printed, performed, and sold by piazza peddlers and charlatans. These focus on rural poverty and on the position of the *villano* who has come to the city either temporarily to sell his produce or as a desperate immigrant seeking a new life.

Derived from a satirical medieval tradition, the *villano* poem was carried into the age of print by piazza *canterini* and displayed the usual urban prejudices against the peasant for being backward, stupid, bestial, or (in contradictory fashion), scheming and deceiving.[25] Emilio Lovarini argues that the anti-*villano* poem was taken up by early modern *canterini* who had a certain affinity for the conditions of the peasant. Transforming the monovocal anti-*villano* satire into the popular *contrasto* genre, the singers gave voice and sympathy to the peasant as he defended himself against the attacks of the landlord and the city dweller.[26] Because the *villano* is almost always identified with the state of poverty, the poems provide more evidence of the multiplicity of attitudes toward the poor.

The undated, late fifteenth-century or early sixteenth-century *Contrasto del cittadino el contadino*[27] consists of alternating stanzas in *ottava rima* that pit a representative peasant, or *contadino*, designated as

"El lavoratore," against an innkeeper ("L'oste"), who represents the city dweller, or *cittadino*. The *contrasto* provides a lively instance, common to oral culture, of festive insult: the two protagonists hurl threats, insults, and accusations at each other in the public sphere of the piazza, with the public treatment of the immigrant *villano* in the piazza itself raised as an issue. The dramatic form of the *contrasto* formally translates the monovocal insults of the anti-*villano* poem into the dramatic and perspectivized context of the dramatic two-person *contrasto*. It is a particular person who is telling us, conventionally, that the *villano* (the Lavoratore) is a lazy, tricky, clever, lying, bestial, and stealing scoundrel—and this person (as we learn from the Lavoratore) happens to be both wealthy and uncharitable, wear fine clothes, and practice usury. If the next pamphlet we'll examine revolves around price wars between the *villano*-vendor and urban artisan consumers, here the debate centers around food distribution: the Lavoratore accuses the Oste of hoarding, and the Oste charges that the Lavoratore has been stealing. For the Lavoratore, the finely clothed Oste consumes and spends in great excess: "Et tutto el giorno / in cose inique bestiale et atroce" (2v; And you spend the entire day devouring sinful, bestial, atrocious things). All the advantages—money, written legal codes that the Lavoratore cannot read, and power—create a distinctly unlevel playing field, on which the Lavoratore sees nothing less than class warfare: "un ricco sempre il povarel vuol morto" (3r; a rich man always wants the poor dead). The rich Oste, complains the Lavoratore, has less compassion than those who live in hell (2v). The Lavoratore laments the numerous evils of poverty: the poor die in prison (2r), die from thirst (2r), and do all the work while the rich idly reap the benefits.

Here, the Oste gives a new, suspicious twist to the pietistic notion that the poor must bear their inequality patiently in the hope of future reward: according to him, poverty is sent by heaven to punish the *villani* for their vices (4v)—and particularly for their ingratitude toward heaven and incapacity to accept their fate. As the Oste sanctimoniously declares,

> L'uomo che è da qualche affanno tribolato
> Ricorre al ciel per aiuto e consiglio
> Ma il villan micidiale crudele ingrato
> Chiama el dimonio in ogni suo periglio
> Bestemmia il cielo e chi l'ha ingenerato[.] (3v)

> The man who is tested by some affliction trusts in heaven for help and counsel, but the murderous, cruel, and ungrateful peasant calls on the devil in every time of trouble, cursing heaven and he who created him.

In other words, the Lavoratore's complaint against rich landlords is inspired by the devil and provides the very sign that he deserves to be afflicted with poverty. The argument is strained, and at this point it becomes clear that the formally even-handed *contrasto*—allotting equal *ottave* to both parties on the rhetorically level playing field of the piazza—is decidedly tilted in favor of the Lavoratore, whose targeted, detailed complaints against the wealthy ring much more true than the formulaic, repetitive, and unreflective charges of mendacity and thievery against the poor. When, near the end of the poem, the *villano*-Lavoratore declares that "sempre fu il pover huom da Dio amato / el ricco havuto in odio e in dispetto" (4v; the poor man was always loved by God, and the rich man hated and despised), this anti-anti-*villano* poem has framed its attack against the wealthy with a Chrysostom-like spiritual perspective.

Class antagonism is somewhat less pronounced in a pamphlet "composed for Lorenzo Piccinini": the *Astuzie de' villani*, divided into two parts. The first, a diatribe against *villani*, is spoken by a collective of urban artisans, and is counterpointed by the *Risposta de villani*, representing the peasants' perspective.[28] The complaints levied by each group against the other center on the prices demanded by working-poor peasants as they sell their foodstuffs in the public piazza. The peasants defend their prices, as compensation for the many injuries they suffer, which mostly derive from the landlords and not their interlocutors, who are their working-class counterparts. The artisans, however, fling the usual epithets at the country folk: they have mouths like dogs (1v), resemble the very animals that they have slaughtered and bring to the city (1v), and are full of tricks and not to be trusted. Other, more particular complaints—that they don't let one touch the food they are selling; that they don't play fair and straight while selling the wood desperately needed by the urban artisans (2r)—have the ring of actual encounters in the piazza. In the *Risposta*, the *villani* direct some of their complaints against the artisans—mostly for verbally abusing them in the marketplace—but reserve their chief complaints for the rich landlords. The illiterate peasants are the victims of clever legal maneuverings (3r); they are squeezed out by greed and avariciousness; they do all the work, but the owners, as Marx would put it, extract surplus labor: they "toglian tutta la raccolta, / E ci votano il granaro" (3v; take away all the harvest and empty the granary). To be sure, they are not beggars—they survive precariously as food vendors—but they do elicit compassion as they directly address their audience: "Ascoltate la ragione / Ci havereste compassione / Da che viene che siamo mal trattati" (3r; Listen to our reasons; you will have compassion for us, when you see how badly treated we are).

The *Alfabeto dei villani* (1517–24), a text in Paduan dialect that appears in manuscript and in several printed editions,[29] similarly transforms the anti-*villano* satire into a lament and complaint. Alluding to the foreign wars that devastated northern Italy in the early sixteenth century, the speaker decries the soldiers who have marauded their farms, raped their women, and forced them to leave the land (ll. 28–30)—a significant form of capital-destroying "negative labor," according to Carlo M. Cipolla.[30] Tax and rent collectors beset the peasants, waking them up in the middle of the night to collect money (ll. 10–12), and the priests are even worse: "E canta i preve sora i cuorpi e sberga, / po' ne castra i borseti a man a man. / Ge vegna 'l lango mo sotto la chierga" (ll. 16–18; The priests sing and lament over our dead bodies, and they steal our money little by little. Curses on the whole lot of them!). The endless, grinding labor of the peasants is all extracted for the benefit of others: they sow grain and raise animals for others and are left with nuts and turnips to eat (ll. 22–24). We sleep on filthy, putrid beds of straw and hay, declares the speaker (ll. 31–33); if we are accused of being like animals, it is because we eat like them, sleep on the same surfaces, and are haunted by animal, not human sounds: "Luvi de note sì è nuostri segnore; / rospi e ranuogi sì ne fa el biscanto; / d'aseni e gagii aldom sonar le ore" (ll. 34–36; The wolves of the night are our lords; toads and frogs are our evening choir; our clocks are asses and roosters). Unlike the agonistic *Contrasto del cittadino el contadino* and *Astuzie de' villani / Risposta de villani* examined above, even in its very complaint the *Alfabeto* seems to internalize some of the anti-*villano* discourse: if we sleep and eat like animals, we are no smarter than they (l. 54); we are all false (l. 53) and deserve to be judged by God (l. 75); "we are really the scum of the world!" (l. 82; A' seom pruoprio la schiuma de sto mondo!). It is likely that this piazza performance of self-loathing, however, when combined with complaint would not tend to elicit the derision and scorn of the anti-*villano* poem, but rather something like compassion and even anger against those who have put them in that position.

Itinerancy and Poverty: Zanni on the Road

The anti-*villano* satire—as well as the agonistic rejoinders that we have examined above—finds a home in Pantalone's litany of insults levied against his servant Zanni, originally a *villano* who was forced to travel from Bergamo into Venice, where (to again quote Marx) he "found his master waiting for him." Adjacent to the commedia dell'arte proper, possibly performed on a few occasions by *canterini* who may also have acted in commedia troupes, are several cheap print poems representing the *zanni*'s exhausting, degrading, and perilous voyage from his native land, sometimes to a specific destination (usually Venice) and sometimes just adrift in the no-man's-land of the road. There, he is equally beset by the perils of lawlessness (e.g., bandits) and of law, in the form of the surveillance of itinerant "foreigners" that significantly increased from the late fifteenth century onwards. As Giovanni Liva has demonstrated in the case of early modern Milan, officials stationed at ports and other border zones of cities were increasingly required to monitor the coming and going of foreign itinerants, due especially to fear that they might be importing infectious diseases.[31] Ferrymen and boatmen who worked rivers and canals bordering the state were enjoined to monitor foreigners, and innkeepers, under threat of penalty, were required to supply the names of foreigners lodging with them "specifying their names, and the nation the foreigner comes from, and whether or not they are bearing arms, and whether or not they are traveling by horse."[32] The three Zanni-as-traveler poems we shall consider do not figure the *zanni* as the codified *Arte* servant; but the culture of the organized companies and that of these piazza songs are adjacent, reciprocally influential. If the canonized theater of the Gelosi and other highly successful troupes tends to marginalize (but not eradicate) its own connections with poverty, the pamphlets can amplify the social context of the commedia dell'arte, known in some early texts as the *commedia degli zanni*. In these *zanni* poems of what we might call "degraded travel," we may then connect the actual travel of commedia actors—a source of frequent complaint for its perils and discomforts—with the legend of the displaced, itinerant, and poor *zanni*.

In the late sixteenth-century Bergamask text *Viaggio di Zan Menes,*[33] a vicious winter storm drives the desperate inhabitants of a Bergamask village to sleep in barns with animals and compels the narrator to travel forth in search of lodging and food, "ch'em reparas dal fred e dalla fam" (1r; so that I could recover from cold and famine). He describes himself as homeless: "che a no trove ledam / casa casina log stalla o teg / ch'am tegnis covert mi poveret" (1r; for I couldn't find a manure heap, a house, a hut, a place, a stall, or a roof, that would keep my poor self covered). Exhausted, he travels and arrives at an inn where, desperately banging on the door with both his feet and his hands, he is met by a surly innkeeper. Quickly sensing that this dubious client doesn't have the money to pay, the innkeeper sardonically insults him in the way of rogue's cant, as a "segnur" (lord), a "baru" (baron), and a "canoneg de doana" (1v; canon of the customs house). He threatens to beat him up and finally casts him outside, where the embattled Zan Menes is forced to sleep in an animal stall with a disorderly group of other abject travelers: "ilo tra sta canaia / ul me laghe e senza lum al scur / che quella stalla e chigadur" (1v; there, among these dogs he abandoned me in the dark, in this shithouse of a barn). A fight breaks out among Zan Menes' unfortunate bedmates, foreign refugees from diverse Italian towns. Relief for the bedraggled *zanni* only comes in the morning, after a night that seemed as long as three years (3v; che cert me pars che la dures tre an).

The undated but probably late sixteenth-century *Disgrazie del Zane* similarly brings its degraded protagonist to an inn, where the tensions generated by the increased surveillance of foreign itinerants nearly burst into violence.[34] Night has fallen, and the speaker, beaten down by fortune (1v; zani sbattut da la fortuna), is traveling through the forests and countryside with his *putta* (woman), looking for shelter, when he is suddenly attacked by bandits, who take his *putta* away from him and send him into a desperate search through the multiple travails of the road: "cerchevi boschi, vai, groti, e campagn / castei, ville, e caso, et, e montagn" (1v; I searched through woods, valleys, grottos, fields, castles, villas, houses, and mountains). Proceeding on foot, he suffers from the twin evils of terrible weather (1v) and maurauding bandits. He arrives at what he thinks to be an inn, but an old man in his nightshirt violently opens the door and, after examining him, sends him rudely away. Back on the road, the disconsolate *zanni* sees a light in the distance and arrives at what truly is an inn. There, however, he is assaulted by the suspicious innkeeper and serial representatives of different regions or countries—a Mantuan, a Ferraran, a Greek, a Venetian, and so on—who are possessed by fear that he is a spy sent to identify "foreigners" such as themselves, along the lines discussed by Liva. Most of the foreigners (much of whose function is to provide the poem with linguistic variety, along the lines of the *maridazzo*), threaten to beat up the *zanni* and send him away; but one or two vouch for him, and he ends up persuading the innkeeper and the foreigners that he can stay. As if the entire poem is structured by the insistent tempo of hunger, the poem ends with the famished *zanni* sitting down to consume a meal.

In another cheap print work, the 1579 *Viaggio del Zane a Venetia,*[35] the Bergamask *zanni* is so pinched by hunger at the end of the year that he leaves his native land to try his fortunes in Venice. The point of this poem is not so much the *zanni*'s own poverty, which is real enough, but the poverty that he witnesses in Venice. He has been starving and makes sure to pack his bag "perche fam ne sit no me fes dan" (2v; so that neither hunger or thirst afflict me), carrying a *bastone* (club) for protection on the road against bandits and thieves. Traveling by boat on a canal, he finally reaches the Serenissima, whose concentration of vendors, buyers, goods, and beggars overwhelms him: "restè balord e mut / a veder tan confet da i spiccioler" (3r; I was astonished and dumb-struck seeing so many things sold by peddlers). But what might have been merely a hymn to Venetian commerce abruptly changes when very different voices of the street are interpolated: the cry of a blind man and the plaint of a woman with four children, one blending into the next: "A chi signori ve paisa / Soccorrer sto meschin orbo ch'è privo / De la luse, del mondo a pena vivo, / Signori no habiè a schivo / Mi grama con sti Quattro fantolini / Chi vuol dai da farina" (3v; Which of you gentlemen can help me—a wretched blind man who has been deprived of the light, and is barely alive? Lords, don't treat me with scorn; I am miserable, here with my four children / Whoever wishes give me some flour). The voices of the poor modulate from one to the next, as if invoking a collective presence, juxtaposing the material excess of early capitalism to its dark side.

Gluttony and Famine

Shakespeare's *The Merchant of Venice* evokes the ghostly vestige of the Pantalone-*zanni* agon in what Gobbo and Shylock say about each other at the point when the servant is leaving one master for another. For Shylock, Gobbo is a gourmandizing idler, who will not be able to live the "high life" as he ostensibly has been doing with the Jew: "Thou shalt not gurmandize, / As thou has done with me . . . / And sleep and snore, and rend apparel out" (2.5.3–5). Via dyslexic malapropism, Gobbo invokes the topos of the stingy master: "I am famish'd in his service; you may tell every finger I have with my ribs" (2.2.106–7). The binary of the starving/gluttonous *zanni* and his master is structured between the poles of scarcity and plenty, and animates the very core of the *Arte*. In the "non-Euclidean" phantasmagoria of popular culture, the immoderate gluttony of the *zanni* functions as the photographic negative of his starvation. The trope of exaggeration, as we shall also see in the Cuccagna texts, both distorts and reveals.

If the starving and gluttonous *zanni* does not figure center stage in "golden age" commedia publications such as Flaminio Scala's scenario collection, piazza pamphlets antedating Scala amply represent the "archaic" *zanni*, still tied to his rural Bergamask roots, the hardships of travel, and the elemental agon of survival with his stingy and verbally abusive urban master. Three works of cheap print bound together as Miscellanea 2223 in the Biblioteca Nazionale Marciana of Venice nicely feature the *zanni*-Pantalone *contrasto* and show in particularly clear ways the organic relationship between gluttony and hunger.[36] All published in the same year (1576) and by the same press (unnamed, but with the same typographic mark of a clover leaf on the frontispiece), the works appear to be related to a common set of performance conditions, featuring one particular Pantalone piazza actor and one particular *zanni*. The titles declare that the works were either composed by or for (the language is ambiguous) two recognized piazza performers of the day: Fortunato, a master or Pantalone figure, mentioned by Tommaso Garzoni in the 1585 *Piazza universale*; and Zanni Bagotta, a *zanni* whose name appears in other popular pamphlets.[37] Fortunato is mentioned in the first pamphlet and Zan Bagotta in the second and third; in all three pamphlets, there is a mixture of *lingua Veneziana,* the idiom of Pantalone, and *lingua Bergamasca,* the language of the *zanni.*

In the second of the three pamphlets grouped as Miscellanea 2223[38] is the "Dialogo del Patrone e del Zane." The poem, filled with multiple internal rhymes created as often by nonsensical homonyms as by sense (e.g., "mio caro ninato bufato"), provides a paradigmatic example of the encounter between Pantalone and Zanni and demonstrates the close connection between gluttony and famine. Zanni's importunate supplications for food meet the firewall of Pantalone's perception (parallel to the new official critiques of the poor as spongers and moochers) of Zanni as a rapacious glutton threatening his hard-won capital. To Zanni's "Mi voref . . . che non fosseu avaro, in darme da magnar" (I wish that you were not so stingy in giving me food), Pantalone responds as the responsible capitalist: "Zane mio tu sei si ingordo ninordo balordo con convien far il sordo, se non me voi rovinar" (4r; My *zanni,* you are so greedy and silly and stupid that I must be deaf to your begging, unless I want to ruin myself). Pantalone goes on to claim that he couldn't feed the gluttonous *zanni* if he had enough food for an entire city. To his avaricious master, Zanni comes back: "Designeme la mia pitanza ninanza a bastanza chem porsi impi la panza" (4r; Give me my pittance, enough that I can fill up my stomach). Pantalone's repeated denials, homologous to the more stringent poor laws, elicit from Zanni a rhyming gastronomic litany: "Ogni past un polastrel, un agnel, ò un vedel e un baril de moscatel . . . e un ster de macaro" (4r; For every meal a hen, a lamb, some veal, and a bottle of muscatel . . . and a plate of macaroni). The paratactic enunciation of foods, so common to *zanni* discourse, achieves a kind of virtual, compensatory power: a magical nominalism that has to make up for the material scarcity reaffirmed by Pantalone, under penalty of being whipped with his *bastone.*

A poem connected to Zan Bagotta from the first pamphlet in Miscellanea 2223 places the *zanni*'s gluttony in the context of a mass famine.[39] Much of the mock-heroic poem celebrates the heroic *deeds* of the *zanni* at table, where, gifted with powerful jaws, strong teeth, and an iron stomach, he can consume astounding quantities of food and drink.

Ho pur da render gratie a la natura
Che mi ha fat si valente magiador[.]

No ghe, nog fu, ne sara creatura
Che habi budel che fia dol me mazor
Ganas si larghi, e bona dentatura
Che mena zo a frachas con tal furor. (2v)

> I must give thanks to nature for making me such a valiant eater. There never was, is, or will be a creature who has such large guts, such powerful jaws, and such a good set of teeth that chomp down with such great fury.

This paean to the feats of the table is conventional enough (though given particular poetic energy in this collection), but it acquires more pointed social resonance in the following stanza:

L'an me recordi de la carestia
Che nos podiva avi pa per daner
Un di me imbat che andam per la via,
A incontram ol famei del nos former
Cargat da pa che eu zur la fede mia
Che crez che ie era plu, de do bei ster
Ge mangi tut ol pa perque ol bravava
E manivi ach alu sel no scapava. (3r)

> I remember in the year of the famine when bread was like money. One day it fell out that I was walking on the road and I ran into the servant of our local baker loaded up with bread, I swear. Who do you think was the stronger of the two? I ate all of the bread, and made such a scene that I would also have eaten him up if he hadn't escaped.

If cannibalism, which Piero Camporesi sees as a leitmotif in the popular literature of starvation, is rhetorically invoked rather than physically realized here, violence runs through the poem, unfortunately directed more against fellow proletarians than against the wealthy. The omnivorous *zanni* terrifies all who behold his gigantic jaws and hear the deafening sounds of his gastronomic conquests: "Tut quel ches ved in mi da gran segnal / che sia 'l prim mangiador de tut ol mond" (3r; Everything about me shows that I am the primal eater in the world). But occasionally the cannibalistic fantasy is realized: in another poem, a sequence narrating the rise and fall of Zan Falopa da Bufeto's amorous fortunes ends with a commemorative sonnet, after his death from a broken heart, reaffirming the life force of this gastronomic appetite in the strongest possible terms. Speaking from the grave, he boasts that he will eat the earth, the walls, the stage, the charlatans—and everyone in the piazza listening to him.[40] In the Zan Bagotta poem, when the *zanni* encounters a peddler carrying a load of meat, he orders the peddler to stop. The terrified peddler races away, "pensat de scapula la furia mia" (3r; thinking that he'd escape my fury). But chasing him down, the *zanni* devours, in the "bat of an eye," the bread, the meat, the fish—and, in this case, the peddler as well.

The first piece in the third pamphlet in this collection, the "Insonio" of Zan Bagotto, follows the "dream vision" motif pursued by the early sixteenth-century *buffone* Zuan Polo and others, in what appears to be a parodic rendering of Dante's *Inferno*. There, in the cruel logic that blames the poor for their own fate, gluttony and famine are related as a zero-sum game. In the fantastic time of grotesque culture ("Nel hora che'l ventru commanda a i pet" [1v; In the hour when the stomach makes us fart]), the *zanni* dreams that a devil hovers over him and summons him to hell:

> Leva sus, ò poltronaz
> trist, lecard, ingord, e mangiador,
> e ven con mi, se non ti rompo i braz
> Innanzi al tribunal nel nos Segnur
> Re del Inferno addomandat Plutu. (1v)

> Get up, you lazybones, pathetic, ass-kisser, fatso, glutton and come away with me, unless you want me to break your arms before the tribunale of our Lord. The King of Hell is calling for you.

Replicating the self-loathing of the anti-*villano* poem, the abuse and blame are all turned upon the *zanni* himself (rather than the hoarders and usurers). In a Dantesque world in which everyone is "paid according to [his] work" (1v; pagat secondo el to lavor), the *zanni* has to empty out all the shit of hell: "tu vod tug quanti canter de chiga" (2v). The charge against the *zanni*, preposterously, is that his gluttony has been the sole cause of the famine: "che da ti sol ol nas la carestia / com hom che mangia senza discretio" (1v; the famine was born from you alone: a man who eats without discretion). The *zanni* therefore functions rather like a scapegoat, onto whom the greed of the hoarders is displaced.

These particular gluttony texts are cognate with Cuccagna literature:

in one of the "Fortunato" pamphlet poems on the "Magnar del Zane," the city is carnivalized, rendered as so many pieces of food: "Se le città fus pezze de formai, / e le vile castei fus macharò / noi basteria per impirme ol ventro" (Marciana Misc. 2223.1.4v; If the city were pieces of cheese and the [vile] castles were macaroni, it would be enough to fill our stomachs). Just as tropes of gluttony spring forth as reverse distortions of hunger, so the delectable laziness of the Cuccagna poems, in the popular poetics of reversal, plays the unrelenting, crippling labor that we have seen in the *villani* poems in a negative key. Not only is the new capitalist unable to extract surplus labor from the peasant, but the latter is paid for sleeping and imprisoned for working. Nor is exchange value abstractly extracted from labor-produced commodies; there is no commerce or exchange of any kind: the earth easily yields its fruit into one's hand.[41] As with the gluttony poems, the magical, incantatory naming of foods (whether they are being banished in "Death of Carnival" poems or celebrated in Cuccagna), provides a compensatory pleasure for audiences who have known scarcity much more often than excess.[42]

Travel itself, which was such a perilous affair in the *zanni* poems discussed above, is suddenly effortless: one can go where one pleases, and the inn—frequently a place of surveillance and violence—is rendered as a carnivalesque paradise, as in *Il piacevole viaggio di Cuccagna*:

> Larga è la strada, e molti troverai
> Che s'aggiran per essa volentieri,
> E senza piu temer d'affanni e guai
> Lassan gir hoggi 'l Mondo come hieri,
> Tanto che al hosteria tu giongerai
> De i Spensierati, dove a i forestieri
> Si fa grata acccoglienza col Boccale[.] (IV)

> Wide is the road, and you will find many who travel there gladly, without fearing trouble and woe, letting the world go on today as it did yesterday, so that at the inn you'll find carefree folk, where foreigners greet you with a jug.[43]

With the conspicuous enjoyment of foreigners at the inn—a group that would have been under particularly close surveillance, the poem provides a resolutely topsy-turvy vision. But as with tropes of gluttony, we can only understand the social resonance of the poem by figuring in the aesthetics of distortion.

Whether they put poverty front and center or refract it through the various tropes of distortion, the songs that we have examined in this chapter provide a palpable link between poverty and performance, staging destitution in the anarchical, centrifugal Italian piazza that, if less rational than Jürgen Habermas' coffeehouse, still functioned as a public sphere. This theatrical arena reveals how poverty was actually experienced on the ground—and how others may have responded to it.

4 Ruzante
Necessity and Invention

Poet of Hunger

No early modern playwright addressed the problem of poverty and hunger in such direct, sustained, and complex ways as did the Paduan Angelo Beolco, known as Ruzante (b. 1496–1502, d. 1542). In a series of astonishing plays written in the crucial decade of the 1520s, in the very years of a catastrophic famine in the Veneto and a series of new municipal laws designed to discipline the widespread practice of begging, Ruzante's actor-centered, visceral, and embodied theater stages the agon between the raw, material reality of poverty and a series of desperate but inventive responses to it: tragicomic gags stabbing at hunger.[1] Like Shakespeare's *As You Like It* and *King Lear*, written in the aftermath of the 1590s Midlands famine and the turn-of-the-century English poor laws, these works of Ruzante stage the "play" between official policy and actual practice, between authoritarian discourse and lived attitude.

On the one hand, Ruzante keenly represents the ways in which extreme poverty subjects human beings to the laws of force and necessity, as analyzed by Hannah Arendt in *On Revolution*: "Poverty is more than deprivation, it is a state of constant want and acute misery whose ignominy consists in its dehumanizing force; poverty is abject because it puts men under the absolute dictate of their bodies, that is, under the absolute dictate of necessity."[2] In plays from *La pastoral* (1520?) to *Moscheta* (1529), external biological, economic, and social constraints inexorably press upon the deracinated peasants—the abject heroes of Ruzante's plays. A brilliant poet of material force, Ruzante finds apt metaphors to evoke such constraint working upon the body, ranging from farming (e.g., the pull of oxen) to metallurgy (e.g., hammers striking anvils). Not unlike Homeric characters under the weight of force and the necessity of war, as analyzed in Simone Weil's brilliant essay "The Iliad, or the Poem of Force,"[3] the souls of Ruzante's characters become things.

On the other hand, in agonistic struggle with necessity, Ruzante's protagonists demonstrate an inexhaustible capacity for invention and autopoesis. The very constraint that forces Ruzante's peasants from country to city is offset, as if according to a hidden law, by the inventive mobility of Ruzante's little heroes. The fictionalizing, distorting, sometimes hallucinogenic imagination that we have seen at play in the piazza pamphlets is here brought to bear in plot-driven, dramatic situations, against obdurate antagonists. Such mortal tension between constraint and invention sometimes strains the limits of dramatic form, allowing the centrifugal energies of the stand-up performer more license than can be disciplined by dramatic form. But given the sheer richness of the performing body that emerges through Ruzante's dramatic text, this is no loss. The "fictions of poverty" improvised by Ruzante's desperate protagonists function like the lying truths of Poor Tom and the distortions of the carnivalesque piazza pamphlets, fleshing out the formulaic exaggerations of the beggar catalogues with painful existential truth.

As with Spanish picaresque novels such as *Lazarillo de Tormes*, at the heart of these works from the 1520s lies *hunger*—alternatively obstacle and engine of plot invention, as it would be for the starving but resourceful *zanni* of the professional Italian theater that emerged just after Ruzante's death. According to Mario Baratto, "il pane" becomes the "primitive and concrete symbol of their [the peasants'] union through the continuity of the seasons."[4] In a kind of "gastronomic humanism," bread (and especially the lack of it) becomes a powerful transregional and transnational bond. In the one-act play *Parlamento*, the protagonist "Ruzante" speaks to his kinsman Menato of his travel to Agnadello and other "distant" places in wartime, asserting com-*pan*-ionship, etymologically speaking, with peasants there despite cultural differences such as their "slurred speech." Claiming the need to eat to be a fundamental ground of human identity and thus productive of a "poor theater" that can translate well across national boundaries, Ruzante asserts that the Agnadello peasants are "uomeni de carne, com a' seóm nu" (flesh-and-blood men, just like us), who "make bread like we do, and they eat like what we do, too" (2.48; e sí fa pan com a' fazóm, e sí magna com a' fazóm nu).[5] Ruzante's first play, *La pastoral*, carries the temporal structure of a deferred and finally consummated meal, since it begins with the character "Ruzante" complaining of his agonizing hunger and ends with him devouring the meat sacrificed for the god Pan (heard by the peasant Ruzante as "Pane"). For Giorgio Padoan, the hunger, or "mal de la loa" (evil of the wolf) invoked in Ruzante's work is no longer a mythic trait of the folkloric peasant but a phenomenon of real social life.[6]

If great works of art are "many people deep," the peculiar brilliance of Ruzante's work may well result from his capacity to straddle and absorb socio-economic worlds that were normally sharply delineated. A combination of necessity and natural invention probably formed Ruzante's ability to negotiate different settings, for he seems to have been both insider and outsider in the three worlds that he inhabited: aristocratic, agricultural, and university.

Owing to land purchases dating back to his grandfather, Beolco had access to his family's considerable holdings in the country, where he gained a rich appreciation of the countryside and enjoyed living in the fine Paduan house purchased by his successful father. However, because he was illegitimate—probably the son of a family maid whose father was an "operarius"[7]—he inherited only a small sum. Because of his grandfather's connections with the early Venetian printing industry and the University of Padua, as well as his father's prestigious position as dean of the Faculty of Medicine and Arts at the university, Beolco had strong ties there, taking classes and probably using the university as the initial venue for *La pastoral* and other early dramatic ventures, but he was never able to take a degree—also probably because of his illegitimacy. Thanks to the patronage of Alvise Cornaro, Ruzante gained access to a vital center of culture, art, and power in the Veneto; Cornaro himself, however, felt marginalized and excluded from the inner circles of the Venetian patriciate.[8] Ruzante also performed in Venice with the Compagnie della Calza, groups of young Venetian patricians given to *momarie* and other kinds of festive entertainments, but along with Cornaro himself Ruzante must have often felt shut out from the real centers of Venetian power.

As an intimate member of Cornaro's privileged circle, as well as Cornaro's paid intermediary (*nuntius*) with the Paduan peasants, Ruzante lived comfortably, representing his employer in collecting taxes, fines, and supervising the peasants. At the same time (and this is perhaps why he was hired by Cornaro to mediate between the court and the country), Ruzante was thoroughly acquainted with the life of the countryside; and his work for Cornaro only deepened his understanding of peasants and evident sympathy for their plight in times of crisis such as the 1527–29 famine. Benefiting from his family's extensive landholdings—he is reputed to have written several of his works in the Paduan village of Pernumia[9]—Ruzante makes frequent and extremely specific references to birds, flowers, plants, farming procedures, and the like in his plays. Several early plays, such as *La pastoral*, *Betía*, and *Dialogo facetissimo* were set in the countryside, and signature plays such as *Parlamento*, *Bilora*, and *Moscheta* represent peasants forcibly displaced to the city, represented both through literary prisms and with what impresses us as the "reality effect," to no small degree evoked by his use of the Paduan dialect. Ruzante's choice of the pastoral genre for his first play, *La pastoral*—unusual when compared to the generic panorama of contemporary playwrights Ariosto, Machiavelli, and Aretino—allowed him to contrast the mode of literary pastoral absorbed from Sannazaro and the Venetian aristocrat-turned-actor Francesco de' Nobili with the lives of real country dwellers.[10]

Ruzante's dramatic representation of peasants, as performed before the elitist circle of Paduan courtiers and patricians and in various Venetian venues, poses complex and interesting questions. From university, amateur theatrical, and literary milieux Ruzante knew and absorbed traditional anti-*villano* satire, and the peasant is often the object of mirth and mockery in his plays. We must remember that his primary audience was Cornaro's aristocratic circle, even though the plays were performed in other venues as well. Still, just as Ruzante transformed every popular genre that he touched—the *bulesca* (based on street toughs and prostitutes), the *mariazo* (wedding celebration interrupted by lower-class strife), the *buffonesca* (based on comic buffoonery)—he clearly rewrote the *villanesca* (the theatrical representation of peasants [*villani*]) toward a more complex and often sympathetic treatment of its protagonists.[11] For one thing, Ruzante possessed a natural skill for impersonation, or *contraffare*. This skill for mimicry, shared by the great Venetian *buffoni* Zuan Polo Liompardi and Domenico Taiacalze, with whom he worked, may have linked him physically and emotionally with his subjects. The contemporary testimony of Bernardino Scardeone, a Paduan chronicler and author of *De antiquitate urbis Patavii*, that Beolco used to mix with peasants from the countryside outside of Padua, imitating their speech and even exchanging clothes with them,[12] bespeaks the extraordinary facility for mimicry that he brought to his famous character of the peasant, or *villano maschera*, "Ruzante." According to the contemporary Venetian chronicler Manin Sanudo, it was the creation of this role that distinguished him in his first recorded performance in 1520 with the Immortali, one of the Compagnie della Calza.[13]

Appointed Cornaro's delegate to "riscuotere crediti e fitti dei contadini" (collect debts and rents from peasants),[14] Beolco was in an ambiguous position: he was obliged to enforce official policy and defend the grand land-reclamation projects of Cornaro but also witnessed, at close hand, the desperate circumstances of Paduan peasants, compelled by market forces like so many other small farmers throughout Europe to sell their land. One such peasant, Michele Polato from the village of Codevigo, was described in a notarial document dated June 15, 1529:

> [V]olens sibi succurrere in tanta penuria victus ne fame pereat, cum iam duobus mensibus publice mendicare sit coactus, prout aput omnes de eo notitiam habentes notissimum est, et non habens alim modum sibi facciendi et substentandi pauperam vitam nisi per venditionem.

> Vanquished by such great need, and wanting to help himself so that he would not die from hunger, and having already for two months been driven to beg publicly, as was known by everyone aware of recent events, and not having other means of making and sustaining his poor life except by selling his land.[15]

The best evidence that Ruzante would have been capable of great sympathy for the plight of peasants such as Michele Polato comes from the plays themselves. As a man of the theater, Ruzante was certainly not above exploiting the pleasure deriving from anti-*villano* satire in times of comfort, but in periods of crisis and famine, especially in the years 1527–29, his allegiances seem clear enough.

La pastoral

Ruzante incorporated his capacity to impersonate peasants, as described by Scardeone, in the signature role of "Ruzante" that he took on as an actor in his first play, *La pastoral*, and sustained through much of his career. We cannot recover much in the way of specific details of his ongoing performance in this role, but it is worth remarking that impersonating a peasant required Ruzante to understand his subjects in specifically corporeal, gestural, kinesthetic, and emotional ways. The genre of pastoral is a telling choice for his first play, which may have emerged from amateur theatrical circles at the University of Padua, where he had attended classes. Even more than comedy, the genre of pastoral was extremely fluid and negotiable in the early sixteenth century. Whether approaching literary tragedy in style and *gravitas*, as in Poliziano's late Quattrocento *Orfeo*, or being a capacious instrument for mythological devices of a rough and popular strain,[16] pastoral drama in the late fifteenth and early sixteenth centuries had not yet achieved the literary codification that would be forged in the Estense court of Ferrara between the 1550s and 1580s, from Agostino Beccari's *Il sacrificio* to Battista Guarini's *Il pastor fido*. Although the idea of pastoral, from Vergil if not Theocritus on, proposes the possibility of a unifying relationship between the country and the city or court, versions of pastoral most congenial to our own modernist and post-structuralist tastes tend to render this relationship complex and vexed. If for William Empson pastoral "puts the complex into the simple," reconciling the complex court with the presumably simple representative pastoral figure becomes, in the hands of complex writers, a vexed but generative poetic undertaking.

What Ruzante stages in *La pastoral*, written between 1517 and 1521, is the incommensurability of the courtly/literary pastoral genre and the radically materialist world of the peasant. The "Proemio alla villana" (Peasant Prologue) begins with a gag, recycled in later plays, that nicely stages the counterpoint between material reality and (often desperate) invention that we have proposed as a formative principle in Ruzante's work. The peasant Ruzante, hunting for his starving family, is loaded down with bird traps and complains that he has just sprained his foot in the thick brush. Additionally frustrated that no birds are in sight, he decides to go to sleep. Upon waking he wonders if he is really alive, if he hasn't died instead—suggesting the fragility of existence itself for Ruzante's emaciated peasants. Then follows a brilliant, poor man's version of Descartes's methodical refutation of skepticism, *avant le mot*. The first sign that he might be alive rather than dead is his latest injury, his sprained foot. Next, he recognizes his overcoat and two objects of everyday life: his red cap and a piece of bread. Coming to his own body, he pulls his hair and squeezes his hand. Finally, he arrives at the ground zero of human existence—bread:

> Questi è pur i miè cavigi;
> a' m'i toco pure.
> Pota, a' aén pur dure
> le mie man.
> A' vuò pur tuor fora el pan,
> ch'a' verò
> s'a' magnerò.
> [*Riprende il pane e si prova a mangialo, stupito perciò di essere vivo.*]
> Pota de San Ragno
> mo a' magno.
> An, a' me ho insuniò.
> ("Proemio alla villano," 26–32)

> This is really my hair; I can even touch it. Damn, I still have my good, solid hands. I'm going to take out the bread and see if I can eat. (*He takes the bread out and starts to eat it, amazed that he is still alive.*) Well I'll be damned, I can still eat. So I must have been dreaming.

As in almost all of the plays written in the 1520s, these kinds of virtuosic one-man performances lie at the heart of Ruzante's dramaturgy, coexisting with dramatic structures of plot and character.

The first, Tuscan half of the play absorbs strains of recent literary pastorals such as *L'Orfeo* and Sannazaro's *Arcadia,* basing its plot on lovelorn shepherds and nymphs. When an older shepherd, Milesio, commits suicide out of love grief, a younger shepherd (Mopso) faints at the sight of the dead body. What shifts the play out of a monologically pastoral world is the very material reality of burial. Taking both Milesio and Mopso for dead, the shepherd Arpino seeks help in burying Mopso from none other than Ruzante. But Arpino interrupts the desperate and famished peasant just as he is trying to shoot birds in order to feed his impoverished family—which includes a sister whose husband has been killed by German soldiers. With his intended prey scared off by Arpino's voice, the starving Ruzante furiously demands reparations: "[O] pota, c'a'no digo, di San Loro! / A' me smaravegiava infin damò / che te no me daïssi un po' di sboro" (11.10–12; O damn, by Saint Loro! It would be wonderful if you could give me a bit of compensation). Ruzante, here and in every scene, is beset by the terrible "hunger of the wolf" (*mal de la loa*).

The encounter between literary courtliness and crass materialism is comparable to the witty dialogue between Touchstone and Corin in Shakespeare's *As You Like It*, except that the worlds of Arpino and Ruzante are so incongruous as to render any real communication impossible. The scene turns on sharp misunderstandings, as in the following exchange between Arpino and Ruzante:

> Arpino: O sacro Pan, pietà d'i servi toi!
> Ruzante: Tu me vuò dar del pan? Mo su, anagún. (11.40–41)

> Arpino: O, sacred Pan, have pity on your servants!
> Ruzante: You want to give me some bread. Sure, go ahead.

The laughter at Ruzante's taking Arpino's "sacro Pan" as "pane," knowingly registered by the Paduan patriciate watching the play, pleasurably short-circuits the incommensurability of the two worlds and of literary pastoral and materialist comedy. Seeing Mopso's presumably dead body, Ruzante's mind immediately turns to the material reality of infectious disease, thinking that Mopso has died from the plague—a very real fear in the early sixteenth-century Veneto, on account of which the Sanità had recently been founded. Fearing contagion, and resuming his desperate search for food ("ch'a' vuò anare a magnare, / ch'a' muor da fame" [11.55–56; I've got to go eat; I'm dying of hunger]), Ruzante is lured back when Arpino offers him him bread, and the Arpino-Ruzante exchange becomes something like a begging scene, as elsewhere in Ruzante's work. His hunger momentarily stayed, Ruzante sees another opportunity for material exchange and asks if he can have Mopso's clothes after he is buried, including a fine *gabbana*—an important material commodity in an artisanal economy in which clothes would have been made by hand.[17] When Ruzante discovers that Mopso is not in fact dead, Arpino goes off to fetch a doctor, and Ruzante is left to reflect on his situation, disconsolately holding the second piece of bread that Arpino has given him:

A' sun pur stò el gran mato
a dirghe che 'l sia vio:
s'a' l'aessàm sepelío,
arave abú il gaban.
Mo a ogni muò a' he abú el pan;
Laga anare!
An, pota de me pare
co' a' l'abia magnò,
da lí a un puoco a' 'l cagherò
e sí n'arò fato niente.
(12.5–14)

I was a real idiot to tell him that he was alive. If they had buried him I could have had the overcoat. So I got some bread—big deal. As soon as I eat it, I shit it out, and I haven't gotten anything.

This is not exactly cannibalism, but Ruzante's cold-blooded yet entirely rational calculus—all I would have had to do to get the overcoat was to have buried an upper-class person alive—conjures up the cannibalistic fantasies belonging to popular literature. Consoling himself by voraciously eating his bread, he reflects, "L'è pur un gran impazo / sto magnare. / Ogni cossa se pò portare, / fora la fame" (12.35–38; This eating business is a big drag. I can put up with everything else except hunger). Then, demonstrating the very same relationship between the tropes of gluttony and hunger that we have seen in the piazza literature, Ruzante finds his lost purse and with the money inside gorges himself at the local tavern, bragging, "Non c'è boaro / che magne pí di me" (19.31–32; No cow eats more than I do). The arrival of the "Medico"—strikingly similar to a piazza charlatan—introduces an extended gag of comic, cross-dialectal misunderstandings between the Bergamask-speaking Medico and the Paduan dialect of Ruzante, in the course of which Ruzante manages to extract from the Medico a nefarious "remedy" for his ailing father, whom Ruzante has earlier cursed for making continual demands on him and keeping him from his beloved Betía. In the final scene of the play, Ruzante joyously returns with a present of ricotta cheese for the Medico, thanking him for the success of the remedy that has, in fact, killed his father off, enabling Ruzante to possess his father's animals and fields. The dimly concealed patricide—one would be hard-pressed to find another in Italian early modern pastoral drama, is smoothed over by the final sacrifice and feast to the doubly-valenced "Pan."

La Betía

La Betía is Ruzante's baggy monster, a wild, sprawling gallimaufry that, at various points, incorporates *villanesca, contrasti, mariazo,* mock widow's lament, *giullare* monologues, *buffonesca, bulesca,* song and dance, and rich folkloric motifs from the Veneto.[18] As with many of Ruzante's plays, none of which were published in his lifetime, dating poses challenges. Some scholars, such as Linda Carroll, have argued for an initial draft from the period of 1517–18, with several references to recent wars and people who had recently died.[19] Lovarini and Zorzi argue that the reference to "l'ano da la fame" (the year of the famine) points to the famine of 1522[20]—an allusion, to be sure, that could have been layered into an earlier draft. Ronnie Ferguson argues that this and other references to food shortages are "not severe enough to be the great famine of 1528–29 . . . possibly referring to the shortages of 1522."[21] As an almost certainly early play, with food shortages part of the Venetian landscape but probably not yet at crisis levels, *La Betía* introduces motifs that will be explored in more depth in later plays. Structurally, this sprawling play rather absorbs other forms without developing a properly dramatic form itself.

A simple plot loosely ties the play together. After an extended, pastoral-style *contrasto* debating the nature of love between sharply differing perspectives, Nale convinces his disconsolate—and poor—friend Zilio to try his amorous chances with Betía, with the ulterior aim of a ménage à trois that will gain Nale himself access to her (Nale's marriage to Tamia hardly rules this scenario out for him). With Zilio's initial wooing of Betía less than successful, Nale must convince Betía to proceed with him, with the understanding that Betía will secure his own services as well as Zilio's if she consents. A planned elopement goes awry, first from Betía's hesitations and then when her mother, Dona Menega, discovers the plan. Conflict ensues between Zilio's armed friends and Dona Menega's, only resolved by the innkeeper, Taçio, who then presides over the *mariazo* wedding. Nale continually provokes Zilio with open declarations to Betía that their marriage will merely provide him a sexual cover. Zilio finally erupts in rage, knifing Nale so as apparently to have killed him. Nale's wife, Tamia, engages in an extended peasant-style wife's lament, but Nale, who is still alive, then pretends to be a ghost and tells his wife tales and visions from the afterlife. But when Tamia, thinking her husband is dead, promptly runs off to marry her lover Meneghelo, Nale quickly abandons his plan and declares himself alive to Tamia. The entire play ends with a kind of reconciliation among all parties, but with the promise of a ménage à quatre including Betía, Zilio, Nale, Tamia, and possibly also Meneghelo—a kind of sexual communism.

The basic conditions of *La Betía* aptly reflect the impoverished and constrained existence of the kinds of Paduan peasants supervised by Ruzante. Peasant society is sharply hierarchical, depending on the holy grail of land possession. The wealthy peasant and petty capitalist Barba Scati, who owns extensive landholdings and farm products, dominates landless peasants such as the day laborer Bazarelo, who asserts that love is only possible with a substructure of material sufficiency. The gluttonous pleasure that the poor peasants have enjoyed at Barba Scati's great feasts, which almost split their stomachs open (1.133–34), merely represents the tantalizing counterpoint to the hunger that torments them on a daily basis. The prodigious teeth and jaws that Dona Menega proudly attributes to her daughter Betía at the wedding ceremony, worthy of a commedia dell'arte *zanni*, derive from a culture in which good eating amounts to nothing less than survival: "Oh, la par pur bon a menare / le massele e i dente!" (5.265–66; Oh, she is very good at moving her jaws and her teeth). Although, notwithstanding Bazarelo's example, it may be possible for Zilio to love and be poor at the same time, his indigence does not argue his advantage in love, not to Betía herself and not to her mother Dona Menega, who voices her concerns about the impending marriage in a public speech to her daughter:

> . . . int'ogne muò
> te sganghiré da fame.
> Ché a' sè che l'ano da la fame
> sto to marío andasea a Pava,
> per tuor una scuela de fava
> in Vescoò o a Santo Urban,
> e mezo un pan.

Pènsate mo com l'andasea;
che a' no sè com el vivea
da tanta povertè.
Orsú, te 'l proverè.
(4.493–503)

At any rate, you are going to die of hunger. I know that during the year of the famine this husband of yours went to Padua in order to get a bowl of beans and some bread at Vescovado or Saint Urban. Just think how that was for him, when he couldn't figure out how to manage because he was so poor. Now then! This is just what is going to happen to you.

The specter of the peasant Zilio being forced to trek into the city for church-sponsored public assistance is not a point in his favor for the concerned potential mother-in-law. For her, and presumably for Betía as well, who frequently voices concern about Zilio's poverty, it is a mark of shame rather than an invitation to compassion. As is the case in the next four plays we will examine, all written in the context of the great famine of 1527–29, economic destitution quickly becomes aligned with sexual impotence in the world of Ruzante.

Dialogo facetissimo

The first, 1554 edition of Ruzante's *Dialogo facetissimo* explicitly connects the play to the terrible Venetian famine of 1527–29: the title page reads "Dialogo Facetissimo et Ridiculosissimo di Ruzzante / Recitato à Fosson alla caccia, / l'anno della carestia. / 1528 (Witty and Ridiculous Dialogue of Ruzante / Performed at Fosson during a hunt, in the year of the famine). "Fosson" refers to Ruzante's patron Alvise Cornaro's property on the border between Venetian and Ferraran lands, where Cornaro owned a hunting lodge. This *villanesca* play was thus written for Cornaro's elite circle of intimates for an occasion of recreation, but the short play was also apparently designed to transform aristocratic mirth at their peasant inferiors to sympathy for their plight in a period of extreme suffering. In fact, it might be possible to view the entire play as a vehicle of charity, a plea by a courtier (Ruzante) with close links with peasants to treat them with compassion and largesse beyond that mandated by official policies.

Further tying the play to occasion, *Dialogo facetissimo* begins with the starving peasant Menego (almost certainly played by Ruzante) literally counting the months until the next harvest, re-creating in the monotonous reiteration of the months a sense of "hunger time" for those without food: "Zenaro, fevraro, marzo, avrile, mazo, e an mezzo zugno al fromento. *Sospira.* Poh, a' no gh'a' riverón mé! Cancaro, mo l'è el longo ano, questo. A' sè che 'l pan muza da nu, mi, mo sí, pí che no fè mé le çéleghe dal falchetto" (1.1; January, February, March, April, May, and even half of June until harvest. *Sighs.* Damn, this year has been a long one. It looks like bread is escaping us just like sparrows flying from falcons). As Ronnie Ferguson argues, the play was probably actually performed in January of 1529 and written shortly before that,[22] and so Menego's iteration of the months would have further linked the audience to the situation of the peasants, desperately trying to survive until the next harvest.

For Menego's peasant companion Duozo (probably played by Ruzante's patrician friend Marco Aurelio Alvarotto) hunger is a real material force, squeezing or pinching him ("strenzere") like a wedge (1.2). To the obdurate reality of hunger, Menego invokes a series of fantastic "solutions" for their hunger, desperate inventions laughing in the dark. The peasants, Menego observes, have taken to eating "rape" (turnips) of the kind usually fed to the animals, but their laxative effect renders this counterproductive, emptying their bowels and making them all the more hungry. Eating a diet of sorb apples (later herbs and flowers), as Duozo proposes, would painfully pinch the stomach. Then, as a kind of perverse appropriation of the Venetians' grain hoarding, Menego suggests tightening up the anus in order to buckle the food within his body, so that "le buele starae pine, e sí no vegnerae pí tanta fame" (1.5; the bowels will stay full, and there won't be any more hunger). Duozo's objection that such a desperate measure will not be very healthy prompts Menego's next fantastic proposal, namely, to become sick, so that one will not have to eat, to which Duozo objects that dying is not an optimal way of defeating hunger. As foil to his desperate comrade, Duozo recites a series of anodyne proverbs, such as "l'ano fa con quelo che l'ha" (1.9; the year produces what there is), of the kind that characterize the quietistic, orthodox point of view that endorses the "natural" order of things. In this particular dramatic context, the proverbs are meant to feel banal and sharply out of place given the urgent nature of the famine. Menego objects that in fact the natural order of things might be enough to guarantee enough food for everyone, except for pernicious human intervention that stacks the odds in favor of those with capital: "El provierbio è ben vero . . . [m]o gi usulari el fa falare, perché i no vò vendere né dar fuora la biava. . . . [G]i è pí bramusi de sangue de poveriti, che no è cavala magra de erba nuova" (1.9; The proverb is true . . . except that the usurers mess it up because they are not willing to sell or give away the harvest. . . . They are hungrier for the blood of the poor than are horses for new grass). Here, the "usurers" are pointedly the Venetian authorities who hoarded grain harvested from the Paduan countryside for their own citizens, at the expense of peasants such as Menego and Duozo. Because such practices were also clearly disadvantageous to people like Cornaro who supervised Paduan farms, we can understand the particular alignments of allegiance that Ruzante constructs in this play: the peasants and their Paduan masters on one side, the Venetian centers of power from whom Cornaro felt excluded on the other. In this and the other Ruzante famine plays, therefore, anti-Venetian sentiment can be nicely wedded with traditional compassion and charity for the poor and hungry. The quasi-hallucinogenic quality of Menego's fantasies is displaced onto the impoverished peasants themselves, whom Duozo compares to mad and rabid dogs "amazè per bel comun" (1.10; killed for the common good)—for the common good of the hoarders, that is to say. Then Menego expresses his fear that they will become so thin that they will be like smoked meat, hung up to dry (1.13). In general, although we should not underestimate the period's capacity to laugh at social inferiors, the sympathy elicited for the peasants in *Dialogo facetissimo* casts their fantastic schemes as not merely ridiculous and pathetic but as inventions of necessity not devoid of a certain strain of courage.

As in *La Betía*, *Parlamento*, and *Bilora*, male poverty is explicitly linked with sexual performance. Declares Menego, "[A]' giera squase tolto zó, mi, per ste carestie, intendíu, compare? Menar femene a ca' con sta valúa de pan, l'è el cancaro: l'omo che magna puoco no pò . . . intendíu con a' dighe, compare?" (1.19; I've been just about knocked down by this famine—do you understand what I mean, comrade? To have a woman in the house with this little bread, it's the worst: a man who doesn't eat enough cannot . . . do you understand what I'm talking about, comrade?). The bravado displayed by Menego (which seems to be a standard aspect of the "Ruzante" stage persona) inevitably leads to its quick deflation, as Nale, Menego's rival for Gnua's affections, arrives and beats him to a pulp. When Duozo comes onto the scene to assist his wounded friend, Menego plays what might be called the "*lazzo* of a hundred," as replayed later in *Parlamento*: the crazed fantasy that, since he is so valiant and has suffered so many wounds, he must have been assaulted by not one but a hundred men. Absurdly fearing that he is going to die (he has merely injured his hand), Menego has Duozo run off to fetch a figure who will also appear, as a positive agent of transformation, in the pastoral world of Shakespeare's *As You Like It*: a hermit-magician, "uno a muò omo salbego" (a kind of savage man) who serves as a priest of Diana.

Upon Duozo's departure, Menego-Ruzante performs one of the great monologues in the corpus, an extended meditation on suicide anticipatory of the famous suicide gag of the Italo-French Harlequin Domenico Biancolelli. Despairing that his "crippled" hand will not allow him to perform farm labor, the next alternative after dispossession from agriculture—wage work—seems equally impossible to him: "Chi me vorà mé pí a vuòvera?" (5.76; Who will want me for day labor?). It would therefore be better for him to kill himself, since he is going to die of hunger anyway. The ensuing stage psychomachia, a comic version of "To be or not to be," explores the alternatives of the materially destitute. On the side of not killing himself is the prospect of surviving as a beggar, since with a crippled hand he would not even have to devise the simulated wounds described in the *Liber vagatorum* in order to be perceived as a legitimate recipient of charity. On the side of suicide is the prospect of revenge on his rival Nale, since the latter would then be prosecuted as a murderer. Having resolved to kill himself, he first laments the lack of a suitable instrument, but then decides that he can eat himself and at least die having finally been well fed: "E sí sera an miegio, ché a' me magnerè da mia posta, e cossí a' morirè pur passú, e despeto de la calestia" (5.80; It would be better if I ate myself, because that way I could die well fed, despite the famine). Just before he prepares to commit the horrible act (at the very last moment he decides to strangle himself because auto-cannibalism would take too much effort), he confesses his sins, revealing that earlier in his life he had resorted to stealing in order to survive.

Duozo hurredly enters with the hermit-priest, who heals his hand in the manner of the pastoral *mago*, then grants the peasants a wish. They elect to speak with a deceased companion, who tells them of his present existence *outre-tombe*, describing two different kinds of paradise (the peasants vote decidedly in favor of the version that allows one to eat normally rather than fast). The play ends with the hermit-priest reconciling Menego with Gnua and Nale and promising the peasants that they need have no fear of the famine, owing to the help of the goddess Diana. Like the soothing frame endings of Citaredo's piazza songs that we examined in Chapter 3, the fideistic ending takes away the sting of famine, while not negating the plaint of hunger that had resonated before the ending. Like the one-act plays *Parlamento* and *Bilora*, this occasional play relies on the stand-up routine of the virtuosic solo performer. The energy generated by the one-man show cannot be contained by a plot-based dramatic resolution but rather is resolved by an arbitrary, outside force: a hermit-priest, or Diana.

Il parlamento

The 1529 *Il parlamento de Ruzante che iera vegnù de campo*, according to Ronnie Ferguson "the most effective demystification of war and heroism in Italian theatre,"[23] takes as its background the famine and the ensuing forced migration of peasants into Venice, with the additional evil of war compounding the problems of poverty and vagabondage. Fictionally (with the problems of 1529 layered in), the play is set in 1515, when the Venetian republic, with the help of loyal Paduan peasants, managed to recoup some of the considerable losses to the French king Louis XII they had suffered in the disastrous defeat of Agnadello in 1509. Peasants living in a ruined agricultural economy, like this play's protagonist, volunteered for the army less motivated by patriotism than by the need to earn wages.

As the play begins, the peasant Ruzante, who had fought for Venice but then deserted the army and lived by his wits for the last four months, slouches into St. Mark's Square, glad to be back but in desperate search for his wife Gnua, who in the meantime has had to move from Padua to Venice because of the famine. Penniless, homeless, emaciated, hungry, filthy, and lice-infested, he typifies the common plight of the former soldier, whether honorably or (like Ruzante) dishonorably discharged. In regard to charity, his status is provocatively ambiguous: as a former soldier, he would be considered a legitimate object of poor relief, but not if it were known that he was a deserter and hadn't done any real fighting. After a virtuosic opening monologue, Ruzante meets his "kinsman" Menato, who skeptically hears and interrogates the latter's tales of the front. As boasting *alazon* to Menato's sceptical *eiron*, Ruzante joins fecklessness and braggadocio—a comically incongruous blend that makes up the heart of the *maschera*. Ruzante's initial joy at seeing Gnua suddenly appear quickly diminishes when he learns that she has taken to prostitution under the protection of a Venetian *bravo*. As with the impoverished Menego in *Dialogo facetissimo*, Ruzante's failure in the economic sphere entails impotence in the sexual arena, as Gnua tries to make clear to him. But only the appearance of her *bravo*, who wordlessly beats Ruzante senseless, momentarily shuts him up. Alone again with Menato, Ruzante elaborates the "*lazzo* of a hundred" introduced in *Dialogo facetissimo* and also deployed in *La Moscheta*: he imagines in his delirium that he has been beaten up by not one but one hundred men.

Arriving in the piazza, Ruzante declares himself gladder to be back in the Veneto than a skinny, weak horse is to find new grass—thus projecting his destitution onto an animal, as Shakespeare does in a scene from *Henry IV, Part I* we shall examine later. Desperately happy to have escaped the guns and drums of war, he brags of the distances he has traveled since he deserted the army, only lamenting the price his precious (and stolen) shoes have had to pay. Reiterating a gag that we have seen deployed, with greater elaboration, in the prologue of *La pastoral* (and typical of the "hallucinogenic" tropes of early modern popular literature), Ruzante suddenly fears that he may be just a ghost, having been killed in battle. But he refutes his own skepticism by eating a piece of bread, declaring, "No, cancaro! Spiriti no magna. [*A bocca piena*] A' son mi, e sí a' son vivo" (1.6; No, damn it! Ghosts don't eat. It's me, and I am alive). But as if excessive invention must compete in a zero-sum game with material reality, he then describes himself as constrained by necessity: "tirò da i can" (1.7; pulled by dogs).

Menato appears and confirms Ruzante's utter destitution. His kinsman declares that his ugly face looks worse that that of a hanged man: Ruzante is pale, thin, and "afumò" (smoked)—like the smoked meat to which the emaciated peasants compare themselves in *Dialogo facetissimo*. Much of the dialogue turns on what constitute the legitimate signs of war, which would enable one to qualify as an object of charity: Ruzante claims that his "mala ciera" (ugly face) results from wearing cramped iron helmets and from the bad drink and worse food of the front. When Menato suddenly notices the lice teeming on Ruzante's head and body, the victim invokes the grotesque trope—common to the popular imagination, according to Zorzi—that crumbs of bad bread transform themselves into lice and rotten wine mutates into scabs, mange, and pimples. Anticipating the gastronomic feats of the commedia *zanni*, always just this side of starvation, Ruzante boasts of having in desperation eaten his weapons and clothes. Nevertheless, in a point later reiterated by Gnua, Menato declares that Ruzante does not bear the legitimate external signs of a soldier (indeed, the kinds of signs that an imposter from the beggar catalogues might adopt): "el volto tagiò, o sturpiò d'una gamba, o de un brazo, o senza un ogio" (2.27; a slashed face, lame in the leg or the arm, or missing an eye). Later, Menato and Gnua attempt to demonstrate how Ruzante might slash his own face, like the figures in the beggar catalogues, so as to gain more credibility: "A' vossevu un signale che 'l foesse sto ananzo: almanco cossi, una sfrisaúra. *Accenna a descriverla sul volto di Ruzante*" (3.83; You'd want a sign that you were at the front; at least, like that, a scratch. [*He makes motions marking Ruzante's face.*]). Just as English authorities marked vagrants' bodies with a "V" for vagrant or "R" for rogue, the dispossessed could "write" on their own bodies, as Poor Tom does, or as Menato here urges Ruzante to do. To be sure, on the field Ruzante did prove himself adept in some respects at manipulating external signs: he abandoned his sword at the right moment because the enemy pitied those without weapons, and he deftly knew when to switch from one side to another a special shield that carried the insignia of both armies. But mainly his fictions and inventions are desperate ones, if admirable in the metatheatrical sphere.

Gnua, when she appears on the scene, also doubts that Ruzante has seen any real military action and particularly laments his failure to retrieve plunder. Suffering from a ""gran paura de morir da fame" (3.73; a great fear of dying from hunger), after the collapse of her and Ruzante's farming livelihood she had taken to selling vegetables in Padua markets (3.73) before she was forced to break with her country roots and take up urban prostitution (and ironically, in so doing, possibly gain more sexual freedom than she had had in what appears to have been a ménage à trois with Ruzante and Menato). Love is all well and good, she declares, but when one has to eat each and every day, love is best expressed in concrete, material benefits. She declares, "A' te vorae ben mi, intiènditu? Mo com a' penso che te si' pover'om, a' no te posso veere. No che a' te vuogie male, mo a' vuogio male a la to sagura" (3.68; I like you well enough, do you see? But when I consider that you are poor, I cannot see you. I don't think badly of you, but I think badly of your disgrace). The specter of "disgrace" extends to the possibility, at least in Gnua's eyes, that Ruzante has been forced to seek recourse to public assistance: "Te si' stò in qualche ospedale" (3.80; You've been in some hospital). This scene, along with Ruzante's other treatments of the problem in *La Betía, Dialogo facetissimo, Bilora,* and *La Moscheta,* provides one of the most striking portraits in Western literature of the ways in which poverty insinuates itself into sexual relationships.

The invention of Ruzante's exaggerations, wit, and braggadocio, nicely dilated in the extended dialogues with Menato and Gnua, appears to die upon contact with the fists of Gnua's bodyguard. But he rises from the dead, metatheatrically at least, with the most elaborated version of the "*lazzo* of a hundred" in the Ruzante canon. Only Orlando, declares Ruzante, could have held off so many. As with Falstaff's multiplication of "buckram men," such bravura fictional poesis constitutes a certain kind of triumph, displacing the grim existential truth of the peasant's poverty, dispossession, and sexual defeat onto the metatheatrical plane that the performer shares with the spectators. Like Quixote with the "evil enchanter" (the reference to Orlando signals a similar parody of chivalric mythos), when the skeptic Menato reduces the hundred men back down to one, Ruzante's imagination is fit to the task: he was made to see one hundred men because of the "incantason" (enchantment) practiced by the "strega" (witch) Gnua. Of course, if he had only known that it was just one man attacking him, he would have handled him easily. The play ends, appropriately enough, with metatheatricality, with the actor-based verve programmed into Ruzante's own performing body trumping, if not negating, material reality. Commenting on Ruzante's final fantasies of tying Gnua and her *bravo* together and watching them squirm, Menato observes that it would have been "com è le comierie che se fa" (5.103, 543; like those plays that they put on).

Bilora

A companion piece to *Parlamento* as the second of two *dialoghi*, the one-act play *Bilora* replicates the basic context of the first play: the forced migration of Paduan peasants into Venice with ensuing struggles over sexual power. But *Bilora* (the name is taken from the protagonist, roughly translatable as "weasel"), even darker than *Parlamento*, does not climax in a display of stand-up, metatheatrical glee but in a singular and highly disturbing "resolution" of what might be called tragicomic form.

Like *Parlamento*, *Bilora* begins with the filthy, destitute Paduan peasant Bilora straggling into Venice in search of his wife Dina. Impoverished herself, she has followed the money into the comfortable house of Andronico, a wealthy but elderly and unattractive Venetian businessman. Like Ruzante in *Parlamento*, Bilora desperately wants his woman back. Although Dina first mistakes him for a beggar when he knocks on her door in an attempt to get her to return to him, she finally begrudges him a few coins for the local tavern and tells him to return, saying that she will give him her answer at that time. Returning drunk from the tavern, Bilora gets his older friend Pitaro to plead with Dina on his behalf—an intervention that only results in Dina's resolution to stay put and Andronico's sending Pitaro away. Bilora, who has overheard everything, seethes with rage. In a mounting, drunken fury outside Andronico's door, he fantasizes killing the old man, acting out his rage on a wine jug. When Andronico suddenly appears, Bilaro confusedly—and shockingly—knifes his rival to death.

If, as we have argued, Ruzante's work is normally characterized by a continual counterpoint between invention, usually in a fantastic and hyperbolic vein, and the kind of unyielding necessity that Hannah Arendt sees as the telling index of poverty, Bilora's opening monologue is decidedly tilted toward necessity, an imbalance that continues throughout this bleak play and foreshadows its bloody ending. *Tirare* (to pull) is the operative word of the monologue and perhaps the entire play, collapsing the forces of hunger and sexual desire into one. Bilora complains that he, even though no longer young, is "tirò" (pulled) by love to endure the harsh and difficult voyage from Padua to Venice in pursuit of Dina. Utterly devoid of romantic veneer, love is an unpleasant external force that drives one harder than "tre para de buò" (three pairs of bulls). Dina herself has been "pulled" from the country to the city by the inexorable force of Andronico's capital; he is a Venetian *usuraio* (usurer) of the kind that the Paduan peasants and patriciate could join in hating. Bilora, in a desperate attempt to make ends meet, earns a meager living "pulling" (*tirar*) boats along the canals of the Veneto—the kind of day labor that was the first, precarious recourse after losing one's land. Unsurprisingly, this stopgap measure has not forestalled his inevitable migration to the city.

After an exchange with Pitaro in which he absurdly threatens to inflict various injuries upon his rival, Andronico, Bilora finally approaches the Venetian's house. Dina answers the door, thinking at first at the sight of the emaciated Bilora that he is a beggar: "Chi è quello che sbate? Siu poereto? Andè con Dio" (3.27; Who is that knocking? Are you a poor man? Go with God). Extreme poverty has reduced the husband-wife relationship to a beggar-almsgiver encounter. At the end of their tense scene, which only gains him a slight reprieve (she tells him he will have his answer later, but we sense that she is just buying time), he implores her: "Mo, a' dighe mi, arístu mé un pezato de pan da darme? Ché, a la fe', a' muoro da fame" (3.42; Listen, I'm telling you, you wouldn't have a piece of bread to give me? Because I'm really dying of hunger).

Not only can the hapless Bilora not manipulate the "war of signs," as Ruzante in *Parlamento* sometimes could, he can't even decipher them. He is unable to pronounce Andronico's Venetian name, takes the canals of Venice to be ditches, and cannot count the strange Venetian coins that he has won by begging from his wife. Returning drunk from the tavern, he avoids direct confrontation with Dina and Andronico, preferring to work by proxy through Pitaro. As if, in this bleak play, his powers of invention and impersonation are a diminished thing, he outsources them to Pitaro, imploring his friend to plead on his behalf and invoke the fictions of the beggar catalogues at one narrative remove: "E dîghe ch'a' son stò soldò, che fuossi aràlo paura. . . . [D]îghe pur ch'a' son sbraoso, e biastemè" (6.59; And tell him that I am a soldier—that'll scare him. . . . Tell him that I'm a real tough shit).

Such mediated disguises, of course, have no effect (and in *Moscheta* we shall see the disastrous failure of disguise even when the protagonist assumes it himself), and we are left with the devastated peasant alone onstage, stewing in his own juice. Predictably, he rehearses various fantasies of braggadocio, imagining how he will pummel the old man to a pulp. He will, he thinks, take on the proto–commedia dell'arte role of a Spanish soldier, performing it so well that now his antagonist will imagine there is not just one but multiple enemies. He places a wine jug before himself to stand in as Andronico, works himself into a fury of grandiose imprecations, and in what would appear to be a ritual act of violence homeopathically relieving him of the need for actual violence, he breaks open the jug with his knife, imagining the dead Andronico splayed out like a sacrificial cow (*un gran boazon*). Continuing the fantasy of escaping his miserable existence, he plans to steal Andronico's clothes, buy a horse, and go off to the wars. Like the end of *Parlamento,* the scene stages a metatheatrical play within the play—but this grim staging presses so forcefully at the bounds of its own fiction that it quite naturally spills over into Andronico's death. Here, the play is not resolved so much by framing dramatic structure with one-man virtuosity, as is the case with *Parlamento,* but by striking out into the terrain of dark, tragicomic form—not Renaissance tragicomedy with its felicitous endings but something anticipating twentieth-century experiments.

Moscheta

Moscheta, the last in the series of peasant plays written in the decade of the poor laws and famine, reestablishes the hierarchy among peasants characteristic of *La Betía.* Menato, a prosperous peasant who has moved in next door to his "kinsman" Ruzante precisely in order to be close to the latter's attractive wife Betía, is caught in the painful throes of love, and by the end of the play appears to have managed a successful ménage à quatre among himself, Betía, Ruzante, and Tonin, a Bergamask soldier on leave from duty who in the course of the play also has his way with Betía. Given their impoverishment, we may assume that Ruzante and his wife have followed the demographics of the earlier one-act plays, in which the peasants have been forced to move into the poor suburbs of Padua. Ruzante's destitution is demonstrated by his frequent recourse to petty crime: he has stolen some money from Tonin, and he later attempts to cheat Menato out of the clothes that Ruzante, as directed by his treacherous kinsman, foolishly used to disguise himself in order to test his wife's fidelity. (As in *La pastoral,* when the character "Ruzante" laments a missing *gabbana,* we see the enormous value that fine clothing must have had for the poor.) As in all of the peasant plays, and as Menego expressed so clearly in *Dialogo facetissimo,* material poverty translates immediately into sexual impotence. Menato's utter sexual mastery of Betía seems to follow inevitably from his economic superiority relative to Ruzante. Money and sex make up a zero-sum game: When Ruzante begs Tonin to give him back his wife, Tonin declares that he will return the woman if Ruzante returns the cash that he has stolen from him. When Ruzante complains that he is too poor to return the money, Menato brokers the deal, paying off Tonin, but apparently with Betía's assurance that the deal will also be sexually advantageous to Menato. The "inventions" of Ruzante, in this play, are at their most pathetic and least productive, even on a metatheatrical level. In the famous nocturnal scene of act 5, Ruzante fecklessly stands before his house as, unbeknownst to him, Menato assaults first Tonin and then Ruzante himself. In the darkness and confusion, Ruzante believes he is being attacked by a terrible, fiery ogre growing progressively larger before his eyes. But this apparition—cognate with the "*lazzo* of a hundred" that we have seen before—not only provides little theatrical release but is strategically used against him, as Betía claims that it was Ruzante who unknowingly assaulted Tonin while he (Ruzante) was desperately fleeing the monster. Forced then to make peace with Tonin, and utterly unaware of Menato's treachery against him, Ruzante unsuspectingly settles into a hierarchical arrangement of sexual power, with Menato ranked first, then Tonin, and last of all the hapless peasant.

Still, Ruzante does bring off a few virtuosic and tragicomic stand-up performances that carry the theatrical day. Most noteworthy is the extended "suicide" scene of act 3, scene 6, after Tonin has demanded his price for the return of Betía and the penniless Ruzante has resolved that his only end is despair. First he seeks a knife to stab himself; lacking that, he resolves to punch himself to death, which develops into the idea of auto-strangulation, with the added benefit that his eyes would pop out and terrify anyone passing by. (Ruzante's sense of his own body as an autonomous site of performativity, even postmortem, seems peculiarly postmodern.) Next he reprises, and elaborates, the *lazzo* of auto-cannibalism initiated by Menego in *Dialogo facetissimo*:

> A' me vuò magnare. Betía! [*Si trascina davanti alla casa del soldato*] Vien almanco, da' mente, che con strapasse de sta vita a l'altra, te puossi criare: "Iesò" [*Steso in terra considera la propria persona*] Da che dego mo scomenzare a magnarme? A' vuò scomenzare da i piè, perché, s'a' scomenzasse da le man, a' no porae po aiarme a magnare el resto. [*Alza il capo verso la finestra*] Betía, di'almanco un paternuostro per me. Orsú, sta' con Dio, ch'a' scomenzo. [*Si morde un polpaccio e si fa male*]. A' no me porè miga magnar tuto. Mo a' me magnerè tanto, ch'a' creperè . . . [*altro morso*]. E co' a' sea crepò, che arètu guagnò? [*Abbandona la gamba e guarda in su*]. Deh, butame zó una sogheta, cara Betía, che m'apicherè, che no me staghe a stentare . . . [*si accascia*][.] (3.6.49–51)

> I want to eat myself, Betía! (*He drags himself in front of the soldier's house.*) Come outside for a moment and pay attention, so that when I pass from this life to the next, you can cry out "Jesus!" (*Lying on the ground he considers himself.*) What part of myself shall I begin to eat? I want to begin with my feet, because if I start with my hands, I won't be able to help myself eat the rest. (*He raises his head toward his window.*) Betía, say at least an Our Father for me. Come on! Go with God, because I'm starting. (*He eats part of his calf and gets sick.*) I won't be able to eat myself completely. But I can eat enough so that I kick off . . . (*another bite*). And when I'm dead, what will I have gotten from it. (*He drops his leg and looks upward.*) Oh, throw down a rope for me, dear Betía, so that I can hang myself and not suffer any more. (*He collapses.*)

Greatly developed from the nascent *lazzo* of the early *Dialogo facetissimo*, the hapless peasant eats himself, just as the grain-hoarding Venetian authorities were cannibalizing the Paduan peasants. Again, paramount to the performance is the intended effect that it will have on others; Ruzante imagines a shocking spectacle offered to Tonin as revenge; a pitiful sight, inviting charity and prayer, to Betía. As so much in Ruzante's tragicomic theater, the grotesque gag of auto-cannibalism hovers uneasily (and simultaneously) between the ridiculous and the terrible in this theater that performs poverty through the forms of exaggeration, projection, distortion, reversal, and hallucination.

We may observe Ruzante throughout his career experimenting with different formal possibilities, and with different ways of ending his plays. As Ferguson has aptly demonstrated, the most pertinent formal characteristic of Ruzante's plays is their virtuosic generic hybridity: the playwright's capacity to meld the popular genres of *villanesca, bulesca, buffonesca,* and *mariazo* with the New Comedic forms that increasingly hold sway in the plays of the 1530s (not discussed in the current study). In a rough and ready vein, *La pastoral* evokes the pastoral mode's idea of a "beautiful relationship between rich and poor" only to conclude rather ironically. The unwieldy, brilliant *La Betía* never strays far from its base in all four popular forms mentioned above; with the ambiguous sexual communism ending the play, there is a sense that it could begin all over again. The obdurate conflicts of *Dialogo facetissimo* are magically conjured away by supernatural—and neo-feudal—fiat, from the hermit-priest's healing of both Menego's hand and his bitter rivalry with Nale, to a vision from the deceased "Zacarotto," to the utopian ideas of the great landowner Cornaro with which the play ends. *Il parlamento* ends with a virtuosic and solipsistic one-man gag, and *Bilora* with the virtuosic extension of rehearsed into actual violence. *La Moscheta* tilts back toward comedic form, but of a quite literally dark variety, with the ménage à quatre between Betía, Tonin, Ruzante, and Menato made possible under cover of the darkness that cunningly enshrouds the whole of act 5. Any formal critique of these plays must also acknowledge both their humane, existential power, and their dazzling theatricality.

5 The Commedia dell'Arte
Poverty at the Margins

The Underside of the *Comici*

Whether or not a given commedia dell'arte troupe or actor directly experienced or even cared about poverty, famine, destitution, or other social issues, by the time of the commedia's "golden age" between 1560 and 1630, these themes had become part of the actors' repertoire, much more central to their performance tradition than they were in English and Spanish early modern theaters. The hungry servant, stingy master, and related tropes became hardy perennials in the *Arte* repertoire, infused with new life in the late seventeenth century *Comédie-Italienne* and in the eighteenth-century theater of Carlo Goldoni. Especially because of the strong presence of itinerant mendicant orders in Italy, the commedia dell'arte inherited a culture in which poverty, begging, itinerancy, and a certain disposition to perform degradation were in the air, and this was absorbed into the grammar of their performance. Not only were tropes and gags of hunger and destitution continually deployed in the commedia, but some of the actors assumed for their own rhetorical purposes the histrionic pose of destitution. In other words, whatever their professional fortunes, they "played" poverty both onstage and in their offstage personae.

Whether or not this social dimension of the commedia dell'arte had political implications is difficult to answer from the available evidence. In many cases, it is probable that the actors were exploiting gags and themes that, simply put, played well. According to the traditional Aristotelian notion of the comic protagonist as someone socially and morally inferior to the spectator, poverty, hunger, and degradation were funny to the early modern spectator. But if we establish that poverty was a central and persistent topos in the commedia, it is also possible to imagine representations of poverty that could pass beyond Aristotle's limitation of the comic to that which does not cause pain—in other words, representations that could approach the pathos of Ruzante's suffering peasants.

Flourishing in the period of the Italian Counter-Reformation, arguably more closely tied to aristocratic patronage than the English and Spanish professional players, the commedia dell'arte could not claim to be directly "political," or at least not in a contestatory manner that engages matters of state. When the theater was attacked, as it often was by ecclesiastical and municipal critics, it was not on political but on moral and sexual grounds. Churchmen decried the perceived pernicious effect of the sexually alluring actress on her audiences. When actor-authors such as Adriano Valerini, Pier Maria Cecchini, and Giovan Battista Andreini vigorously defended their art against the charges of moral corruption, their defenses frequently invoked orthodox theological and political principles, which did not challenge the status quo. Poverty, however, was one of the few social issues addressed by the church. If the church did not systematically address, or challenge, the real economic roots of poverty, it did speak out against the harshness of the new poor laws and against the sins of greed and excessive consumption. Italian preachers invoked patristic and medieval texts such as Chrysostom's homilies on Dives and Lazarus and Aquinas' critiques on hoarding.

The great Harlequin Domenico Biancolelli, a contemporary of Molière, was rather well off, with a nice paunch to prove it. His repeated performance of hunger gags does not appear to have drawn from his own immediate experience. But it is certainly the case that many of the actors *could* have experienced poverty firsthand. Itinerant actors across Europe were often associated with vagabond beggars and other transient performers, such as minstrels, acrobats, and bearwards—and for good reason. The traveling actors of the commedia dell'arte must have shared some of the same roads as vagabonds. To be sure, the successful *Arte* troupes did enjoy certain advantages from their patrons: boats to convey them along the canals and waterways of the Po Valley; humble one-animal carriages, horses, and mules as they carried their costumes and simple stage apparatuses from town to town. But water travel itself was dangerously vulnerable to bad weather. Animals of transport frequently became ill or injured and would have been too expensive for many actors to afford (renting a mule for two days would have cost an entire week's salary for an artisan).[1] Even with a horse or a mule, travel was difficult because paved roads were extremely rare, making rain a major problem, as Tristano Martinelli complains to a ducal secretary in Mantua on 19 September 1609:

> I wasn't able to arrive earlier because I fell into the water with my horse, who I think is going to die. . . . With a great deal of trouble, I was able to borrow a horse in order to come to Mantua. I made it, thank God, but I'm half-ruined and I've become sick from those terrible roads. . . . Well, here I am: soaked and smeared with mud.[2]

Domenico Bruni, in *Le fatiche comiche*, describes how thin the line might have been between actor and beggar:

> If I were to tell you about the misadventures that happened to me and the dangers that I underwent in the three days that it took us to get from Bologna to Florence, it might seem like a fairy tale and yet it's true, because in Savena we almost drowned, and in Scarico l'Asino the wind knocked me off my horse, or mule, or whatever. We had to descend the Giogo by foot, and in Florence no one was willing to take me in that evening because I looked too much like a beggar.[3]

Since the pan-Italian commedia dell'arte companies were continually passing from one political entity into another, they were subject to the surveillance of "foreigners" at inns, borders, and waterways. And in addition to the dangers and impediments of bad weather, border controls, patronage disputes, and other problems, famine itself, such as that of the 1590s that ravaged northern Italy, could have a direct effect. A letter from Pirro Visconte Borromeo to Ferdinando I dei Medici on 3 November 1590 states that the Gelosi company, intending to travel to Florence from Milan, were, however, "astretti per la presente carestia a fugire la spesa di così longo viaggio" (constrained by the current famine to avoid the costs of such a long voyage).[4]

Furthermore, even the famous and successful troupes of the commedia dell'arte had some relationship to the poor theater of the piazza examined in Chapter 3. Troupes like the Gelosi and the Fedeli held contradictory postures regarding this undeniable kinship. Ambitious actor-writers such as Isabella Andreini and Pier Maria Cecchini strove to distance the *Arte* as much as possible from their piazza brethren; Isabella Andreini even promulgated a petition to suppress piazza performers in Milan.[5] The true actor, for Cecchini and others, was defined as whatever the piazza and banquet *buffone* was not. Other actors, especially the anarchic *secondo zanni* and the Dottore, who could play a kind of piazza charlatan, fairly brandished their affiliations with early modern street theater. A few of the established actors, such as the early seventeenth-century Dottore Giovanni Rivani (Dottore Campanaccia), were known to have performed in streets and halls just the kind of cheap print texts that we have examined in Chapter 3.[6]

The legendary history of the *zanni* tells a story of demographic displacement triggered by agricultural crisis. The *zanni* is said to come from the agricultural region of Bergamo and the surrounding country. Bergamo, which was annexed to the Venetian Republic in 1428, suffered both from the historical economic crisis described above and from the agricultural ravages of the Italian wars (1494–1559): the plundering of crops by foreign troops and the difficulty of sowing and transporting new crops in a time of war. Large numbers of Bergamask peasants and mountain dwellers actually did flee to the large cities, either Milan or Venice. Having sold, for a pittance, his small farm in Bergamo to his brothers, Stefano Sartorello came to Venice in 1545 (the year of the first extant commedia dell'arte contract) and took up as a beggar.[7] Andrea Zannini argues that many Bergamask immigrants may have actually had some success, although they were probably never very far from poverty: befitting their future fictional role of servant, they dominated the lists of porters at the Venetian Dogana, or Customs House, as they did in Milan, and many did take up employment as servants.[8] It may in fact have been precisely resentment toward their relative, if certainly not spectacular, success that spawned the anti-Bergamask literature that emerged in the late fifteenth and early sixteenth centuries, upon which the commedia dell'arte drew as it codified the figure for the stage in the 1540s and 1550s. The Bergamask *zanni* did come to typify the new immigrant craftily shifting for his life, living on the edge of poverty. He finds some security in binding himself to Pantalone, but no guarantee of escape from poverty and certainly not from hunger. As Stefano D'Amico has argued, many of the Italian indigent in the sixteenth century were "working poor."[9] Up to 15 percent of the working population were employed as servants, but job security was only as stable as the master's fluctuating fortunes. The commedia gag of the "servant of two masters," which existed well before Goldoni's literary version of it in the eighteenth century, emerges out of the vicissitudes of urban employment after rural exile: one job was never enough.

Tristano Martinelli and the *Maschera* of Arlecchino

No established commedia dell'arte actor had a closer relationship to piazza culture than the Mantuan actor Tristano Martinelli. Scholars have recently demonstrated that Martinelli was the first to bring to the stage the Arlecchino/Harlequin role: a French-Italian hybrid *maschera* that was a non-Bergamask version of the *zanni*.[10] Visual and verbal evidence demonstrates that Martinelli frequently deployed onstage the topoi of poverty, famine, and degradation. And as a *buffone*-style actor, Martinelli carried his stage persona into his offstage interactions with ducal and royal patrons, continuing to play the fictions of poverty to kings and dukes well after he had become become fairly comfortable from his professional success.

In a letter written to Alessandro Striggi in Mantua on 21 January 1613, Martinelli defends the right of the piazza performers in Mantua to move around the city as they wish without having to pay an extra fee.[11] In making his case, Martinelli reveals that he too had once worked as a piazza performer, complaining about a time in France when he had been forced to pay for the privilege of moving his trestle stage from one place to another.[12] Because of his previous experience as a piazza charlatan and "information" that he was reputed to have about the hand-to-mouth performers who practiced this trade, the Mantuan authorities in 1599 granted him the authority to supervise, penalize, and when necessary tax the following kinds of performers:

> mercenary actors, jugglers, acrobats who walk the tightrope, those who present demonstrations and structures and the like, and charlatans who put up benches in the piazzas in order to sell oils, unguents, salves, antidotes against poison, perfume packages, musk water, civet, musk, stories and other printed pamphlets, animal claws, and those who put up signs to advertise treatment, and similar kinds of people.[13]

This was the world that Martinelli knew. Insofar as these little performers, like the peddlers of cheap print, were not above performing their very destitution, Martinelli could draw upon the tropes of poverty performed by those who sang for their supper. Although Martinelli, as supervisor of the charlatans, must have exercised his authority at times in punitive ways, the evidence of his letters suggests that he had sympathy for them and could go out of his way to help their cause. In the same letter in which he mentions his former life as a piazza charlatan working in France and elsewhere, he strongly defends the right of the performers, "queste povere gente" (these poor people) to mobility: to be able to move about the city as they wished without having to pay crushing fees. As an itinerant actor himself (albeit by 1613 an extremely successful one), he appears to have identified himself with the condition of vagabondage and itinerancy. On an earlier occasion, Martinelli lamented the penalties inflicted on many itinerant performers, who suffered the same punishments as vagabonds: forced exile from the city, often accompanied by public whipping or other kinds of physical punishment. So Martinelli sympathizes with a certain acrobat named Gasparo and his company, as he complains that the authorities

> banished all of the actors, charlatans, and anyone else who was found in the city they gave only an hour to leave—one has never seen such cruelty. And on top of that, three days ago Gasparo the acrobat, who didn't know about the cruel edict, came with his company, and in order to make an example of these kinds of people they gave them three wrenchings of the rope.[14]

"Wrenchings of the rope" was a form of torture in which the victim's hands were tied behind his back. He was then raised by a rope attached to the wrists and suddenly dropped a short distance, inflicting severe pain on the shoulder joints.[15] When, in performances of Giovan Battista Andreini's 1613 scripted play, *Lo schiavetto*, Martinelli played the role of Nottola, chief of a group of vagabonds, he would have been able to draw on personal experience both for his superiority vis-à-vis the members of his motley cadre and for an understanding of what such a life might have actually been like.[16]

Indirect evidence suggests that Martinelli had frequent recourse to themes of poverty and degradation when he performed as Arlecchino at the Hôtel de Bourgogne in 1584–85. A series of pamphlets published in Paris in 1585 revolves around a quarrel between an Italian Harlequin, now conclusively identified as Martinelli, and a French actor referred to as Robert Triplupart l'Andouiller. Although the French actor has still not been conclusively identified, Virginia Scott has plausibly suggested that he was an actor in Agnan Sarat's rival troupe who dared to steal some of Martinelli's routines and copy the role of Harlequin.[17] The pamphlets are not theatrical texts and so cannot provide direct evidence of performance, but they are highly contestatory and dramatic. They feature several speeches in the vein of the vituperative, agonistic discourse of oral culture, and provide such detailed images of acrobatic, gestural, and other physical routines of Harlequin that they seem to be drawing from what was actually performed on stage.

The first pamphlet, an attack upon Martinelli from the camp of the French *farceurs*, is titled *Histoire plaisante des faicts et gestes de Harlequin commedien italien* (The Pleasant History of the Deeds and *Gestes* of Harlequin, Italian Actor)[18] and recounts the voyage of Harlequin to the underworld, in a parodic version of the descent of Orpheus, in order to win back the poem's "Eurydice": a famous Parisian bawd named Mère Cardine. The madame has appeared to Harlequin in a dream vision, beseeching him to come rescue her from hell, which is figured as a kind of state prison where she suffers for the crime of having given Parisians the pleasures of Venus. Deciding to respond to Mère Cardine's request, Harlequin dons his pouch, mask, slapstick, and belt—as if he were an itinerant actor preparing for just another voyage—and descends into hell.

Unlike the accompanying poem in this first pamphlet, the *Histoire* may appear to us as more a celebration than a defamation of Harlequin. As in the "voyage to hell" poems featuring the early sixteenth-century Venetian *buffoni* Domenico Taiacalze and Zuan Polo Liompardi,[19] Harlequin literally clowns his way through hell, performing virtuosic acrobatic feats in Charon's boat and dazzling Pluto with a revue-style medley of a Bergamask dance, a clownish harangue worthy of piazza charlatans, and a spectacular leap: "[A]lor il feit un sault / En arriere courbe de quatre pieds de hault" ([T]hen he made a backwards somersault, leaping four feet into the air).[20] The extremely detailed account of Harlequin's acrobatic and gestural skills, replete with numerous technical distinctions for different kinds of leaps, bespeaks the knowledge of an insider—in fact, perhaps an insider who was beginning to copy Martinelli's routines for Agnan Sarat's troupe.

If the *Histoire*, for someone not concerned that another actor might be stealing his routines and thus his livelihood, could be taken as flattery in the form of imitation, the accompanying poem written from the French quarter is pure invective: *La sallade de Harlequin a luy envoiee par le Capitaine le Roche, appotiquaire luquoys, pour la guarison de sa malade Neapolitaine* (The Salad of Harlequin, Sent to Him by Captain le Roche, Apothecary, for Healing His Neapolitan Disease). The implicit defamation by association with a famous madame in the *Histoire*—which matches a persistent connection in later scenarios between Arlecchino, prostitution, and lower-class crime[21]—and the consequent inclusion of tropes of poverty are carried much further in the vituperative *Sallade*. In the persona of Captain le Roche, the poem's author facetiously offers his services as piazza charlatan, or "apothecary," to Martinelli/Harlequin, to whom the defamatory poem attributes the "Neapolitan malady," that is, syphilis. Harlequin, the poet declares, will undergo public humiliation and punishment for having served as a pimp to Mère Cardine: he may have to carry a collar around his neck in a public market or be "whipped and banished" like vagabond beggars.[22] Worse, he may go to hell for it, where he will have to empty the chamber pots in which Proserpina has defecated (397)—a typical punishment for the degraded *zanni* in hell, as we have seen in the "Insonio" poem in Chapter 3. Harlequin's syphilis, the effects of which are described in graphic detail, will be healed by the grotesque "sallade" proposed by the poet-apothecary, a disgusting, intensely insulting charlatan's "remedy" of the kind described in cheap print and performed in piazzas (a horrible concoction of human feces, thistles, harsh herbs, slugs, and other ingredients).

Harlequin's proxy poet comes right back at the French "apothecary" in the 1585 *Response di gestes de Harlequin au poete fils de Madame Cardine* (A Response to the Poet of the *Gestes* of Harlequin, Son of Madame Cardine). The poem is written more in the vein of the slanderous *Sallade* than that of the lighter-hearted *Histoire*. A pleasant meal with his neighbor cannot keep Harlequin from working himself into fury at the libelous French pamphlets—a fury that generates another dream voyage into hell. Tossing a leg of lamb to Cerberus, who is "dying from hunger," Harlequin forges ahead, where he discovers his enemy, the "son of Cardine," just about to pass into the flames of hell. Suggesting that the rival French troupe members have fallen into the ranks of the disgraced poor, the son of Cardine is accompanied by "une troupe de coquins et gueu" (402, l. 35; a troupe of rogues and beggars). Here, "buffone" also becomes a loaded word for one's theatrical adversary. Although later Martinelli would accept and even embrace the terms, here he declares, "Je ne suis point bouffon, fils de Cardine, / Comme l'escrit ton histoire badine" (403; I am not a buffoon, son of Cardin / As is written in your moronic story). Pathetically, the son—or pimp—of Cardine laments his punishment in the flames of hell, and abjectly beseeches Harlequin to deliver him. Harlequin merges his personal attack on the poet who has maligned him with a critique against mother and son for exploiting their employees, pocketing half of their profits. Raising the possibility that "prostitution" in these pamphlets serves as a metaphor for theatrical thievery (stealing material from a rival troupe), Harlequin issues this threat to "Cardinon" (as he is called): "Cardinon, / De ce pays jamais ne sortiras / Si tu ne rens cela que tu robas / E plus trompé tu as / Les comédiens de l'Hostel de Bourgogne" (402, ll. 45–49; Cardinon, you will never leave this country unless you return what you have stolen. What is more, you have cheated the actors at the Hôtel de Bourgogne). What especially infuriates the Italians is that the rival poet has recorded his routines on paper: "Ce sot poet qui mes gestes a imprimé" (401; This stupid poet who has printed my gags). Interestingly, Harlequin's proxy pauses the stream of vituperation to acknowledge that both sides in this "war of the theaters" may be driven by poverty: Cardinon is allowed to defend himself (again, within the poem written from the Italian quarter): he only wrote the libelous pamphlet because "je n'avois que mangé" (403, l. 75; I had nothing to eat).

Having won from Pluto the right to punish Cardinon, Harlequin administers a series of harsh punishments to his French rival. On one level, if "pimping" is a metaphor for pilfering a fellow actor's gags, he must stop this immediately ("Je t'ordonne, valet, / De plus ne faire ainsi le maquereux" [404, ll. 134–35; I order you, valet, to stop being a pimp])—and he must pay an entrance fee the next time he watches Harlequin and his company perform. He is condemned to poverty: he cannot eat meat, can only eat rice, and must go naked throughout the city. Being forced to rely on the sixteenth-century equivalent of a soup kitchen, he is constrained to eat directly out of the pot. He will suffer the typical punishments of the vagabond beggar and the common thief: "Je te condamne ester rompu, bruslé, / Et à la galère, et puis ester fouetté" (405, ll. 161–62;

I sentence you to being broken, burned, worked as a galley slave, and then whipped). The same fate that Martinelli would decry fourteen years later, in the case of poor Gasparo the acrobat in Mantua, is inflicted upon the "gueu" (beggar) Cardinon. Tropes of poverty, hunger, and degradation pervade the 1585 French pamphlets, written at the birth of Harlequin.

Martinelli's next performance in Paris, which wouldn't occur for another sixteen years, generated another body of indirect evidence of performance, also disclosing ways in which he might have performed poverty gags. As Siro Ferrone points out, because of the assassination of the Duc de Guise in 1588, the death of the Florentine queen mother Catherine de' Medici the year afterwards, the continual jealousy of the French *farceurs*, and the ongoing obstructionism of the monopolistic Confrères de la Passion, no recorded trips of Italian actors to France occurred until, in 1598, Henri IV invited Martinelli and other actors to Paris to celebrate his impending marriage with another Florentine, Catherine's daughter Maria de' Medici.[23] Stopping first in Lyon during the winter of 1600–1601, Martinelli had printed there a strange publication, as a kind of private gift to the king and queen: the *Compositions de rhetorique*, containing fifty-seven blank pages and thirteen pages of images.[24]

Although by this stage in Martinelli's career he had become successful (in 1602, the same year in which Shakespeare purchased arable land in Stratford, he would buy land outside of Mantua), the *Compositions* demonstrate the way that poverty and degradation had become keyed into his routines, his habits of performance. This bizarre text, designed to advertise the company's upcoming performances in Fontainebleau and Paris, amounts to a wily piece of begging, cognate with the itinerant English players' rhetoric of supplication as they toured from one great house to another. The message of the entire text is that Martinelli and his fellow actors can only perform before the king and queen if they are suitably rewarded. For the Capitano Silvio Fiorillo, who is figured on one page in full costume, they are almost literally singing for their supper: above the image of the dashing Capitano on page 51, it reads, "Vammo à Paris à fé da Cavagler / Que ganneremo aglia bien da comer" (We travel to Paris to play the Knight, so that we can earn enough to eat). Martinelli/Harlequin is more ambitious, explicitly asking for a gold medal and chain, but his rhetoric and posture are servile—or rather, a strange blend of abjectness and cockiness.

On page 5 of the text, he supplicates the king and queen for the gold medal and chain that he requests for his recompense, abjectly crouching on his knees and slumping his shoulders (Fig. 9). He stages destitution, begging for bread, and he riddlingly jests with Henry and Maria (promising to give them "half of nothing" in exchange for his reward) and threatens to return to Italy if he does not receive his medal and chain. On page 48, an Arlecchino who is manifestly on the road carries spurs, a traveling hat, a small sack, a bowl of food attached to his waist with a spoon protruding from it, and in order to protect himself against the dangers of travel (which could include encounters with bandits), a spear and mace (Fig. 10). He travels with his "Allichinaria," a destitute family of little Arlecchini riding in a basket strapped to his shoulders—a motif strikingly similar to contemporary images of familial poverty (see Fig. 11). One of them, crouched on the ground, eats voraciously; another imploringly holds out an empty bowl; and three others are crammed into a basket carried by Arlecchino on his back. He stages here nothing less than hunger, as if to invoke, before Henry IV and in a kind of nostalgic, neo-feudal manner, the medieval notion that it was the duty of the king to feed the poor.[25] What distinguishes this from the classic medieval exchange between king and beggar is that Martinelli, as a "seller of himself," must conjure it up in performance, outside the context of institutional practices established by medieval churches, monasteries, and confraternities to aid the poor.

In Giovan Battista Andreini's 1612 play *Lo schiavetto*, Martinelli played the role of Nottola, the leader of an itinerant cohort of vagabonds.[26] As with his municipal assignment in Mantua, Martinelli is both superior to the others and also one of them. Accompanied by his cohort Rampino and a band of eight other vagabonds, Nottola leads the life of the itinerant charlatan, speaking rogue's cant, or *furbesco*, living a life of petty crime, and surviving by performing the signs of poverty and degradation, which are never conclusively revealed to be either true or false. Like the Harlequin persona of *Compositions de rhetorique*, Nottola stages a peculiar blend of degradation and bravado: he is dressed in rags and plays the part of the destitute, but claims that he is descended from Spanish kings and lords it over his little company.

The role of Arlecchino in Flaminio Scala's 1611 encyclopedic collection of scenarios, *Il teatro delle favole rappresentative*, also draws on material

5

Ha REINE, Colana,   *ROY Medaglia,*
Quantumque donné moy,   *per la morbiu,*
Autrement m'en iray cert'   *in Itaglia.*

ET HARLEQVIN DONNERA A V. M.

Un mezo (C.) Niente,
Con vn (O.) Niente entiero,
Accompagnato con vn (RE.)

FIG. 9. The suppliant Arlecchino/Martinelli. From Tristano Martinelli, *Compositions de rhetorique* (Lyon, 1601), 5. By permission of the Bibliothèque Nationale de France.

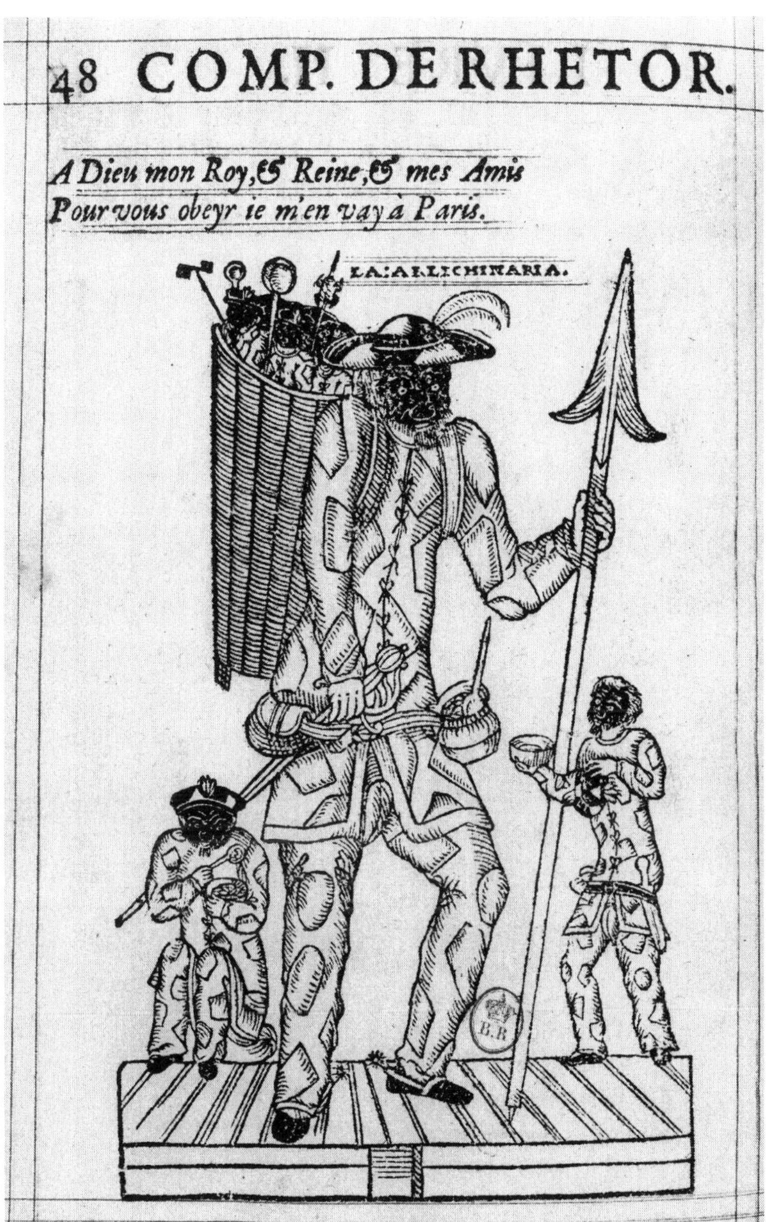

Fig. 10. Arlecchino and His Family. From Tristano Martinelli, *Compositions de rhetorique* (Lyon, 1601), 48. By permission of the Bibliothèque Nationale de France.

FIG. 11. Anonymous, "Beggar Woman." Ferrarese or Paduan, c.1470–80. Photographic Collection ("Beggars"), Warburg Institute, London.

that Martinelli probably performed.[27] Writing with as much of an eye toward the literary consumer as toward the theatrical practitioner, Scala compiled his scenarios well after the cessation of his own active career as an actor, and there is a memorial as well as a literary quality to the collection. The role of "Isabella" clearly celebrates Isabella Andreini, deceased seven years earlier, and the part of "Capitano Spavento" clearly refers to her husband Francesco and conjures up some of his favorite routines, allowing for the patina of Scala's literary embellishment. In the *Teatro*, Arlecchino usually accompanies his master, the Capitano. As in the piazza pamphlets, he is simultaneously famished and gluttonous. Both master and servant are outsiders, even foreigners, and it is possible to glimpse in the pair the two sides of unemployed itinerancy that we have observed in Chapter 3: the counterpoint between *poltroneria* (laziness), and *braveria*, with the volatile and violent Capitano acting out aspects of the vagrant discharged soldier. In Scala's collection, Arlecchino frequents and participates in the particular worlds of petty crime that were aligned with poverty in the period, such as prostitution ("Isabella astrologo" [Day 36]) and thievery ("Il dottor disperato" [Day 13]). He falls into the role of a charlatan dentist in "Il cavadente" (Day 12), plays a rogue in "Il pellegrino fido amante" (Day 14), and frequently projects a persona of degradation.

Poverty in Flaminio Scala's *Il teatro delle favole rappresentative*

The commedia dell'arte character system is organized vertically according to the three status levels of *vecchi* (old men), *innamorati* (lovers), and *zanni*. Usually through their association with one of the *zanni*, a fourth, underground level frequents the pages of Scala's *Teatro*, consisting of beggars, pickpockets, gypsies, card sharks, fugitives, rogues, courtesans, prostitutes, and madmen. These figures represent nothing less than the impoverished underground of Italian cities. If, despite his constant hunger, the *zanni* usually represents an employed servant, reflecting the Bergamasks' relative success in Venice, his service is not secure, and he knows those who have fallen through the economic cracks. The inns commonly invoked in the scenarios often collect various undesirables. Scala himself, in fact, was not far from this world; he owned a *profumeria* on the Rialto in Venice that sold not only perfumes but also oils, salves, and medicaments of the kind hawked by Martinelli's underlings in Mantua. The list of props included in the prefatory material for each scenario suggests that gags involving begging, vagabondage, and hunger were a regular part of the *comici*'s repertoire. Props include bread (frequently given in the scenarios to real or pretended beggars); destitute clothing; begging paraphernalia, such as a stool; and an eye patch for actors either playing a blind beggar or impersonating one within the fictions of the plays.

In fact, each of the three major status levels of the commedia dell'arte could play the "fictions of the poor" that were so ever-present in Italian early modern culture. We shall examine three of Scala's scenarios, each of which focuses on a different character or character group assuming the guise of poverty.

The underworld subplot of "Le burle d'Isabella" (Day 4; The Pranks of Isabella), which dramatizes the tropes of poverty through the figure of the *zanni*, can here be explained without detailing the complicated, erotically driven main plot. (This in itself suggests that the themes of destitution were detachable gags, or *lazzi*, that might stand alone in performance.) The master, Pantalone, has forced himself upon the servant Franceschina and then married her off to the destitute innkeeper Burattino. In order to silence them, he has bought off Burattino with a five-hundred-ducat dowry and the promise that he will give them an additional one thousand ducats for the first male child that they conceive. Burattino shifts into a course of comic obsession (similar to that of Nicia in Machiavelli's *La mandragola*), carrying a urinal with him onstage in order to test his wife's water for her fertility and asking everyone he meets if they know the secret of generating a male child. Pedrolino, Pantalone's servant, is said in the plot summary to praise Pantalone's magnanimous arrangement as a "work of charity" (1:56). And Franceschina sees the arrangement as a welcome opportunity to rise above penury, declaring that "if he [Burattino] were potent enough to impregnate her with a male child, they would escape from poverty" (1:56).

An early scene in act 1, which might be dubbed "fiction for food," dramatizes Burattino's desperation (1:57). Given money by the Capitano in order to buy some food, the famished Burattino begins to start eating the food even before he enters his inn. But two rogues encounter him outside of the inn and accost him. Declaring that they come from the land known as Cuccagna, they transfix the starving Burattino by telling him of this place where there is no hunger, where succulent food fairly drops from the sky, where one is punished for working and one is paid for sleeping. As Burattino achingly listens to one of them dilate on this paradise, the other rogue eats his food. Halfway through (both the food and the story), the two beggars change places until the food is all gone, whereupon they depart, and Burattino awakens to the cruel and pathos-ridden reality of his hunger: "Burattino recognizes that it was a trick. Weeping, he goes inside" (1:57).

In the course of the scenario, Burattino and Pedrolino become at odds. Pedrolino vows to cuckold his antagonist, which he does precisely by deploying the fictions of poverty. Pulling from the *Arte* props storehouse, he dons the disguise of an itinerant beggar with an eye patch and a walking stick (1:61). Pedrolino begs alms of Burattino, who refuses him, and then invokes, for the second time in the play, the land of Cuccagna: he (the disguised Pedrolino) has been exiled from that renowned place because he has committed the unpardonable sin of working. Burattino's attention is again transfixed by the myth, and a *guidone* (beggar), said to be a "companion" of Pedrolino, enters the scene, except that he is now disguised as a merchant. The "merchant" hails Pedrolino and heartily thanks him for having helped him get his wife pregnant with a male child. The rogue suddenly departs, and the gullible Burattino is left marveling at Pedrolino's supposed ability to achieve precisely the thing that, of course, would deliver Burattino and Franceschina from poverty. When asked how he acquired this ability, Pedrolino claims it to be a family secret passed on to him by his father, which he in turn will pass on to his son. Burattino agrees, essentially, to be cuckolded, because it is fairly clear that Pedrolino's "drug" is nothing more than his own sexual potency. However, perhaps experiencing a *crise de conscience* at betraying one of his own class, Pedrolino suddenly abandons the cuckold project just at the point when Burattino is announcing the supposed successful results to Pantalone. Burattino can then only dream of that version of Cuccagna to which he thought he was tantalizingly close: one thousand ducats.

"La travagliata Isabella" (Day 15; The Travails of Isabella), which presents the highest-status-level characters (as well as others) in real or feigned poverty, engages the theatrical poetics we have observed in Edgar's Poor Tom role, where one can never be sure whether the beggar is authentic or performing a theatrical illusion. Invoking the precariousness of early modern capitalist society, in which up to 60 percent of the population were subject to falling into poverty, Pantalone, "a man of rich fortune," effectively becomes Pantalone dei *Bisognosi* (from *bisognare*, "to need") through what is called "perversa fortuna" (1:157; perverse fortune) but can also be attributed to his bad temperment. Enraged by two importunate suitors of his daughter, he hires two *bravi* (the *bravo*, frequently a former soldier in need of work, was often employed by Venetian patricians and could be a highly undesirable social element), with whose help he attempts to kill the suitors, leaves them for dead, and then becomes an itinerant fugitive with his servant Pedrolino, taking to the road with sack and stick. Arriving in Rome, he impersonates the role of a beggar, beseeching alms from door to door. It appears to be mainly a strategic disguise for him, although, as an exiled murderer (as he thinks he is), the fiction borders on truth. Certainly for Pedrolino, who "in the guise of a beggar goes asking alms in a loud voice" (1:159), the theatrical role fits his condition: he is actually painfully hungry in his displaced state. Practically every character in the scenario impersonates a beggar at some point, including Capitano Spavento (one of the suitors, having survived Pantalone's attack), who voraciously devours the food that had been bestowed on Pedrolino. The Capitano's servant Arlecchino (Martinelli), also disguised as a beggar and suffering excruciating hunger, in concert with the Capitano fools the avaricious Dottore out of a plate of food in an extended gastronomic *lazzo* typical of the commedia dell'arte. It is a scenario of displaced persons, in which the fiction of poverty borders on truth, enacting that curious mixture of pain and festivity that so often characterized the Renaissance *beffa* (prank).

In "Il finto cieco" (Day 34; The Fake Blind Man), the *innamorato* is drawn into the fiction of poverty. For betraying Orazio by falling in love with his beloved Isabella, Flavio is forced to wander for three years as a blind beggar, accompanied by his fellow "beggar" Burattino, who actually believes that Flavio is what he pretends. (This suggests that Flavio would have had to immerse himself in the role rather completely.) Flavio's impersonation appears less like the cunning impostures of the rogue books than an actual love penance, practically an amatory version of the mendicant. He enters "a feigned blind man, dressed vilely," and with Burattino "they beseech alms at every door" (2:349). Franceschina gives them bread and wine, but her motives are inflected by the immediate sexual attraction she feels for Burattino—and she asks him to return often for "alms." Attempting to elicit a blend of charity and eros, Flavio declares to Flaminia that his blindness will be healed by the kiss of a young woman, which of course he receives. Within the fictional frame of the scenario, Flavio's status as a blind beggar lies somewhere between fiction and lived experience. On the one hand, he actually has wandered for three years supported by alms with the *guidone* Burattino as his down-and-out companion. On the other hand, it is a fiction that he has adopted—or been forced to adopt by Orazio—and it quickly lifts when the amorous intrigues of the play are resolved. The fiction of the blind beggar is clearly framed by the love story. The device, down to very precise details, is recycled in a scenario from the Venetian "Correr" collection of the same title, with a list of props that includes "da orbo per Orazio con bastone" (clothes for Orazio as a blind man, with stick) and "scanno da tre piedi per l'orbo" (stool with three legs for a blind man). In act 2 of the scenario, precise indications are given for the verbal formulae used by the fake blind man, Flaminio, as he begs with his guide Tartaglia.[28]

Chrysostom dell'Arte

The most thorough treatment of poverty in the important Neapolitan Casamarciano scenarios, newly edited in a fine edition, comes in "Il ricco epulone" (The Rich Banqueter).[29] Melding the biblical parable of Dives and Lazarus with that of the prodigal son, the play provides a striking dramatization of Chrysostom's homilies on the Lazarus theme. Unusually allegorical for a commedia dell'arte scenario, three sons of the Dottore embody distinct traits: Nineusio, the Dives figure, represents greed and excessive wealth; Liberio stands for the attachment to prestige and status (he will become the prodigal son); and Lazarus is the good and humble son. Additionally, three distinct categories of the poor are portrayed: the involuntary, plebeian poor who supplicate Nineusio for alms and are represented with real and compelling needs; the sacred, voluntary poor, as represented by Lazarus, who gives away his wealth to the needy; and the *poveri vergognosi* in the guise of Liberio and his servant Pulcinella, who lose their wealth both by squandering it and by falling victim to thieves. Poverty-induced crime occurs on an individual, isolated level, with the servant Pulcinella stealing from the Dottore in order to go gambling. And it also emerges in the form of organized crime, more akin to the picaresque novel, with the servants Tartaglia and Coviello fleecing Liberio and Pulcinella out of all their belongings—including their clothes—on behalf of the brothel for which they work.

Much of the dramatic power of the scenario would have come from scenes of actual supplication: the cries of the poor beseeching the avaricious Nineusio first offstage and then onstage—only to have Nineusio furiously reject them. A poor woman entreats Nineusio to loan her twenty ducats to pay off a debt that is detaining her husband in prison. Then a husband abjectly begs Nineusio for some money to bury his deceased wife, a kinswoman of the rich man. In the vein of Chrysostom's homilies, striking visual images of Nineusio's gluttony sharply contrast with those of scarcity and want: "[Nineusio] dice esser straqquo, ma non stufo de suoi godimenti, dice volersi ristorare con cose dolci . . . lui mangia e beve smoderatamente, e poi fa sonare, e si adorme" ([Nineusio says] that he is exhausted, but never tires of taking his pleasure with her. He says he wants to restore himself with sweet things . . . he eats and drinks gluttonously, and orders that some music be played. Then he falls asleep).[30] After Nineusio, predictably, refuses each of the deserving suppliants and Lazarus steps into the breach on behalf of the poor, a low cry from the crowd goes out on behalf of Lazarus—an interesting case of a resonant, and potentially political, *Arte* representation of the plebeian class.

In strongly siding with voluntaristic, individual charity, which may also be considered "indiscriminate" because the generous Lazarus does not interrogate his suppliants, the play counters the gist of the poor laws. Still, it does voice alternative viewpoints and explore different kinds of responses to poverty. When Liberio and Pulcinella, reduced to extreme poverty, encounter their virtuous brother Lazarus, he recasts his voluntary poverty as "wealth" because the needy to whom he has given his goods have become "mercadanti che vendono la gloria del cielo" (merchants who sell glory in heaven).[31] In response to this neo-medieval praise of almsgiving, in which capitalist terms ("mercadanti") are cunningly transposed to heaven, the more worldly Liberio and Pulcinella offer a skeptical riposte, deeming Lazarus a "bacchettone" (pious hypocrite).

The two parables draw to their proper conclusions. The dissolute Liberio, after having prevailed over his father, the Dottore, to grant him his share of the estate, travels to Turin, where along with his servant he is robbed and despoiled of his clothes, his nakedness a powerful visual symbol of poverty as judgment—visited upon the dissolute and immoral as in *Barzelletta de' falliti* and the fictional *antefatto* of Poor Tom. The newly destitute master and servant are constrained to beg for alms and then work in the woods tending pigs with Tartaglia and Coviello (who used to work for the brothel before they were discharged). Returning to Rome, still naked, they prostrate themselves before the Dottore's feet, who responds with the largesse of the prodigal son's father. Employing exactly the same kind of grotesque make-up used by the fraudulent beggars of the *Liber vagatorum* and the like—an *impiastro* (poultice) made to simulate body sores—Lazarus appears at the feet of his heartless, gluttonous brother. Spitefully and grotesquely licking his dishes so that the poor will not receive any leftovers and pushing the abject Lazarus away toward the dogs, Nineusio suddenly feels a pain in his chest and dies the death of the wicked, as the play ends with the rich man's lament in hell. All told, "Il ricco epulone" is an extraordinary *Arte* document, which gives theatrical flesh to a parable that for St. John Chrysostom had carried great dramatic power.

Domenico Biancolelli

Much in the same manner as Martinelli's Arlecchino, Domenico Biancolelli demonstrates the vestigial power of hunger gags in the age of Molière. An Italian actor born in Bologna in 1636, Biancolelli came from a long line of actors and was trained by his stepfather, the famous *zanni* Carlo Cantù (in *arte Buffetto*). He moved to Paris and because famous playing the role of Harlequin for the Comédie-Italienne from 1662 to 1688, when he suddenly died at the age of 52—according to one report from excessive dancing. By the time he became established in Paris, all indications are that he did not suffer from poverty, but that did not prevent him from staging it.

During his career, Biancolelli kept an extensive written record, the original of which is now unfortunately lost, of the typical plots, routines, and *lazzi* that he performed with his troupe. He directed that the manuscript be bequeathed to his actor son Pierre-François. When the son died in 1717, the manuscript was passed on to the magistrate Thomas-Simon Gueulette, an eighteenth-century chronicler of the Comédie-Italienne. Sometime probably between 1750 and 1753 Gueulette made a French translation of the scenario, adding some commentary, cutting some of the original, and making some emendations. Given the complicated textual history of the original manuscript and the fact that Gueulette undoubtedly made some changes, the surviving text must be assessed critically, with Gueulette's interventions taken into account. Still, scholars do accept the text as a fairly reliable record of what Biancolelli actually performed.[32]

Biancolelli's Harlequin, in relationship to poverty and hunger, recalls the virtuosic invention and dazzling fiction-making of Ruzante. The Harlequin of the Comédie-Italienne, however, is considerably more protean, and more successful, than Ruzante, whose fictions and inventions take the form of delusions and hallucinations operating only (if virtuosically) in the plane of the individual performer. "Baroque" is in fact a rather apposite term for Biancolelli, who manages to transform himself into multiple shapes and roles that, despite their zaniness, exercise more power and agency than the brilliant but hapless fictions of Ruzante. Class appears more malleable in the world of Biancolelli (and Molière) than it is for the abject peasants of Ruzante's Padua: when Harlequin dresses up and impersonates a gentleman, as he does in the scenarios "Le capricieux" (1:159–68) and "Le baron allemand" (1:177–81)[33] he does not go crashing to defeat as Ruzante does in *Moscheta*. In his routines, Harlequin impersonates a Turk, a German, a charlatan doctor, a necromancer, a Capitan, and deploys (if maladroitly) various bits of foreign and professional language in order to do so. Although most predictably linked romantically with the servant Diamante, he flirts with the *innamorate* and even has some success with them.

Many of the plots, in fact, revolve around Harlequin's complex love entanglements, so that romance becomes a staple of the character, as it had not been for the first Arlecchino. And much time is taken up with knockabout physical routines between Harlequin and another actor, sometimes involving props such as ladders. But although the zodiac of Harlequin's wit and theatrical virtuosity takes him well beyond his immediate surroundings, hunger and poverty are omnipresent and often staged at the beginning of a scene as a datum, a point of departure. Harlequin begins "L'innocence persecutée" (1:267–70) in an acute state of hunger, competing with his master Fabrizio as to who is more famished. "Les maisons devalizées" (1:285–88) begins with Harlequin's lament of hunger, to which his fellow servant Trivelin proposes a crafty plan. "La fille desobeissante" (1:127–32), which we will examine in more detail below, begins with Harlequin taking on the role of a discharged soldier so that he can beg for food, which he does in his own persona in "Les trois faux Turcs" (1:227–30), knocking from door to door. Sometimes, however, Harlequin finds himself in the position of almsgiver. In "Il Basilisco di Bernagasso" (1:139–44), the character Bernagasso, for whom a beggar costume is designated in the scenario, asks charity of Harlequin, who first responds, "Le Ciel t'assiste" (May Heaven help you)—code for refusing a beggar. Certainly Bernagasso takes it as a no and thwacks Harlequin on his head, declaring in a menacing voice, "une petite charité" (1:140–41). Bernagasso's violent response ends this elastic gag and initiates another, as Harlequin suddenly shifts into a hyperbolically generous mode, giving Bernagasso the large sum of one-quarter of an ecu. Bernagasso quickly becomes unhappy, or rather feigns it, declaring that he is going to be ruined with so much money and that the devil will inspire him to spend it at brothels; a sol alone would suffice. Harlequin is so impressed by his honesty that he gives him a sol, but without taking the earlier amount back. Bernagasso then explicitly performs his part of the traditional medieval exchange, praying for the bounty of heaven to descend upon his gracious almsgiver, which in turn so impresses Harlequin that he gives him more money, and the *lazzo* elastically expands. Cognate to this is the scene in Molière's *Tartuffe* where Orgon recounts the pitiful, desperate spectacle of Tartuffe when he first encountered him as an abject beggar seeking charity in a church: "Je lui faisois des dons; mais avec modestie / Il me vouloit toujours en render une partie. / 'C'est trop—me disoit-it / c'est trop de la moitié / Je ne merite pas de vous pitié'" (1.5.293–96; I offered him gifts, but he modestly kept asking me to take part of it back. "It's too much," he said; "it's too much by half—I don't merit your pity").[34]

Perhaps the richest scenario featuring hunger as a *point de départ* is "Le voyage de Scaramouche et d'Harlequin aux Indes (2:669–74)," which begins thus:

> J'arrive et je dis: je suis perdu dans ces bois où il y a trois jours que je n'ay mangé. Oh mes chers boyaux, autrefois labirinthes delicieux où coulloient les souppes succulentes, où passoient les jambons accompagnés d'un cortege de saucisses et de pigeons qui s'y promenoient à droite et à gauche, et erroient dans vos spacieux destours, à present tristes et abandonnez, on entend vos faible murmures qui font *flu, flu, flu,* cauzés par un jeusne trop long! Oh destin cruel pourquoy pourvioir un aussy petit homme que moy d'un aussy grand appétit? Et puisque je devois avoir une faim aussy violente pourquoy ne m'as tu pas fait un animal vorace, qui trouve à vivre aux depend des autres? (2:669)

> I arrive and I say, I am lost in these woods and it's been three days since I've eaten. Oh, my dear intestines, which once were delicious labyrinths where succulent soups flowed, where hams passed accompanied by a parade of sausages and pigeons which walked right and left, and wandered in your spacious environs, which are now so sad and empty, and where one hears faint cries of "flu, flu, flu," caused by too long a fast. Oh, cruel destiny, why grant such a tiny person as myself such a big appetite? And if I am to have such a violent hunger, why didn't you make me into a voracious animal, who can live at the expense of others?

Despite the occasional efficacy of magic in these scenarios, Harlequin's subsequent supplication that an Ovidian metamorphosis might transform the "pierres en pain, cette eau en vin, ces papillons en poulardes" (these stones into bread, this water into wine, these butterflies into fat chickens) does not come to pass. Few passages in the commedia dell'arte and related popular literature demonstrate the close connection of gluttony and hunger as much as this one, as Harlequin's aching and craving bowels become the site of past gastronomic glory, a utopian locus where carnivalesque parades of succulent foods pass in review. Although Biancolelli was diminutive in height, the reference to his "tininess" is a gastronomic in-joke about an actor already grown corpulent by the 1660s, and the joke nicely demonstrate the vestigial, sedimented nature of poverty gags with Biancolelli.

As with Ruzante at the beginning of *Il parlamento,* hunger in the scenarios becomes a sign of one's human existence. In "La fille desobeissante," Harlequin is poisoned along with Eularia by her lover Octave, and left for dead next to her in the tomb. When asked by Eularia's servant Diamantine who he is, he declares, "[J]e suis un mort qui se meurt de faim" (1:131; I'm a dead man who is starving from hunger), only to realize that he is alive. Macaroni amounts to a kind of coin of the realm for Harlequin.[35] A common gag becomes the recitation of the names of succulent foods;[36] and the scenarios are full of kitchen utensils, often used as implements of battle in a carnivalesque mode.

Hunger is often perceived as a Tantalean experience. We meet the actual Tantalus in a vision-of-hell scene in "Le voyage de Scaramouche et d'Harlequin aux Indes" (Harlequin emerges from a cave which he has been forced to enter and tells Cinthio that he has been to hell and back): "Ensuite je vis dans la rivière un homme qui, lorsqu'il vouloit boire, voyoit l'eau s'abbaisser[;] un diable malicieux luy avoit mis un morceau de lard sur le nez et quand il elevoit sa bouche pour le manger, ce mesme diablotin le levoit en l'air de façon qu'il mouroit de faim et de soif" (2:670–71; Then I saw in the river a man who, when he wanted to drink saw the water lowered out of reach; a malicious devil placed a piece of bacon on his nose and when he raised his mouth to eat it the same devil lifted it in the air so that Tantalus was dying from hunger and thirst). For his part, Harlequin repeatedly comes tantalizingly close to the utopian meal, only to see it snatched away from him, as in "L'innocence persecutée," when Angiola inadvertently knocks over a succulent stew that he is carrying and about to eat—whereupon he tries to lick it off the floor (1:268). In an even more abject version of this gag, in "La hotte" (1:197–202), Trivelin reads a list of food expenses, tearing off each item as he reads it and throwing it on the floor, only in sudden regret to eat the pieces of paper (1:197).

Alternatively, Harlequin may become a delectable food object himself, just as the peasants imagined themselves being at the beginning of *Dialogo facetissimo*. In "Le voyage de Scaramouche et d'Harlequin aux Indes," in the descent to hell that he recounts to Cinthio, Harlequin is captured by Pluto, whom we meet wearing a pair of glasses and reading the gazette while being fanned by two devils. Pluto orders Harlequin to be boiled in a cauldron. (Readers of Rabelais will recall Panurge being roasted on a spit by Turks.) As Proserpine looks at the delectable meal as if it were a "un petit cochon de lait à la broche" (1:671; a nice pig roasted on a spit), Harlequin narrowly escapes what amounts to a cannibalistic fate by promising the king and queen of hell that he can lead them to someone much fatter than he: another actor in Biancolelli's troupe (but probably another ironic self-reference to Biancolelli's own corpulence). The scene ends with a ridiculous *lazzo* of eating, with Harlequin's and Scaramouche's arms attached to each other, both having to perform ridiculous gyrations to get to tables of food placed behind each of them.

To be sure, there are long stretches in the scenario when, caught up in Harlequin's inventions, disguises, and romances, we momentarily forget about his hunger and poverty (as we never do for a moment with Ruzante in the hunger plays that we have examined). But if Harlequin is not hungry, he is persistently drawn to the "culture of the poor"—the world of petty crime, roguery, charlatanry, and even prison. He frequently steals or intends to steal;[37] he is either put in prison or threatened with it;[38] and he takes on the shady role of the piazza charlatan, offering dubious nostrums to naïve customers.[39]

And he was adept at playing the role of the fraudulent beggar that we have examined in Chapter 2. One of the greatest theatrical turns ever on the trope occurs in "La fille desobeissante" (1:127–29). Here, Harlequin assumes the disguise of a destitute and famished discharged soldier who had fought at Porto Longone on the island of Elba. As we have seen in Ruzante's *Il parlamento*, this was a relatively legitimate object of charity to whom one might feel justified in dispensing individual charity even in cities and periods when the poor laws officially forbade it. Approaching the *amoureux* Cinthio, Biancolelli/Harlequin first declares, after a ceremonious verbal greeting, that he is mute. When Cinthio laughs and asks him how it is possible that he can speak, Harlequin first replies that he has been brought up to always respond to gentlemen, only to recognize his obvious absurdity and declare that he is actually deaf, eliciting an even louder guffaw from Cinthio. Confessing again to his mistake (he claims that hunger keeps him from thinking clearly), he announces that he is blind, to which the now extremely skeptical (but well-entertained) Cinthio aggressively thrusts his fingers toward Harlequin's eyes. After the latter instinctively recoils, to Cinthio's insistence that blind men do not react in that way Harlequin claims that he is only able to see in cases when people try to harm him, only to confess his stupidity again and assume yet another guise that, effectively, could be taken straight from the pages of the beggar books: he is lame. But when Cinthio lures him into running by showing him money and quickly pulling it away from him, then denouncing him as a *fourbe* (rogue), Harlequin pulls out the last stop: "Ouy, Monsieur, c'est ce que je voulois dire, je ne pouvois pas trouver le mot, je suis un fourbe" (1:128; Oh, yes, sir, that's what I really wanted to say but I couldn't find the word: I'm a rogue!).

Another version of the fraudulent beggar may be found in "Harlequin dogue d'Angleterre et medecin du temps" (2:797–807). Here Harlequin enters hungry (again at the beginning of the play, as if this were his customary state) and disguised as a lame man, with two false legs, one of which he declares he will use as a bed frame and the other as a fan. He begs alms of Octave and reciprocates the latter's generous gift of thirty sols with a pietistic benediction, even as he steals his handkerchief. Octave sees him do it and declares that it is shameful that a lame person should steal, to which Harlequin responds that his hands work just fine (2:797). An argument with a *capitano* figure named Spezzafer generates what must have been a hilarious scene of stage combat, with Harlequin using his fake legs as weapons, until he is knocked over to reveal his real legs as well. Spezzafer asks how it is that a man should have four legs, and Harlequin replies, "Une mouche en a bien six" (2:798; Well, flies have six). Although by the eighteenth century, in the hands of Marivaux and others, Harlequin would become so protean as to resist any sort of definition, ranging in the zodiac of his theatrical wit from beggar to emperor, in Biancolelli's Harlequin we find a particular negotiation of stupidity and shrewdness, as exemplified in this scene—especially when we remember that it is the supremely clever actor Biancolelli who is playing the role.

Whether rendered with baroque sophistication as in Biancolelli, refracted through a carnivalesque lens as with Martinelli, or literally marginalized as in Scala, poverty remained a crucial theme in the commedia dell'arte, no matter if for the actors themselves it remained an existential problem or had become a vestigial trope.

6 Shakespeare

Complexities of Response

In *Henry VI, Part 2*, during the first scene of act 2, King Henry VI, Queen Margaret, Gloucester (the king's uncle and the powerful lord protector), and Gloucester's fierce rivals for power Cardinal Beaufort and Suffolk have all come to St. Albans to divert themselves with some hunting and hawking recreation. What transpires at the sacred site of St. Albans, shrine to the first English martyr, demonstrates the ways in which Shakespeare articulates ambiguous and nuanced thoughts and feelings regarding poverty and charity.[1]

We have learned in act 1, scene 3, that the local commoners strongly favor the "good man" Gloucester over Suffolk, whom they accuse of enclosure. The high-soaring flight of Gloucester's falcon, straightforwardly praised by the pious but politically naïve king, is aggressively seized upon as political allegory by the hostile Suffolk and the cardinal, who interpret the high-flying bird as emblematic of Gloucester's overweening pride and ambition. In a series of fierce asides Gloucester and the remarkably secular cardinal challenge each other to a private duel to be held later on that evening.

Their vicious squabbling, decried by Henry, is interrupted by a townsman who cries "A miracle!" and breathlessly tells the court party that a man blind from birth has just received his sight at St. Albans' shrine. The holy king, seconding the townspeople's belief in the "miracle," declares, "Now God be prais'd, that to believing souls / Gives light in darkness, comfort in despair!" (2.1.64–65). As a parodic "triumph," the mayor of St. Albans, a group of townsmen, the "healed" man Simon Simpcox, and his wife process in. As if to double the comic effect (and anticipating Biancolelli's virtuosic routine of multiple disabilities), Shakespeare adds to the source the extra gag of lameness, so that Simpcox (with one disability left) is borne in on a chair. Gloucester, who in some other versions of the story initially rejoices in the miracle, is in Shakespeare's version neutral enough that he grants the beggar the extraordinary privilege of an audience with the king. This initiates the first of several dramatized or imagined encounters in Shakespeare's work between the "king" and the "beggar."

King Henry begins to ask questions of Simpcox, not as a skeptical examination but as prompts aimed at confirming the formulaic narrative of the medieval miracle story: "Good fellow, tell us here the circumstance, / That we for thee may glorify the Lord" (2.1.72–73). By revealing that he does not come from the local surroundings but rather from Northumberland, Simpcox begins to arouse concern regarding itinerant beggars who have traveled far beyond their place of birth. Differentiating himself from the exultant credulity of the townspeople, Henry soberly counsels humility for Simpcox. Presumably from a skeptical stance, Queen Margaret asks the beggar whether he has traveled to St. Albans "by chance / Or of devotion, to this holy shrine?" (2.1.85–86). In the vein of the *Liber vagatorum*, Simpcox tells a narrative of mystic faith and devotion. The martyr himself has spoken to him in his dreams "A hundred times and oft-ner" (2.1.88)—a claim promptly seconded by his wife, as partner in comedy as well as crime. As Simpcox tells it, the oneiric voices of St. Alban invite the reciprocal exchange of medieval charity: "'Simon, come; / Come offer at my shrine, and I will help thee'" (2.1.89–90).

As the scene proceeds, Gloucester's skepticism builds, but his response is characterized by measured rationality rather than instinctive hostility. In fact, Gloucester's attitude might be likened to the posture of Sir Thomas More himself (the source's author)[2] in *Utopia*, where through the persona of Raphael Hythloday he registers both compassion for the plight of new-made beggars dispossessed by enclosure and the determination to respond to poverty in a rational and effective way, ensuring that idlers and dissemblers will not divert legitimate charity. (Gloucester, we recall, is beloved of the commoners because he is thought to oppose Suffolk's enclosure policies.) Simpcox' story explaining his lameness arouses suspicion: he claims that he became lame by falling out of a tree. That a blind man should take to tree climbing completes, in the now increasingly skeptical Gloucester, the conversion of the exchange from a miracle narrative to a municipal examination. He tricks Simpcox into identifying particular colors as proof that he can actually see, and the beggar is convicted as a fraud, since if he were truly blind from birth he would not be able to match the name of colors to objects; and even the pious Henry begins to have doubts. If *Henry VI, Part 2* continually subjects the concept of "providentiality" to rational critique (without altogether dismissing it), the very humanly constructed nature of Simpcox' "miracle" is exposed.[3]

Gloucester himself generates the next "miracle," which is to cure Simpcox of his lameness by having him whipped and thus forcing him to run away. The complete punishment is to have husband and wife whipped back "through every market town" to their native home in Berwick, fulfilling the 1576 amendment to the 1572 act *For the Punishment of Vagabonds and for Relief of the Poor and Impotent*: "[E]verye suche person shall for his or her suche firste offence bee whipped and so retourned Home againe unto his her or their Parishe."[4] Notwithstanding the cruelty of whipping as a public and shaming ritual, especially to our twenty-first-century sensibilities, the punishment enforced by the friend of the commoners is in fact lenient. Execution, branding, or mutilation would have also been possible legal responses to Simpcox' deceit, especially if it could be identified as a repeated offense. Gloucester's response, much like that of More/Hythloday in *Utopia*, is for its time rational and moderate.

The whipping and entirely manmade "miracle" of Simpcox' swift flight elicits four distinct responses. The credulous townspeople, when they see the suddenly mobile Simpcox scamper away, foolishly cry out, "A miracle!" Henry VI, though surely no longer believing in the beggar's ruse, laments what from his idealistic perspective is excessive and cruel punishment: "O God, seest thou this, and bearest so long?" (2.1.151) That God would take such profound interest in this everyday and relatively moderate punishment, as if it were the very emblem of human suffering, seems slightly ridiculous and ironizes the king. But Margaret—a genuinely unsympathetic character in the play as Suffolk's unscrupulous lover and co-conspirator—goes too far toward the other extreme, which is to laugh heartlessly at the exposed rogue: "It made me laugh, to see the villain run" (2.1.152). This puts the theater audience, which has been groomed to laugh at this comic exposure scene (with Shakespeare adding an extra disability), in the uncomfortable company of Margaret. Gloucester finalizes his judgment by naming Simpcox and his wife as "knave" and "drab," fixing the errant beggars with typological terms in the manner of the continental catalogues. But the scene remains unstable to the end, with the surprising turn that Simpcox' wife is afforded her own voice: "Alas, sir, we did it for pure need" (2.1.154). Does the actual need and driving hunger of these two wretches, signaled in this line, offer a different perspective on their deceit? Is it impossible to imagine, insofar as literature invites us to extend fictional worlds beyond the manifested plot or narrative, that Simpcox and his wife have traveled to St. Albans both for the sake of devotion and to trick others into giving them bread or money? Of the two parties traveling to the holy site—the two beggars and the court entourage (gone there for a hawking recreation but dragging their internecine disputes to the holy site)—could one argue that the beggars' purposes, if dubious, might carry more in the way of piety? Perhaps. But neither can this sympathetic view of the two itinerants—who have just, after all, committed a gross imposture—securely stand. Naïve credulity, whether baldly foolish as with the townspeople or in the more sober vein of the king, does not seem to elicit admiration in the world of this play: if the state cannot control hordes of itinerant beggars, it will not be able to restrain the anarchic and disruptive insurrection of Jack Cade that will dominate act 4.[5]

This scene presents the divergent responses to the beggar as a revelatory litmus test for the ethical-political stances of the powerful figures in the court party: it is important to see how one responds to a beggar, for it indicates how one will probably respond to other things. Responses fall out according to a spectrum, ranging from the exultant credulity of the townspeople; the more dignified faith of Henry VI, followed by pity for what is perceived as a cruel penalty; the initially neutral, progressively skeptical, and rational examination, conviction, labeling, and punishment of Gloucester; and the mocking, cruel delight of Queen Margaret, devoid of both faith and pity. A theatergoer, in the course of the scene, might identify with each of the responses—except possibly the simplistic credulity of the townspeople. The beggars themselves, through most of the scene, are objects of discipline and mockery, but at the end they are briefly given voice. Gloucester may be most linked to Shakespeare as a kind of moderate *raisonneur* figure, between the extremes of the king and the queen, but the life and energy of this "trickster tricked" scene probably tends to oscillate, in the theater audience, between the responses of mirth (Margaret) and disapproval of excessive cruelty (Henry). Ostensibly, the scene appears to debunk traditional Catholic charity and devotion in the form of both exchange-based charity and saint worship; certainly the Protestant ideologue John Foxe found the story apt for inclusion in *Acts and Monuments*. But in Shakespeare it is not so simple.

Christopher Sly, listed as a "beggar" in the stage directions and stage prefaces of the Folio edition of *The Taming of the Shrew*, similarly provides unstably alternative responses that make it extremely difficult to locate Shakespeare's own position.[6] Whether he is seen as an outright beggar or granted his claim to have worked as a peddler, cardmaker, bearward, and now tinker, a member of the "working poor," Sly would probably have been associated in Shakespeare's mind with some of the beggars and marginally employed figures he observed in Warwickshire; he comes, after all, from Burton and has run up drinking debts in Wincot—both villages close to Stratford.[7] That he may actually be, in his own words, "the lying'st knave in Christendom" (Induction 2.24—the very phrase used by Gloucester in his denunciation of Simpcox [2.1.123–24]), is entirely possible. Depending upon our assessment of the "lord," his disgusted description of the drunken Sly asleep before him may stand on its own, un-ironized, as an emblematic designation of both idleness and ugliness: "O monstrous beast, how like a swine he lies! / Grim death, how foul and loathsome is thine image!" (Induction 1.34–35). Did Shakespeare's own father, as town bailiff, respond in such a way to the many drunken Warwickshire beggars that he would have seen in Stratfordian streets and taverns?

The lord's response to Sly both resembles and differs from that of Gloucester to Simpcox in interesting respects: whereas Gloucester wishes to brand Simpcox as a dissembling beggar, depriving him of any spiritual aura in a harsh application of the reality principle, the lord enchants rather than disenchants. He devises his fanciful scheme of fine clothing, a sumptuous banquet, attendants, and an Italian play precisely in order to transport Sly to a fictional world: "Would not the beggar then forget himself?" (Induction 1.41). The tantalizing and ephemeral fantasy that the lord perpetrates on Sly resembles the Cuccagna fantasies of the Italian piazza pamphlets, except that Sly is in no way the agent of the compensatory fantasy, as the piazza singers are, who usually register at the end of the song the painful gap between desire and reality. The transvestite page who is to play the role of Lord Sly's wife is instructed to address Sly as a kind of *povero vergognoso* fallen into poverty and then risen back to his proper rank: he (she) is to "shed tears, as being overjoyed / To see her noble lord restor'd to health, / Who for this seven years hath esteemed him / No better than a poor and loathsome beggar" (Induction 1.120–23). Sly's dream might possibly be construed as a "good man's feast" charitably dispensed by the great lord to the poor, but his contempt and scorn for the drunken beggar make this unlikely. His avowed reason for casting Cuccagna upon Sly is nothing more than sport, as a "pastime passing excellent" (Induction 1.67). His willingness to draw mirth from the poor connects him with Margaret's heartless laughter at Simpcox' expense. Does our critical assessment of the lord, dallying with the poor, defuse the possible contempt that we ourselves might feel for the Warwickshire beggar? Might then our critique of the lord's prank (to be administered, he repeatedly insists to his servants, with moderation) lead us to the reverse effect of some compassion and sympathy for Sly? But if we in the twenty-first century are troubled by the lord's treatment of Sly, would a sixteenth-century audience have been as sensitive? As with the exchange between the king and the beggar in *Henry VI, Part 2*, the exchange in this early comedy between the rich man and the beggar is complex, channeling into the dramatic medium nuanced possibilities of feeling and response regarding the poor.

Neither the Simpcox scene from *Henry VI, Part 2* nor the Sly induction of *The Taming of the Shrew* conclusively reveal the playwright's own stance. To complicate matters, most current editors argue that *Henry VI, Part 2*, if perhaps written with the "overall shaping spirit" of Shakespeare, may well have included plot and dialogue from Robert Greene, George Peele, and Thomas Nashe.[8] Three other plays that address begging and poverty, *Timon of Athens*, *Pericles*, and *Henry VIII*, were also coauthored.[9] What does seem clear is that in both his sole-authored and collaboratively composed plays, the issues of begging, poverty, and charity were certainly important. We might side with the Marxist playwright Edward Bond in censuring Shakespeare for contradictions between his art and his life, but we cannot accuse him of avoiding the issue in his plays.[10] And what emerges in his plays is not just random heterogeneity but a persistent structural opposition, characteristic of both *Henry VI, Part 2* and *The Taming of the Shrew*, that seems to encourage a complex critical sensibility regarding poverty. Shakespeare continually offsets the ideal beggar and the ironic beggar, the sympathetic and the repulsive, the sacred and the profane.

Kinds of Poverty

Shakespeare describes, evokes, and represents poverty in many kinds and guises. He evokes poverty, particularly in the form of hunger, in strikingly graphic detail. The word "beggar" appears frequently in his work, in metaphorical, rhetorical, descriptive, and dramatized ways; it both functions metonymically for poverty in general and is structurally set against the king or the rich man, but often with the effect of blurring boundaries between those at the top and the bottom of society's ladder. Not only outright beggars but the "working poor," often inventing their lives by a variety of legal and illegal activities and fictions, abound in the plays.

As arguably the early modern English dramatist with the most direct agricultural experience (like Ruzante in comparison to Ariosto, Machiavelli, and other urban Italian early modern playwrights), Shakespeare tends to showcase rural rather than urban poverty. And the economic concerns of penurious urban dwellers in his plays often revolve upon issues directly related to agricultural crisis, chiefly the hoarding and exorbitant pricing of grain—the angry plebeians' complaint in *Coriolanus*. Rarely in Shakespeare are the specifically urban conditions of living in poverty evoked, such as the rotten tenement buildings and putrid beds described in the Giulio Cesare Croce pamphlets. The strikingly urban picture of Subtle's destitute origins that Face derisively paints in Jonson's *The Alchemist* seems slightly foreign to Shakespeare, notwithstanding the degraded Vienna of *Measure for Measure*. So Face:

> But I shall put you in mind, sir, at Pie Corner,
> Taking your meal of steam in, from cooks' stalls,
> Where, like the father of hunger, you did walk
> Piteously costive, with your pinched-horn-nose,
> . . .
> When you went pinned up, in the several rages
> You'd rakd, and picked from dunghills, before day,
> Your feet in mouldy slippers, for your kibes,

A felt of rug, and a thin threaden cloak,
That scarce would cover your no-buttocks[.]
(1.1.25–28, 33–37)[11]

In Shakespeare, by contrast, we tend to see pictures such as Titania's description of devastated crops in *A Midsummer Night's Dream,* written by Shakespeare in the midst of the horrendous crop failures of the mid-1590s that directly impacted the fortunes of lower- to middle-class Londoners:[12]

The ox hath therefore stretch'd his yoke in vain,
The ploughman lost his sweat, and the green corn
Hath rotted ere his youth attain'd a beard.
The fold stands empty in the drown'd field,
And crows are fatted with the murrion flock[.]
(2.1.93–97)

As a realistic rather than idyllic pastoral play, *As You Like It* stages exiled courtiers encountering Corin, a smallholding shepherd about to be dispossessed by a churlish and greedy landlord, at the same time when the cruel and jealous Oliver evicts Orlando from his farm. The itinerant Simpcox and the Bedlam beggar Poor Tom, discussed earlier, are rural, not urban, beggars.

Strikingly detailed, graphic, and shocking descriptions of poverty, hunger, and material degradation abound in Shakespeare's works, comparable in their specificity and evocativeness to Ruzante's grim "poetics of hunger." In some cases, direct, painfully exact depictions of hunger wrought upon the emaciated body offset evocations of superfluity, excess, and greed expressed in the same scene or play. Alternatively, as we have observed in the Italian piazza pamphlets, the poetics of destitution works *obliquely,* like Freudian dream work, by condensing, exaggerating, or displacing the material images of poverty.

In the Q1 version of the "To be or not to be" speech" in *Hamlet,* more politically and socially inflected than the Q2 and Folio versions, Hamlet invokes (as reasons to escape our mortal coil) the "taste of hunger," along with "the widow being oppressed, the orphan wrong'd . . . or a tyrant's reign" (Q1 7.126–27).[13] In *Romeo and Juliet,* when the apothecary at first refuses to sell the desperate Romeo his "mortal drugs" for fear of the death penalty, Romeo reflects his destitution back to him, allegorizing "Famine," "Need," and "Oppression" as body parts of the poor:

> Art thou so bare and full of wretchedness,
> And fear'st to die? Famine is in thy cheeks,
> Need and oppression starveth in thy eyes,
> Contempt and beggary hangs upon thy back.
> The world is not thy friend, nor the world's law;
> The world affords no law to make thee rich;
> Then be not poor, but break it, and take this.
> (5.1.68–74)

Although the distracted Romeo's response to the emaciated apothecary is closer to contempt than charity, his graphic account puts the impoverished subject directly before our eyes and perhaps recalls in counterpoint Capulet's lavish feast earlier in the play.[14] In *Pericles*, severe grain shortages attack the recently prosperous but now starving citizens of Tarsus with "hunger's teeth" (1.4.45) so that their "cheeks and hollow eyes" (1.4.51) powerfully bear witness to their want:

> Those mothers who, to nousle up their babes,
> Thought not too curious, are ready now
> To eat those little darlings whom they lov'd.
> So sharp are hunger's teeth, that man and wife
> Draw lots who first shall die to length life.
> (1.4.42–46)

As with the starving, deranged peasants of Ruzante's *Dialogo facetissimo*, hunger drives the citizens of Tarsus to the edge of cannibalism, even as they recall their recent plenty and abundance, which in retrospect now appears "superfluous." Reflecting the binary structure of the Dives-Lazarus story and English homilies written in periods of dearth, stark poverty intervenes as a grim corrective to excess, a *lex talionis* punishing greed and superfluity. Cleon describes pre-famine Tarsus as a place

> Whose men and dames so jetted and adorn'd,
> Like one another's glass to trim them by;
> Their tables were stor'd full, to glad the sight,
> And not so much to feed on as delight;
> All poverty was scorn'd, and pride so great,

The name of help grew odious to repeat.
(1.4.26–31)

In *Timon of Athens,* when Timon fulminates with a diatribe against charity, his misanthropic extremism tends to make us sympathize with the opposite view, especially when the beggar is presented before our eyes with such graphic power: "Hate all, curse all, show charity to none, / But let the *famish'd flesh slide from the bone* / Ere thou relieve the beggar" (4.3.527–29; emphasis mine). As with the excess-to-want structure of *Pericles'* Tarsus, Timon's visceral evocation of poverty grimly counterpoints the superfluity and waste of the play's first half, just as the anti-banquet of flung water offsets the opulent feast doled out earlier to the court sycophants.

The Rochester inn-yard scene in act 2, scene 1, of the 1597 *Henry IV, Part 1,* a play written in the aftermath of the bad harvests of 1595–96, conjures a picture of acute and disgusting poverty and degradation that employs both "direct" and "oblique" representation. The highway robbery perpetrated by the prince, Falstaff, and Poins does not stand on its own as merely a flamboyant and playful "education of the young prince" episode but is linked to the scene in a way that connects poverty and criminality.

The scene of poverty takes place in the town of Rochester, an important post station about halfway between London and the pilgrim site of Canterbury, and is evoked by two food carriers readying themselves in the early morning to transport their foodstuffs to London. Again, graphic images of poverty counterpoint references to material abundance. We have learned in act 1, scene 2, that Poins has proposed to Falstaff and Prince Hal that they intercept and rob a group of "pilgrims going to Canterbury with rich offerings, and traders riding to London with fat purses" (1.2.126–27). The robbery performed by Falstaff, Poins, and the young prince as "St. Nicholas' clerks" will take place at Gadshill, just east of Rochester. Poins has learned of this opportunity from his informant, the chamberlain at the Rochester inn, where a wealthy franklin, carrying three hundred marks in gold, plans to travel from Rochester to Canterbury through Gadshill to make some kind of religious and charitable offering at the cathedral. The chamberlain has overhead the franklin sharing his plans with one of his companions, an accountant "that hath abundance of charge too" (2.1.58). Somehow Poins has also learned of wealth moving through Gadshill in the opposite direction (eastward, toward London), of the wealthy traders riding to London. At Gadshill, therefore, will cross two versions of wealth: one "sacred" in nature (the franklin's "rich offerings") and one profane (the traders' fat purses).

The carriers living at the Rochester inn paint a very different picture. What they prepare to carry to London are a "gammon of bacon," "two razes of ginger," and some "starv'd" turkeys (2.1.24–25, 26–27). The projection of human hunger onto animals, the key "oblique" conceit in the scene's poetics of hunger, also applies to their destitute horse. The "poor jade," suffering from a worn-out saddle that cuts through its hide, has contracted intestinal worms from moldy food. The carriers simultaneously voice nostalgia, sorrow, and social critique when they allude to happier times under the previous ostler, who was apparently so keenly attuned to the welfare of his animals that the rise in the price of oats—an incendiary issue in the 1590s—hastened his early death.[15] Just as the character Ruzante in *Il parlamento* has brought back lice as his only trophy from the wars, the carriers are infested with fleas, and for reasons that Shakespeare chooses to make particularly explicit and disgusting. Because their superiors do not provide them with chamber pots, they are obliged to urinate in the chimney, drawing fleas which then turn back to feast on them as if they were rotting fish. This repulsive food cycle, reminiscent of Hamlet's subversive jibes to Claudius after Polonius' death, returns humankind to the lowest level of animal existence.

Criminal activity in *Henry IV, Part 1* may be considered the roguish tertium quid to superfluous abundance and the powerless lament of the poor. The chamberlain living in the destitute inn overhears the wealthy franklin plotting his "pilgrimage" to Canterbury; the chamberlain conveys this information to Gadshill (the character), who relays it to Poins, who informs Falstaff and the prince. The franklin's magnanimous gesture of charity is tainted by the fact that he is accompanied by a wealthy accountant and by the prevalence of prosperous merchants traveling the same road. The extreme poverty of the inn dwellers casts such "superfluity" in an ironic light. Poins and company, engaged in redistributing wealth, may initially suggest a gang of Robin Hood brigands, but they are less a socialist band (half of them turn on the other half) than a criminal network in which the tricksters become the tricked.

Crucial to Shakespeare's detailed and comprehensive descriptions of poverty is the extensive and variegated invocation of the word, idea, and figure of the beggar.[16] Characters may use the term metaphorically to insult their enemies; "beggar" figures among the long litany of colorful insults hurled by Kent at Oswald ("knave, beggar, coward, pandar, and the son and heir of a mungril bitch"; *King Lear* 2.2.21–23) and is invoked by Shylock against Antonio in the third person: "a beggar, that was us'd to come so smug upon the mart: let him look to his bond. He was wont to call me usurer, let him look to his bond" (*Merchant of Venice* 3.1.46–48). (Here the beggar counterpoints the usurer, which for someone opposed to lending with interest would ironically reflect back upon Shylock: does usury produce beggars?) Hamlet refers to himself as a beggar, in a manner that at least poses as self-deprecation, when he says to Rosencrantz and Guildenstern, "Beggar that I am, I am even poor in thanks—but I thank you . . ." (*Hamlet* 2.2.272–73). Hamlet's use of "beggar" here simply means the lowest of the low; it is related to the use of the verb *beggar* to mean "to sharply reduce in value." Frequently, aristocratic characters refer to themselves as beggars when they are forced into a suppliant position, for example, Portia-as-male-judge suing for Bassanio's ring (*Merchant of Venice* 4.2.439–40); the Duchess of York beseeching Henry IV to spare the life of her son Aumerle in a scene Bolingbroke calls "The Beggar and the King" (*Richard II* 5.3.80); and Clarence desperately appealing for his life: "A begging prince what beggar pities not?" (*Richard III* 1.4.267).

But in a world in which a large percentage of the population were vulnerable to poverty, the use of the word by upper-class characters often has a way of sliding into the factual, as does the very word "poor." Prosperous bourgeois, gentlemen, aristocrats, and even kings come to experience either the threat of actual poverty or even some material aspects of it, if usually only temporarily. Edgar as Poor Tom provides the supreme example of this, as his assumed role of mad beggar matches much of his current condition. Stumbling into Arden in *As You Like It*, the exiled courtier Celia, accompanied by Rosalind and Touchstone, "faint[s] almost to death" with hunger (2.3.65–66), and both Orlando and Adam "almost die for food" (2.7.104). Another comedic representation of the aristocrat-as-beggar (its shorter duration alone signals a difference between comedy and tragedy) is the starvation trial imposed by Petruccio on Kate in *The Taming of the Shrew*. Tantalized, like Biancolelli's Harlequin in hell, by succulent food dangled before her eyes and pulled away, she declares:

> What, did he marry me to famish me?
> Beggars that come unto my father's door
> Upon entreaty have a present alms,
> If not, elsewhere they meet with charity;
> But I, who never knew how to entreat,
> Nor never needed that I should entreat,
> Am starv'd for meat[.]
> (4.3.3–9)

The tragicomic gag of tantalizing the starving may be found in the commedia dell'arte "magical pastoral" scenarios that provide a deep source for *The Tempest*, where it appears when Ariel-as-Harpy snatches the appetizing banquet away from the shipwrecked and bedraggled court party.[17] As double-edged pastoral heterotopia, in both the commedia scenarios and Shakespeare's play, the island suggests either foison or famine, depending on one's perspective. Antonio's plot against Prospero quickly casts him from duke to beggar, his destitution only mitigated by Gonzalo, who "out of his charity" bestowed upon him food and water (and to be sure, such "necessary" luxuries as garments and books). To Miranda, Prospero bitterly recalls his experience of penury, projecting a lived sense of poverty onto his decrepit, rat-abandoned raft, just as the carriers in the Rochester inn projected hunger onto their animals: "A rotten carcass of a butt, not rigg'd, / Nor tackle, sail, nor mast, the very rats / Instinctively have quit it" (1.2.146–48). The marvelous Masque of Ceres, with its happy union of country and the court, its fantastic winter-free annual cycles, and its bounteous harvests, may function as an apotropaic ritual to ward off the hunger to which even courtiers may be subject.

In his misanthropic retreat from the world, living in his austere cave, Timon is not exactly a beggar—he neither seeks nor wishes any charitable assistance from detested humankind—but he has surely taken on the life of a Cynic in the philosophical/economic as well as the obviously attitudinal senses of the word.[18] In their extended scene, Apemantus and he may disagree in perspective, but to a large degree they have both followed Diogenes as they share a meal of roots. Timon's precipitous fall from his life as a rich man is due to several factors: his lavish spending, waste, and what amounts to excessive "charity" to his flatterers; the exorbitant rates of interest that his creditors have charged him; the utter lack of generosity, or "charity," that his former friends bestow upon him; and his voluntary choice to live on nuts and berries, far from the haunts of men. One of his servants decries "his [Timon's] poor self, / A dedicated beggar to the air, / with his disease of all-shunn'd poverty" (4.2.12–14). He is a direct victim of usury, which is figured as cannibalism. Timon's faithful (and frugal) steward Flavius lashes out at a group of servants trying to collect the debts of their masters, who "fawn upon his debts, / And take down th' int'rest into their glutt'nous maws" (3.4.51–52). Like the landless Lear, Timon has "no house to put his head in" (3.4.64); he must sell his land in order to meet his debts (2.2.145). Timon's poverty (not essentially changed by his discovery of buried gold) clearly counterbalances the excess, greed, and waste in the first half of the play, as mathematical *contrepasso*.

Shakespeare was fascinated, perhaps even obsessed, with the king/beggar (or rich man / beggar) dyad. The binary may be evoked rhetorically; or by having actual kings encounter actual beggars, as in *Henry VI, Part* 2 and *King Lear*; or by having kings themselves imagine or even partially experience the condition of a beggar. The trope evokes the relativity and ephemerality of wealth and fortune, either philosophically and neutrally (as in Calderón's conservative, quiescent opposition of the "rico" and the "pobre"), or with the subversive suggestion that kings may be no better than beggars. Additionally, as in the economically zero-sum games of *Timon of Athens* and the Tarsus scene of *Pericles*, the coupling of king and beggar may suggest that the very condition of destitution is generated by unequal distribution.

Frequently, references to the king/beggar dyad in Shakespeare simply stress the incongruity and disparateness of the two opposing states. Mercutio takes the well-known tale of the African king Cophetua, who fell in love with a beggar-maid, to be a case in point of Cupid's irrationality and randomness. In Mercutio's sharp imagination, Cupid's work in yoking kings and beggars is considered to be something worthy of an "Abraham Man," no better than a beggar himself: "Young Abraham Cupid, he that shot so trim, / When King Cophetua lov'd the beggar maid!" (*Romeo and Juliet* 2.1.13–14). In *Love's Labour's Lost,* Don Armado ridiculously models his incongruous courting of the country wench Jacquenetta after the Cophetua legend (1.2.109–11; 4.1.64–87). Disparateness may, in some cases, be not merely incongruous but also reprehensible: Henry VI is deemed to have taken "a beggar to his bed" (*Henry VI, Part 3* 2.2.154) when he married the dowry-less Queen Margaret. Recalling *El gran teatro del mundo*, kings and beggars can merely be juxtaposed as the salient extremes of human typology: the Bastard in *King John* accuses "kings," "beggars, old men, young men," and maids alike of pursuing "commodity" or self-interest (2.1.570).

But at other times, a character's attempt to distinguish sharply between the king and beggar may be subject to ironic reflection, with the effect that boundaries are blurred. Believing that his wife is an adulteress, the deranged Leontes claims that to call her "queen" would indecorously subvert "mannerly distinguishment . . . [b]etwixt the prince and beggar" (*The Winter's Tale* 2.1.86–87). We may reflect that it is King Leontes' outrageous behavior that is testing decorous distinctions between high and low. It is this very slipperiness or contingency between the two states that Richard II explores in his plangent monologue. Having just meditated on "seely beggars / Who sitting in the stocks refuge their shame" (*Richard II* 5.5.25–26), Richard declares,

> Thus play I in one person many people,
> And none contented. Sometimes am I king;
> Then treasons make me wish myself a beggar,
> And so I am. Then crushing penury
> Persuades me I was better when a king;
> Then I am king'd again, and by and by
> Think that I am unking'd by Bullingbrook
> And straight am nothing.
> (*Richard II* 5.5.31–38)

In this highly metatheatrical speech, the sense that an actor can play a king one day and a beggar the next appears to lie behind Richard's "wheel of fortune" motif.[19] The ephemeral glory of acting the role of a king only underscores the transient nature of being a king itself: "The King's a beggar now the play is done" (*All's Well That Ends Well*, Epilogue 1). King Henry VI treats Simpcox sympathetically (most would say too sympathetically) but keeps a decorous distance from him, soberly advising him to give thanks to God. King Lear, on the other hand, begins stripping his clothes off in solidarity with Poor Tom, the "learned Theban." Most subversive of all is Hamlet's carnivalesque leveling of the king and the beggar, with the radical, disturbing suggestion that the king is actually a beggar, when all is said and done, as Hamlet declares: "[Y]our fat king and your lean beggar is but variable service: two dishes, but to one table"; and "[A] king may go a progress through the guts of a beggar" (4.3.23–24, 30–31).[20]

From Pompei the bawd in *Measure for Measure*—"a poor fellow who would live" (2.1.223)—to the shepherd Corin in *As You Like It*—beholden to his churlish master—to the emaciated apothecary of *Romeo and Juliet*, Shakespeare provides many examples of the "working poor" who are not outright beggars, or at least not principally relying on begging for their income. Christopher Sly poses a particularly interesting case because he is designated both as "beggar" (in the First Folio) and as a member of the working poor: peddler, cardmaker, bearward, and tinker. Just as Giovanni Liva has demonstrated how the early modern Italian poor who were subject to border controls and vagabond prosecution had to invent fictive identities in order to survive, Sly and others living on the edge likewise needed to produce multiple working roles and identities in order to survive.

The "masterless man" Autolycus in *The Winter's Tale* provides perhaps the best and certainly the most colorful Shakespearean example of this kind of multiple role playing performed by the poor.[21] Although we never see him engaged in handyman work, he invokes the role of tinker when it serves him to avoid the stocks: "If tinkers may have leave to live / And bear the sow-skin budget, / Then my account I well may give, / And in the stocks avouch it" (4.3.19–22). Behind his jovial and confident exterior, which is crucial to his material success, is the fear of punishment that he expresses repeatedly: "Beating and hanging are terrors to me" (4.3.29–30). If Autolycus has "served" Florizel (4.4.13) in the punning sense of the word, meaning that he has "cheated" him, then he has been "whipt out of the court" for "vices" rather than "virtues," and there is reason enough for his avowed fear of whipping, hanging, and the stocks. If we are to believe this fictional world that he has invoked for himself, it seems sensible for him to resort to petty crime ("knavish professions" [4.4.99]) and travel by obscure "footpaths" rather than open highways, where he might easily be caught.

As an expelled courtier and fugitive, Autolycus compares with Poor Tom, although the worlds inhabited by the two figures contrast sharply. Poor Tom treads the "ferocious pastoral"—or really anti-pastoral—wasteland of a tragedy, with its heaths and hovels; but Autolycus' inventions find favor in a fecund pastoral landscape, cannily managing to appropriate "superfluity" from the sheep-shearing festival, a sign of pastoral abundance. Whereas Poor Tom, like Lear himself, expresses horror in regard to human sexuality, suggesting his fall from prosperity as *lex talionis* for sexual sin, Autolycus celebrates sexuality as the scurrilous variant of the general sexual openness of Bohemia (corrective to Leontes' replaying of *Othello* in Sicilia). Autolycus' songs and quibbles are laced with sexual allusions and innuendos as he celebrates the "summer songs for me and my aunts / While we lie tumbling in the hay" (4.3.11–12). His sexual lexicon ("doxy," "dale," "jay," etc.) both echoes and joyously trumps Harman's repeated criticism of the "merry beggar" for sexual profligacy.

With his pastoral setting, his sexual desire, and especially his virtuosic capacity for fiction making, Autolycus provides a successful variation on the hapless heroes of Ruzante's famine plays. The pathetic inventions of Simpcox and the false bravado of Sly are richly developed in the favorable pastoral setting inhabited by Autolycus. The beggar only vestigially haunts him, in his "rags" and perhaps in the phrase "tirra-lirra," according to one editor evoking the "tirelire," a collection box used by mendicant friars. The variety of his income-generating schemes is impressive. Most conspicuously, he is a peddler, selling cheap print like the Italian piazza singer. He also hawks laces, ribbons, tapes, linens, petticoats, wristbands, cuffs, gloves, bracelets, face and nose masks, caps, and chest covers. He claims to steal linens from hedges at night, a common petty crime; as a "silly cheat" and as the pickpocket of the Clown we may guess that he steals other items (the very wares he is selling?) as well. Whether he is actually a tinker, or is just ready to invoke it when persecuted, is not clear; he does claim to have married a "tinker's wife." And then there is the rich portrait of a man inventing his living by diversification in his comic description to the Clown of the "rogue" Autolycus, that notorious fellow who has beaten and robbed him. This "Autolycus" has run games such as "troll-my-dames" for a living, exhibited monkeys for entertainment, and performed puppet shows on biblical subjects—in all, a rich portrait of a masterless man inventing his living with a canny array of roles and skills.

His fleecing of the Clown replays Simpcox' fraudulence and parody of sacred charity in a successful, exuberant vein, fortunately benefiting from a credulous shepherd rather than a skeptical lord protector as his audience. Clothed in rags, he rolls on the ground before the shepherd, claiming that he has been beaten a million times (comparable to Ruzante's being beaten by a hundred men) and robbed of his money and clothes. By declaring to the Clown, after he has picked his pocket, "You ha' done me a charitable office" (4.3.73), Autolycus registers the scene as a parodic version of charity, especially humorous when the rogue must quickly refuse the Clown's very offer of charity for fear that he will discover the loss of his purse: "Dost lack any money? I have a little money for thee" (4.3.77–78).

Shakespeare's one conspicuous use of the "merry beggar" trope so vilified by Harman neither uncritically celebrates the type nor joins in Harman's stern censure; it is governed by both the dispensations and the limits of the pastoral world it inhabits. On the one hand, Autolycus prospers in a green world that repairs tragedic jealousy and barrenness. On the other hand, Shakespearean pastoral always carries a sense of the real world, and we do not forget the specter of "gallows and knock" for this masterless man.

Kinds of Charity

Although Shakespeare's plays do defy the monolithically negative view of the beggar found in official edicts and the beggar catalogues, hostile attitudes toward beggars and draconian views toward charity may certainly be identified. To insult someone as being a beggar, as Kent does Oswald and Shylock Antonio, clearly displays a negative attitude regarding the figure. Whereas the patent theatricality of Edgar's Poor Tom elicits complex and contradictory responses, the portrait evoked by Speed of a histrionic beggar (as an analogue to his friend Valentine's love-sickness) does not arouse sympathy, especially given what seems to be a Simpcox-like exploitation of a spiritual occasion: "to speak puling, like a beggar at Hallowmas" (*Two Gentlemen of Verona* 2.1.25–26). If Poor Tom manages to elicit charity and compassion from both the duke and the king, his opinion of himself—one who loved wine deeply and dice dearly—is not so favorable. The Fool himself expresses the same moralistic view that beggary results from immoral, specifically sexual behavior: "The codpiece that will house / Before the head has any, / The head and he shall louse / So beggars marry many" (3.2.27–30).

Often, however, sharply negative attitudes expressed in the plays toward beggars, vagabonds, and the hungry poor must be assessed in the light of the character who expresses them and the situation from which he or she speaks. When Richmond's troops approach, just after we have heard a compelling speech from their leader, Richard III desperately vilifies them as

> A sort of vagabonds, rascals, and runaways,
> A scum of Britains and base lackey peasants,
> Whom their o'ercloyed country vomits forth
> To desperate adventures and assur'd protection.
> You, sleeping safe, they bring to you unrest;
> You having lands, and blest with beauteous wives,
> They would restrain the one, distain the other.
>
> . . .
>
> Let's whip these stragglers o'er the seas again;
> Lash hence these overweening rags of France,
> These famished beggars weary of their lives,
> Who (but for dreaming on this fond exploit)
> For want of means, poor rats, had hang'd themselves.
> (*Richard III* 5.4.316–22, 327–31)

In order to slander his enemy, Richard invokes conventional anti-poor discourse, familiar from the official edicts and the beggar literature. The itinerant poor are desperate, seditious, rapacious, and sexually overcharged; they intend to violently "redistribute" both landed and sexual property to their own advantage: "Shall these enjoy our lands? Lie with our wives? / Ravish our daughters?" (5.4.336–37). Richard's skewed perspective in this desperate moment, and our perspective on Richard, must be figured into his fierce diatribe against beggars. It probably resonates for most audiences neither as an objective criticism (we don't have to agree with the desperate tyrant) nor as a sympathetic endorsement of the vagabond beggar. The more ethically complex character Henry IV, responding to Worcester's complaints against the king on behalf of the northern lords, accuses him of stirring up unrest among public mobs of "moody beggars," "starving for a time / Of pell-mell havoc and confusion" (*Henry IV, Part 1* 5.1.81–82). It is the same charge as that beggars foment social anarchy and political sedition, but we must figure in Henry's problematic aloofness and alienation from commoners.

Richard's and Henry's arrogant excoriations of beggars count, so to speak, neither for nor against the poor. Coriolanus' fulmination against the rebellious plebeians may be less neutral. Although the poor in Shakespeare's *Coriolanus* do not speak as directly as they do in the pamphlets of the Italian street singers, they do appear to be "ventriloquized" in Coriolanus' "they said":[22]

They are dissolved. Hang 'em!
They said they were an-hungry; sighed forth proverbs—
That hunger broke stone walls, that dogs must eat,
That meat was made for mouths, that the gods sent not
Corn for the rich men only. With these shreds
They vented their complainings.
(1.1.204–9)

Who is it, we may ask, who says "the gods sent not / Corn for the rich men only"? Coriolanus utters the actual words, of course, in his diatribe against the rapacious mob, but it is not difficult to hear the voice of the plebeians themselves in this Brechtian "quotation." Notwithstanding the representation of the plebeians as unruly, violent, and surprisingly malleable once their petition is granted, their opening cry for economic justice does not appear to be ironized, in what is presented as a zero-sum game between want and surfeit comparable to the *zanni*-Pantalone equation:

> We are accounted poor citizens, the patricians good. What authority surfeits on would relieve us. If they would yield us but the superfluity while it were wholesome, we might guess they reliev'd us humanely; but they think we are too dear. The leanness that afflicts us, the object of our misery, is as an inventory to particularize their abundance; our sufferance is a gain to them. Let us revenge this with our pikes, ere we become rakes; for the gods know I speak this in hunger for bread, not in thirst for revenge. (*Coriolanus* 1.1.15–25)

Coriolanus' representation of the plebeians is considered by most critics to reflect the recent Midlands Revolt in Northamptonshire, Leicestershire, and Warwickshire itself.[23] Notwithstanding Coleridge's conservative critique of the way in which Shakespeare generally portrays plebeians,[24] here they are portrayed quite sympathetically. The play presents perhaps the strongest case in the canon for Shakespeare's taking a side in a contemporary sociopolitical dispute that challenges the government. He seems to make a clear connection between human-induced agricultural crisis and urban famine and protest. To Menenius' blithe claim to the starving and mutinous citizens that the present deaths are caused by the "Gods, not the patricians," who rather have "charitable care" for the citizens, the Second Citizen gives a powerful rebuttal:

> Care for us? True, indeed, they ne'er cared for us yet. Suffer us to famish, and their store-houses crammed with grain; make edicts for usury, to support usurers; repeal daily any wholesome act established against the rich, and provide more piercing statutes daily to chain up and restrain the poor. If the wars eat us not up, they will; and there's all the love they bear us. (1.1.79–86)

Like Menego at the beginning of *Dialogo facetissimo,* correcting Duozo's "natural" understanding of the Venetian famine with incisive social analysis, and like the subversive middles of Italian piazza poems nestled between their conformist frames ("Dio ci manda l'abondanza: / Ma l'huom fa la carestia"), the Second Citizen explicitly connects famine to man-made causes. Recalling the *Dialogo facetissimo,* hoarding is singled out as a particular evil visited by the rich upon the poor. Whereas, in the Plutarch source, the citizens' complaint of the patricians' usury is separated from the problem of dearth, which follows the battle at Corioli, Shakespeare connects them, with "usury" standing metonymically for the "piercing statutes" devised to "chain up and restrain the poor." The "acts established against the rich" that have been "repeal[ed] daily" might readily evoke the royal proclamations against enclosure, which when not enforced by the local authorities were taken by the Midlands rioters as justification enough to break down hedges and fill ditches themselves. During the Midlands Revolt, which drew crowds of protesters as large as five thousand, it was believed that enclosure directly contributed to food shortages.

Other passages in Shakespeare, if less plausibly tied to recent historical events, suggest that laws are biased in favor of the rich. Romeo argues to the emaciated apothecary that he should break the law by selling him the illegal poison because "[t]he world affords no law to make thee rich." In the Q1 version of *Hamlet*, the "undiscovered country" is less a deterrent against suicide than a realm where the injustices of this world—especially the oppression of the poor by the rich—will be rectified:

> The undiscovered country, at whose site
> The happy smile and the accursed damned.
> But for this, the joyful hope of this,
> Who'd bear the scorns and flattery of the world—
> Scorned by the right rich, the rich cursed of the poor,
> The widow being oppressed, the orphan wronged,
> The taste of hunger, or a tyrant's reign
> And thousands more calamities besides[.]
> (Q1 7.121–28)

The afterlife, in the Q1 speech, will redress the injustices of this world, making the "happy smile and the accursed damned." Notably, four-fifths of these wrongs are distinctly social and economic: the poor are scorned by the rich (and thus curse them), widows are oppressed, orphans are wronged, and the poor are hungry. (The calamity of a tyrant's reign may be thought to damage rich and poor alike.) The wrongs of the Q2 version will not be righted in the afterlife, which renders them as unavoidable evils rather than rightable wrongs. Moreover, they are general ("the oppressor's wrong"), and if anything, grievances of the privileged: the "pangs of disprized love," the "law's delay," the "insolence of office." (The Folio version is marginally closer to Q1, by its one major change relative to Q2: "the poor man's contumely" [F] rather than "the proude man's contumely" [Q2].) By claiming that the poor, oppressed, and hungry can only obtain justice in the "undiscovered country," the Q1 speech implies that on this side of paradise the laws favor the rich.

Hamlet's carnivalesque leveling, as he reports to the king regarding the dead body of Polonius, would seem to favor the beggar in relationship to the king, or certainly disadvantage the king by dragging him through the guts of a beggar. And this would resonate with what might be dubbed the "preferential option for the poor" expressed in the Q1 speech. But there are other passages and moments in Shakespeare's corpus that suggest the neutralizing of perspective. The Bastard in *King John*, after he has witnessed the weak king temporizing with France, rails against "commodity," that is, selling out for political advantage. All are guilty of breaking vows for advantage: "kings . . . beggars, old men, young men, maids" (2.1.570). Nor can the Bastard himself claim any superiority, since he is only exempt from "commodity" because he has not yet been tempted by it. The radical relativity of one's position would compromise ethical purity for every station of life:

> And why rail I on this commodity?
> But for because he hath not woo'd me yet:
> Not that I have the power to clutch my hand
> When his fair angels would salute my palm,
> But for my hand, as unattempted yet,
> Like a poor beggar, raileth on the rich.
> Well, whiles I am a beggar, I will rail,
> And say there is no sin but to be rich;
> And being rich, my virtue then shall be
> To say there is no vice but beggary.
> (2.1.587–96)

It is possible to read the *Hamlet* Q1 "scorn'd by the right rich, the rich cursed by the poor" in the same way: the rich scorn the poor and the poor curse the rich merely from their own relative positions, but since the arc of the Q1 soliloquy bends toward the poor, the implication is that the rich deserve to be cursed by the poor. But in the Bastard's version, no socio-economic position can hold any intrinsic ethical advantage. Timon says as much when he declares, "Raise me this beggar and deny't that lord, / The senator shall bear contempt hereditary, / The beggar native honour" (*Timon of Athens* 4.3.9–11). In other words, the vagaries of fortune, which can elevate beggars and debase lords, will then be seized upon by each party as naturally deserved ("hereditary") and not merely circumstantial. At least in these two skeptical speeches (from two highly skeptical characters), beggars are not superior to lords—neither ethically nor in any other way.

Attitudes toward charity and the different kinds of charity dispensed in Shakespeare's play vary in significant ways, but the frequency of traditional, "indiscriminate," exchange-based (alms for prayer) charity belies the notion that England had completely converted to non-voluntary and "discriminate" charity—charity only issued under the discrimination of vested authorites—by Shakespeare's time. The Simpcox episode seems to suggest that examination should precede indiscriminate charity, but the excessive scorn of Queen Margaret, the voice of the beggars, and perhaps the punishment itself renders the scene complex. Edgar as Poor Tom announces that he plans to "enforce charity" with his terrible aspect in a way that is decried in the beggar books, but the sight of "unaccommodated man" is enough to elicit charitable and even redistributional speeches on the part of both Gloucester and Lear. Perhaps even Portia's apparently anti-charity remark, mentioned above ("You taught me first to beg and now methinks / You teach me how a beggar should be answered"), admits of complexity, since the point of the speech is that Bassanio, charitably, ought to give the judge his ring.

Charity may be represented as misplaced, impotent, or a palliative attempt to stave off a more serious reckoning with economic injustice. The "charitable care" (1.1.65) that Menenius claims that the patricians have for the plebeians clearly aims to quell their revolt and is met with scorn by the latter: "Care for us? True indeed! They ne'er car'd for us yet" (1.1.79–80). (We may compare visual images of ostentatious or false charity in the period.) Similarly, in the anonymous play *Woodstock* (c.1591–94) Queen Anne's "charity" is said to have "stayed the Commons' rage / that would ere this have shaken Richard's chair, / Or set all England on a burning fire" (4.2.58–60).[25] The charity of the wealthy Franklin traveling to Canterbury in *Henry IV, Part 1* seems somehow discordant amidst the squalor of fleas breeding in chamber pots, and in *Much Ado About Nothing* the charity invoked by Leonato during his misogynistic tirade against Hero is even more vexed; instead of having a besmirched daughter, he'd rather have "with charitable hand / Took up a beggar's issue at my gates" (4.1.131–32). Or charity may seem merely impotent, as the "devoted charitable deeds" (*Richard III* 1.2.35) performed by Lady Anne in mourning the holy king Henry VI and easily interrupted by the new man of state, Richard.

As with representations of the beggar himself, ostensibly negative remarks about charity may redound in its favor for most audiences. In the "Aristotelian" play *Timon of Athens*, Timon shifts violently from his excessively "charitable" behavior in the first half of the play to an absolute rejection of charity, with his "Hate all, curse all, show charity to none"; the suggestion is that this character who only knows extremes should have been able to achieve a charitable golden mean. The descriptive lack or absence of charity may implicitly suggest that one should, in fact, give. In *The Tempest*, associating beggars with performance, Trinculo speculates on how he might make a profit from the "monster" Caliban if he could take him back to England, where "[w]hen they will not give a doit to relieve a lame beggar, they will lay out ten to see a dead Indian" (2.2.31–33). Notwithstanding Trinculo's mercenary intention, he implies that one perhaps *should* spare a doit for a disabled beggar.

More often than not, traditional, indiscriminate charity carries a positive valence. In *Henry IV, Part 2*, Henry IV praises the Duke of Clarence's brother by claiming that "He hath a tear for pity, and a hand / Open as day for meting charity" (4.4.31–32). In *The Taming of the Shrew*, lamenting the starvation game that Petruccio is playing with her, Kate refers to an informal, voluntary, indiscriminate practice of charity dispensed from the great lord's door: "Beggars that come unto my father's door / Upon entreaty have a present alms, / If not, elsewhere they meet with charity" (4.3.3–5). What Kate describes is hardly what is prescribed in the poor laws.

As You Like It

The two plays that most magisterially evoke indiscriminate, voluntary charity as a positive good, linking it with a critique of economic injustice and a nod toward redistribution, are the works with which this study began, *As You Like It* and *King Lear*. Edgar's fraudulent performance elicits powerful invocations of radical redistributory charity in both Gloucester and Lear. Like Coriolanus, the 1599 *As You Like It* appears to have been influenced by recent agricultural crises. Four bad harvests in a row beginning in 1594 spiked prices for grain from seventeen to forty-seven shillings per quarter, which generated massive suffering and a notable uprising in the form of riots against both grain prices and enclosure in Oxfordshire in 1596. The English forest became a dangerous, liminal place owing to bandits and, in some cases, political subversives opposing emerging forms of agro-capitalism.[26] Charles' merry-old-England portrait of Duke Senior and his companions "fleet[ing] the time carelessly . . . like the old Robin Hood of England" (1.1.117–19) omits, as one would naturally want to do before the acquisitive Oliver, that the English folk hero stole from the rich and gave to the poor. Orlando begins his exilic journey into the Forest of Arden by first relying on the savings of the good old feudal servant Adam, then quickly reverting to a "bold and boisterous sword," until his violence is stayed by Duke Senior's charitable hand.

If the forest can be dangerous, it also functions like a charmed pastoral circle, as it certainly does for Duke Frederick. At the end of the play, a third brother to Oliver and Orlando, Jaques de Boys, suddenly appears with this news of a miraculous transformation wrought by an "old religious man," or hermit:

> Duke Frederick, hearing how every day
> Men of great worth resorted to this forest,
> Address'd a mighty power, which were on foot
> In his own conduct, purposely to take
> His brother here and put him to the sword;
> And to the skirts of this wild wood he came;
> Where meeting with an old religious man,
> After some question with him, was converted
> Both from his enterprise and from the world,
> His crown bequeathing to his banish'd brother,
> And all their lands restor'd to them again
> That were with him exil'd.
> (5.4.154–65)

According to the report, Duke Frederick had amassed an army with the violent goal of putting his brother to the sword. But this tragedically coded plot appears to have dissolved upon contact with the space of pastoral: the "great circle of the forest" and one of its representative figures, the hermit.

The "old religious man" mentioned by Jaques de Boys is connected in crucial ways to other moments in the play. Orlando, attempting to pry out some information about Ganymede/Rosalind's background, notes her fine way of speaking, which Rosalind attributes to lessons from "an old religious uncle" of hers (3.2.344), who had once been a love-besotted courtier, only to reject both love and the court and become an expert in identifying and extirpating the symptoms of love. Rosalind, so her story goes, has learned her hermit uncle's art of disenchantment and promises to help Orlando with his affliction, although of course she does nothing of the kind, enchanting him with her wit, verve, and androgynous beauty.

Near the end of the play, when Orlando can no longer live by thinking or by the imagined worlds of play-acting, Ganymede/Rosalind promises him that she can make Rosalind appear, for "since [she] was three year old [she has] convers'd with a magician, most profound in his art, and yet not damnable" (5.2.60–61). That this magician whom she has known since she was three is one and the same as her "old religious uncle" appears to be confirmed by Orlando just before the mass wedding, declaring to Duke Senior, "This boy is forest-born / And hath been tutor'd in the rudiments / Of many desperate studies by his uncle, / Whom he reports to be a great magician, / Obscured in the circle of this forest" (5.4.30–34). In using the desperate but not damnable arts of her uncle to make Rosalind appear, Ganymede speaks the languages of both disenchantment and enchantment: all she has to do to perform this magical feat is to appear as herself, but on the Elizabethan stage this would require the theatrical enchantment of taking boys for girls. The "belief" that she needs to "in some little measure draw" from Orlando is both belief in the unseen object of one's love—the same belief that Paulina must coax from Leontes at the end of *The Winter's Tale*—and belief in the art of theater.

We might well ask whether Rosalind's uncle, who lives "obscured in the circle of the forest," is one and the same as our first hermit, the one who at the rim of the forest pastorally converts Frederick not only away from fratricidal enmity, but also away from the greed, ambition, and corruption of the court. Certainly we can say that Shakespeare creates a semantic field that links together forests, hermits, magicians, conversion, and even Rosalind herself.

Medieval hermits, wearing rags, sheepskins, and hooded tunics, were indistinguishable in appearance from beggars and vagabonds. Their ascetic existence was meant to manifest the spiritual purity of poverty, and they themselves acted as ministers to the poor. Many of these medieval hermits were extremely charismatic and in their preaching drew audiences of a wide social range, including "men and women of great worth"—like those who flock to the Forest of Arden in *As You Like It.* They were subversive, attracting those with nothing to lose—fugitives and the dispossessed. Whereas Edmund Spenser, via the figure of Archimago in *The Faerie Queene,* warns against fraudulent beggars posing as hermits or mendicant friars (such as might appear in the beggar books), Shakespeare creates a figure of positive moral valence, as did his fellow Warwickshire poet Michael Drayton in *Poly-Olbion.*[27]

The hermit of *As You Like It* thus is linked with both Rosalind's old religious uncle and with Rosalind herself. Both enchantment and disenchantment are possible responses. The hermit's strong association with poverty and charity connects the figure with the speeches of Orlando and Corin that evoke traditional-radical charity. In the epilogue, the boy actor playing Rosalind declares, "I am not furnish'd like a beggar, therefore to beg will not become me. My way is to conjure you" (Epilogue 9–11), as if the summoning of sacred pity by the indigent is similar to the magic of theater and romantic love. To be sure, romantic love is a more continuous theme in *As You Like It* than the theme of poverty and charity. But if Orlando must summon his belief that Ganymede can make Rosalind appear—something that is both obvious and magical—Shakespeare seems also to be saying, in the wake of famines, riots, and the new state poor laws that there are times when we might give the poor the benefit of the doubt.

Shakespeare's plays represent both the poor and responses to poverty in strikingly different ways. Whether imaginatively realized or dramatically enacted, beggars and the destitute can be reprehensibly fraudulent, inventive and scheming to the point of deception, nakedly impoverished, powerful indexes of economic injustice and the need for redistribution, or ministers of sacredness. No single response to beggars seems mandated: every situation must be appraised on its own. Charity itself can be performed in many different ways and for different reasons: to call attention to oneself, as an escapist palliative, as a simple and humble duty, or as as an effort toward economic redistribution. Acts of charity can likewise be perceived in very different ways: as impotent acts of a dying order, as dutiful and appropriate acts that are nonetheless not socially transformative, or as effective means of challenging and transforming the status quo.

Conclusion

From John F. Kennedy's declaration in his Inaugural Address that humankind had by 1961 acquired the capacity to eradicate poverty (if also the means to destroy itself), to Jeffrey D. Sachs' call in his 2005 *The End of Poverty* to "end poverty in our time," the present age recalls the sixteenth-century humanist confidence, expressed by Erasmus and Juan Luis Vives, that the poor need *not* always be with us. But to claim that poverty is not inevitable, not part of the divine order of things, is also to engage it as a question and a problem, which is just what happened in the sixteenth century—and in our own time. What (presumably alterable) conditions and factors cause poverty? How might they be changed? What is the role and responsibility of the poor themselves in this? To what extent is poverty caused by the rich themselves, either by virtue of personal characteristics (greed, selfishness) or by dint of the systems (early capitalism, globalization) by which they have gained their wealth? Proposals for poor relief, such as the 1529 Venetian statutes, certainly responded to a particular emergency, but they also aspired to correct poverty systemically. Shocked and galvanized by the fact of inequality in the "affluent society," as revealed by Michael Harrington's landmark *The Other America: Poverty in the United States* (1962), Presidents Kennedy and especially Lyndon Johnson struggled not only to meet the present crisis but to end poverty in their time. Several recent fiftieth-anniversary reflections on Johnson's War on Poverty have concluded that many of his programs (some benefiting from consultation with Harrington himself) were much more effective than the haze of neo-conservatism has allowed for, raising significant segments of American society up out of the despair, suffering, and tedium of poverty. The rollback of Great Society programs, first by Richard Nixon and then on a massive scale by Ronald Reagan, if occasionally eliminating genuine waste, has generally been catastrophic for the poor, with 15 percent of the American population today living below the poverty line and with the levels of inequality growing each year.

Reagan's folksy, mean-spirited anecdote about welfare queens driving Cadillacs strikingly evokes sixteenth-century diatribes against the poor by Thomas Harman and others. Both Reagan's welfare queen and Harman's Abraham Man are fixed and immoveable ideological types: they arrest the imagination and direct the emotions in monolithic, calculable ways. What we have attempted to explore in these pages is the capacity of early modern theater and performance, in the hands of gifted playwrights such as Ruzante and Shakespeare or rich performance practices such as the piazza singers and commedia dell'arte of early modern Italy, to evoke the poor through nuanced and variegated forms of imagination, thought, and feeling. It is a considerable achievement, alone worth sending us back to Ruzante's *Parlamento*, Shakespeare's *King Lear*, Biancolelli's fantastic inventions, Croce's pamphlets, and the animated mask of the *zanni*. If, as Harrington points out in his opening chapter, a hallmark of poverty in the "affluent society" is its invisibility—poverty being effectively hidden by the flight to the suburbs and economic and educational segregation—early modern poverty was more conspicuous, less avoidable for the middle and upper classes. It was staged on the road, in the street, and in the piazza. And with the mass engines of medieval charity dismantled, such as the systematic almsgiving at the Abbey of Cluny, poverty became more public than ever, up for grabs in the theater of the city. It thus seeped into professional theater—the major artistic form of the day and arguably the first example of Western mass culture—in a way in which it has never permeated a culturally dominant form since.

Early modern theater and performance takes the fixed, two-dimensional type of the Abraham Man and puts it in play, variously interpreted by successive actors playing the role of Shakespeare's Edgar / Poor Tom in *King Lear* and by readers and theatergoers experiencing Poor Tom imaginatively, visually, and orally. Shakespeare seems to have understood this principle of perpetual interpretability in the way in which he drafted the play itself, which is full of divergent internal audience responses (e.g., Lear's and Gloucester's) to the theater of Poor Tom. The false beggar Simpcox from *Henry VI, Part 2*, were he to have been described in a beggar book as the type of the dissembling blind man, is fixed on the page; as a character in a Shakespearean play, he elicits variegated and nuanced responses from other characters in the play, proxies for the theater's external audiences. Ruzante's pathetic, bedraggled anti-heroes, striking out against dispossession and despair with no more and no less than their virtuosic performative inventions, reach a level of artistic irony developed well beyond the stable, one-sided irony of a Harman or a Reagan ("You thought this person was poor, but actually he/she is a fraud"). The character Ruzante and the commedia Harlequin are prodigious liars, and their inventions are the stuff of truth, depending on one's perspective. The Italian piazza singers continually test their audience's temper, inserting subversive challenges to wealth and inequality between the framed gestures of post-Tridentine conformity. Even the outrageous theatricality of the German and Latin beggar books, presumably meant to debunk but potentially translatable to the unpredictable domain of actual performance, places the audience at center stage. Theater and performance, more than any other medium, still can stage nuanced and variegated responses to the poor as well as the poor themselves.

A frequently observed feature of Shakespearean and much other early modern drama is that, written during a period of massive political, economic, theological, scientific, social, and cultural shifts, it holds together disparate temporal layers of cultural experience, as if they were geological sediments. The love poem written by Hamlet to Ophelia and discovered by Polonius ("Doubt not that the stars are fire") invokes a Ptolemaic worldview, but framed to us ironically by the perspectivism of Shakespearean theater. This book has argued that the new, disciplinary discourse about the poor, most prominently featured in official poor laws and in the censorious beggar books, represents only a partial view of actual attitudes and practices in the sixteenth and seventeenth centuries, which could and frequently did draw on medieval and even patristic texts, ideas, and practices. The cheap poems and pamphlets sung and sold by Citaredo, Croce, and countless unnamed *canterini*, many of whom suffered from poverty themselves, drew on long traditions of popular *villano* poetry and complaint literature performed by medieval *giullari*. The piazza itself, a kind of public sphere *avant le mot*, could evoke the memory of pre-print, medieval protests against the usurious rich: a memory certainly enlisted by Croce in his crisis-motivated protests against inequality. Ruzante appropriates several fifteenth-century popular forms such as the *buffonesca*, the *bulesca*, the *mariazo*, and the *villanesca*, that already represented the rural and urban poor in variegated and nuanced ways, and provides more complex representations yet by melding popular drama with new humanist dramaturgies and a sense of Erasmian perspectivism. As at once tax collector for Cornaro and someone deeply attached to the countryside and peasant life, Ruzante himself is an ethically ambiguous figure, but one like Shakespeare who may have been more generous in his art than in his life. The archaic *maschera* of the commedia dell'arte, performed by the new professional actors of the commedia dell'arte, provides another rich example of temporal/cultural sedimentation in theater. Even as the actors presented themselves as men and women of a distinctly new, artistically disciplined theater, the *zanni*, Arlecchinos, and Dottori of the companies (secret sharers of piazza/pamphlet culture) could juxtapose to emerging new dramaturgies primitive structures of thought and feeling that could even link the human suffering levied by poverty to the universal plaint of the starved animal. In his medievally set history plays and throughout his work, Shakespeare staged variegated types of poverty and alternative responses to the poor, which especially in times of famine and economic crisis frequently evoked older forms of charity at once traditional and radical. The "inventions" of poverty that we have seen staged in the audience-centered medium of early modern theater—exaggeration, carnivalization, reversal, displacement, and condensation—provide dialogical, multi-voiced forms of irony that, in an age still beset by both poverty itself and simplistic views about the problem, can still speak to us.

Notes

Introduction

1. All Shakespeare citations are to the *Riverside Shakespeare*, ed. G. Blakemore Evans, et al. 2nd ed. (Boston: Houghton Mifflin, 1997).

2. William Shakespeare, *As You Like It*, Arden Shakespeare, 3rd ser., ed. Juliet Dusinberre (London: Thomson Learning, 2006).

3. For a distillation of the English Poor Laws written between 1531 and 1782, see Paul Slack, *The English Poor Law 1531–1782* (London: Macmillan, 1990).

4. See Carroll's superb study (focused on English early modern theater), from which the present work has greatly benefited: *Fat King and Lean Beggar: Representations of Poverty in the Age of Shakespeare* (Ithaca, NY: Cornell University Press, 1996), 3, 47. For Carroll, "[r]arely has any culture fashioned so wily and powerful an enemy out of such degraded and pathetic materials" (47).

5. Steve Hindle, "Dearth, Fasting, and Alms: The Campaign for General Hospitality in Late Elizabethan England," *Past and Present* 172 (2001): 53.

6. See, for example, the excellent collection of essays edited by Thomas Max Safley, *The Reformation of Charity: The Secular and the Religious in Early Modern Poor Relief* (Boston: Brill, 2003).

7. In his influential book *The Other America: Poverty in the United States* (New York: Macmillan, 1962), Michael Harrington begins by discussing the "invisibility" of the poor in the age of the so-called affluent society.

8. Karl Marx, *Capital: A Critique of Political Economy*, trans. Samuel Moore and Edward Aveling (New York: International Publishers, 1967), 1:716 n.1. In the original, the newly ambulant serf "die neuen Herren fertig vorfindet" (Marx, *Das Kapital. Kritik der politischen Ökonomie* [Frankfurt: Europäische Verlaganstalt, 1967], 1:744 n.189).

9. Siro Ferrone, *Attori mercanti corsari. La Commedia dell'Arte in Europa tra cinque e seicento* (Turin: Einaudi, 1993), 50–88.

10. Annamaria Evangelista, "Le compagnie dei Comici dell'Arte nel teatrino di Baldracca a Firenze. Notizie dagli epistolary (1576–1653)," *Quaderni di teatro* 24 (1984): 50–72.

11. For the Southwark riots, see Ian Archer, *The Pursuit of Stability: Social Relations in Elizabethan London* (Cambridge: Cambridge University Press, 1991), 1–14; and Roger B. Manning, *Village Revolts: Social Protest and Popular Disturbances in England, 1509–1640* (Oxford: Clarendon Press, 1988), 200–210.

12. For a discussion of the 1592 riot, incited by a crowd of apprentices and "masterless men" who were said to have assembled "by occasion and pretence of their meeting at a play," see Carroll, *Fat King and Lean Beggar*, 142–43; and Annabel Patterson, *Shakespeare and the Popular Voice* (Oxford: Blackwell, 1989), 35–36.

13. Luciano García Lorenzo and J. E. Varey document repeated uses of the word "alms" (*limosna*) to indicate the portion of their profits that the companies were obliged give over to the charitable hospitals. See *Teatros y vida teatral en el Siglo de Oro a través de las fuentes documentales* (London: Tamesis Books, 1991), 12–13.

14. W. L. Wiley, *The Early Public Theatre in France* (Cambridge, MA: Harvard University Press, 1960), 223.

15. For the document in English translation, see Kenneth and Laura Richards, *The Commedia dell'Arte: A Documentary History* (Oxford: Blackwell, 1990), 46.

16. Paula Pugliatti, *Beggary and Theatre in Early Modern England* (Aldershot, UK: Ashgate, 2003), 35–54.

17. A modern version of *Le fatiche comiche* may be found in Ferruccio Marotti and Giovanna Romei, eds., *La Commedia dell'Arte e la società barocca. La professione del teatro* (Rome: Bulzoni, 1991); for the quotation, see page 346: "avevo troppo del guidoncello." Unless otherwise noted, all translations from Italian are my own.

18. *La vida de Lazarillo de Tormes y de sus fortunas y adversidades*, ed. Alberto Blecua (Madrid: Castalia, 1972), 139; translated by W. S. Merwin as *The Life of Lazarillo de Tormes: His Fortunes and Adversities* (New York: The New York Review of Books, 2005), 68.

Chapter 1

1. For discussions of the "concentric circles" of poverty, which also included the 4 to 8 percent of the "structural poor," see Christopher Black, *Early Modern Italy: A Social History* (London: Routledge, 2001), 105; and Paul Slack, *Poverty and Policy in Tudor and Stuart England* (London: Longman, 1988), 4.

2. For the argument that poverty was a relative, not absolute, concept, see Bronislaw Geremek, *Uomini senza padrone. Poveri e marginali tra Medioevo e età moderna*, trans. Claudio Rosso (Turin: Einaudi, 1993), 66; Michel Mollat: *The Poor in the Middle Ages: An Essay in Social History*, trans. Arthur Goldhammer (1978; New Haven, CT: Yale University Press, 1986), 5; and Slack, *Poverty and Policy*, 2–5.

3. Lee Palmer Wandel, "The Poverty of Christ," in Safley, *The Reformation of Charity*, 15.

4. Mollat, *The Poor in the Middle Ages*, 74–81.

5. Ibid., 15–18.

6. Ibid., 22.

7. Ibid., 23.

8. St. John Chrysostom, *On Wealth and Poverty*, trans. Catherine P. Roth (Crestwood, NY: St. Vladimir's Press, 1984), 47.

9. Ibid., 49.

10. Ibid., 36.

11. See, for example, R. J. Schoeck, "The Use of St. John Chrysostom in Sixteenth-Century Controversy: Christopher St. German and Sir Thomas More in 1533," *Harvard Theological Review* 54 (1961): 21–27. An important text was the *Opera omnia*, 1530 Basel edition in Latin, in which Erasmus had a hand.

12. Mollat, *The Poor in the Middle Ages*, 104.

13. Brian Tierney, "The Decretists and the 'Deserving Poor,'" *Comparative Studies in Society and History* 1 (1959): 360–73.

14. Bronislaw Geremek, *Poverty: A History*, trans. Agnieszka Kolakowska (Oxford: Blackwell, 1994), 17.

15. Ibid., 20.

16. Ibid., 37.

17. Jean, sire de Joinville, *Histoire de Saint Louis*, ed. N. de Wailly (Paris, 1868), 248.

18. Geremek, *Poverty: A History*, 79.

19. A. L. Beier, *Masterless Men: The Vagrancy Problem in England, 1560–1640* (London: Methuen, 1985), 17–18.

20. Keith Wrightson, *Earthly Necessities: Economic Lives in Early Modern Britain* (New Haven, CT: Yale University Press, 2000), 29.

21. Ibid., 100.

22. Safley, "Introduction," in *The Reformation of Charity*, 4.

23. Wrightson, *Earthly Necessities*, 140–41.

24. Catharina Lis and Hugo Soly, *Poverty and Capitalism in Pre-Industrial Europe*, trans. James Coonan (Atlantic Highlands, NJ: Humanities Press, 1979), 60.

25. On France and Germany, see ibid., 54–55.

26. Ibid., 54.

27. The phrase "seller of themselves" in reference to the "freed" serfs is used by Marx (*Capital*, 1:718).

28. Wrightson, *Earthly Necessities*, 195.

29. Lis and Soly, *Poverty and Capitalism in Pre-Industrial Europe*, 76.

30. Ibid., 77.

31. Ibid.

32. Wrightson, *Earthly Necessities*, 195.

33. Carroll, *Fat King and Lean Beggar*, 21–22; C. G. A. Clay, *Economic Expansion and Social Change: England 1500–1700* (Cambridge: Cambridge University Press, 1984), 1:212.

34. Giovanni Liva, "Il controllo e la repressione degli 'oziosi e vagabondi.' La legislazione all'età spagnola," in *La città e i poveri. Milano e le terre lombarde dal Rinascimento all'età spagnola*, ed. Danilo Zardin (Milan: Jaca, 1995), 303.

35. E. J. Burford, *Bawds and Lodgings: A History of the London Bankside Brothels, c. 100–1675* (London: Peter Owen, 1976), 48. For the licensing requirement regarding discharged soldiers and seamen, see C. J. Ribton-Turner, *A History of Vagrants and Vagrancy and Beggars and Begging* (London: Chapman and Hall, 1887), 108.

36. Ian W. Archer, *The Pursuit of Stability: Social Relations in Elizabethan London* (Cambridge: Cambridge University Press, 1991), 211–12.

37. Burford, *Bawds and Lodgings*, 154–56; Archer, *The Pursuit of Stability*, 211.

38. Nicholas Terpstra, *Lost Girls: Sex and Death in Renaissance Florence* (Baltimore: Johns Hopkins University Press, 2010), 3.

39. Evangelista, "Le compagnie dei Comici dell'Arte."

40. Terpstra, *Lost Girls*, 11.

41. For an English text of the Venetian law, see *Venice: A Documentary History, 1450–1630*, ed. David Chambers and Brian Pullan with Jennifer Fletcher (Oxford: Blackwell, 1992), 303–6.

42. See Brian Pullan, "Catholics and the Poor in Early Modern Europe," in *Poverty and Charity: Europe, Italy, Venice, 1400–1700* (Aldershot, UK: Ashgate, 1994), 15–34.

43. Quoted in Carroll, *Fat King and Lean Beggar*, 28.

44. In *Poverty and Welfare in Habsburg Spain* (Cambridge: Cambridge University Press, 1983), 25–26 and *passim*, Linda Martz gives a good account of early modern Catholic ideas regarding charity.

45. Brian Pullan, *Rich and Poor in Renaissance Venice: The Social Institutions of a Catholic State, to 1620* (Cambridge, MA: Harvard University Press, 1971); Nicholas Eckstein, "'Con buona affetione': Confraternities, Charity, and the Poor in Early Cinquecento Florence," in Safley, *The Reformation of Charity*, 47–62; and David D'Andrea, "Charity and the Reformation in Italy: The Case of Treviso," also in Safley, *The Reformation of Charity*, 30–46.

46. D'Andrea, "Charity and the Reformation in Italy," 35–36.

47. Eckstein, "'Con buona affetione,'" 47, 49.

48. Ibid., 51.

49. Safley, "Introduction," 11.

50. Terpstra, *Lost Girls*, 25–26.

51. Hindle, "Dearth, Fasting, and Alms," 53.

52. Slack, *Poverty and Policy*, 117–20.

53. Steve Hindle, *On the Parish? The Micro-Politics of Poor Relief in Rural England c. 1550–1750* (Oxford: Clarendon Press, 2004), 11.

54. Hindle, "Dearth, Fasting, and Alms," 50.

55. Ibid., 77.

56. Ibid.

57. Ilana Krausman Ben-Amos, *The Culture of Giving: Informal Support and Gift-Exchange in Early Modern England* (Cambridge: Cambridge University Press, 2008).

58. Ibid., 115.

59. For charity within the family, see Ben-Amos, "Parents and Offspring," in *The Culture of Giving*, 17–44.

60. Ben-Amos, *The Culture of Giving*, 242–74.

Chapter 2

1. Awdeley's *Fraternity of Vagabonds* is included in Arthur F. Kinney, ed., *Rogues, Vagabonds, and Sturdy Beggars* (Barre, MA: Imprint Society, 1973), 85–101. For the Abraham Man, see page 91.

2. For Harman on the Abraham Man, see ibid., 127–28.

3. Ibid., 127.

4. Ibid., 128.

5. Stephen Greenblatt, *Shakespearean Negotiations: The Circulation of Social Energy in Renaissance England* (Berkeley: University of California Press, 1988), 94–128.

6. Bronislaw Geremek, *Les fils de Caïn. L'image des pauvres et des vagabonds dans la littérature européene du XVe au XVIIe siècle*, trans. Joanna Arnold-Moricet et al. (Paris: Flammarion, 1988), 68.

7. Debora K. Shuger, "Subversive Fathers and Suffering Subjects: Shakespeare and Christianity," in *Religion, Literature, and Politics in Post-Reformation England, 1540–1688*, ed. Donna Hamilton and Richard Strier (Cambridge: Cambridge University Press, 1996), 46–69.

8. See the discussion of visual representations to beggar books by Lee Palmer Wandel, *Always Among Us: Images of the Poor in Zwingli's Zurich* (Cambridge: Cambridge University Press, 1990), 103.

9. Geremek, *Les fils de Caïn*, 75.

10. Ibid., 77.

11. ". . . fenzendo tremar con una scrufia insanguenata in capo, e pure è sano e gagliardo." Archivio di Stato, Venice, Provveditori alla Sanità, 729, Notatorio V, f. 154v; quoted in Brian Pullan, "Poveri, mendicanti e vagabondi (secoli XIV–

XVII)," in *Poverty and Charity: Europe, Italy, Venice, 1400–1700* (Aldershot, UK: Ashgate, 1994), 1013.

12. Archivio di Stato, Venice, Santo Ufficio, busta 7; cited in Pullan, "Poveri, mendicanti e vagabondi," 1014.

13. Liva, "Il controllo," 311.

14. For the texts of the Augsburg registers, see Friedrich Kluge, *Rotwelsch. Quellen und Wortschatz der Gaunersprache und der Verwandten Geheimsprachen* (Strassburg: Karl J. Trübner, 1901), 1–2. For a detailed account of them, on which I have relied, see Geremek, *Fils de Caïn*, 78–79.

15. Translations from German are my own. For translations from the *Liber vagatorum*, I have consulted the bilingual Thomas edition cited below.

16. Kluge, *Rotwelsch*, 2; Geremek, *Les fils de Caïn*, 78–79.

17. Kluge, *Rotwelsch*, 2–3; Geremek, *Les fils de Caïn*, 79–80.

18. Geremek, *Les fils de Caïn*, 80.

19. Piero Camporesi, *Il libro dei vagabondi* (Turin: Einaudi, 1973), clx.

20. For the German text of the *Basler Betrügnisse*, see Kluge, *Rotwelsch*, 8–16; for a detailed account, see Geremek, *Les fils de Caïn*, 80–84.

21. For bibliographic details, see Geremek, *Les fils de Caïn*, 53. Citations here refer to the German-English facing-page text edited by D. B. Thomas, *The Book of Vagabonds and Beggars* (London: Penguin, 1932).

22. Thomas, *The Book of Vagabonds*, 102–3.

23. Ibid., 74–75.

24. Ibid., 68–69.

25. See Carroll's perceptive discussion of a "war of signs" between beggars and authorities in *Fat King and Lean Beggar*, 44–45.

26. Thomas, *The Book of Vagabonds*, 73.

27. *Tratato contra ceretanos domini thesei de Urbino ad Rev. dum d. Hier.m Sanctutium Ep.um forosempron*. See Camporesi, *Il libro dei vagabondi*, clxii.

28. Ibid., cxiv.

29. Raffaele Frianoro, *Il vagabondo, ovvero sferza de Guidoni* (Viterbo, 1621), collected in Camporesi, *Il libro dei vagabondi*, 78–165. For the *Speculum cerretanorum* itself, see ibid., 5–77.

30. Ibid., 40; hereafter cited parenthetically in text. Translations from Latin are my own.

31. Ibid.

32. Ibid., 44–45.

33. Ibid., 31–32.

34. Ibid., 34.

35. Ibid., 41.

36. Greenblatt, *Shakespearean Negotiations*, 94–128.

37. For the argument that *King Lear* represents an advanced, progressive understanding of poverty and that both Lear and Gloucester develop significantly in regard to charity, see Linda Woodbridge, *Vagrancy, Homelessness, and English Renaissance Literature* (Urbana: University of Illinois Press, 2001).

38. For the close relationship between the disguises assumed by Edmund and Edgar, see Carroll, *Fat King and Lean Beggar*, 185–90.

39. For the antithetical opposition of "king" and "beggar," see ibid., 8–15.

40. Some critics have played down the importance of Lear's speech, as well as the following speech on redistribution uttered by Gloucester, pointing out that because Lear and Gloucester only change their views in regard to justice and the equitable distribution of resources at the point when they have lost all power, the play does not challenge the economic and political status quo. See Jonathan Dollimore, *Radical Tragedy: Religion, Ideology, and Power in the Drama of Shakespeare and His Contemporaries* (Brighton, UK: Harvester Wheatsheaf, 1989), 192–93; and Walter Cohen, *Drama of a Nation: Public Theater in Renaissance England and Spain* (Ithaca, NY: Cornell University Press, 1985), 334.

41. "Poorly led" is from the Folio version, which is cited here (William Shakespeare, *King Lear*, Arden Shakespeare, 3rd ser., ed. R. A. Foakes [London: Thomson Learning, 1997]); the Quarto reads "parti-ey'd," or partly colored (bleeding).

Chapter 3

1. Carlo Ginzburg, *The Cheese and the Worms: The Cosmos of a Sixteenth-Century Miller*, trans. John and Anne Tedeschi (1976; Baltimore: Johns Hopkins University Press, 1980).

2. Piero Camporesi, *Bread of Dreams: Food and Fantasy in Early Modern Europe*, trans. David Gentilcore (1980; Chicago: University of Chicago Press, 1989), 20. Camporesi is actually quoting Sabadino degli Arienti, *Le porretane* (Bari: Laterza, 1914), 242.

3. Melissa Conway, *The Diario of the Printing Press of San Jacopo di Ripoli 1476–1484: Commentary and Transcription* (Florence: Olschki, 1999).

4. Drawing from the traditional association of the Umbrian town of Cerreto with itinerant healers, a *cerretano* was a mountebank-healer. *Curmatore* is a variant of *ciurmatori*, also meaning "charlatan."

5. Susan Noakes, "The Development of the Book Trade in Quattrocento Italy: Printers' Failures and the Role of the Middleman," *Journal of Medieval and Renaissance Studies* 11 (1981): 23–55. The categories are those of Noakes, who addresses them on p. 45.

6. For the background information on peddlers and cheap print, I am indebted to the recent work of Rosa Salzberg, cited below. A quattrino was worth

about a third of a soldo. It cost roughly five soldi (fifteen quattrini) to buy a pair of shoes.

7. Giovanni Pontano, *I dialoghi*, ed. Carmelo Previtera (Florence: Sansoni, 1943), 100–101; cited in Rosa Salzberg and Massimo Rospocher, "Street Singers in Italian Renaissance Urban Culture and Communication," *Culture and Social History* 9 (2012): 13.

8. Tommaso Garzoni, *La piazza universale di tutte le professioni del mondo*, ed. Paolo Cerchi and Beatrice Collina (Turin: Einaudi, 1996), 2:1188–89; cited in Salzberg and Rospocher, "Street Singers in Italian Renaissance Urban Culture," 9.

9. Rosa Salzberg, "Selling Stories and Many Other Things in and through the City: Peddling Print in Sixteenth-Century Florence and Venice," *Sixteenth-Century Journal* 42 (2011): 746, referencing Archivio di Stato Firenze, *Ospedale di Santa Maria Nuova*, busta 195, fol. 20r (15 February 1569). The archival translations in this chapter, unless otherwise noted, are those of Salzberg. All other translations from Italian in the present study are my own. See Salzberg's book-length study of the subject, *Ephemeral Cities: Cheap Print and Urban Culture in Renaissance Venice* (Manchester, UK: Manchester University Press, 2014).

10. Salzberg, "Selling Stories," 747, referencing Archivio di Stato Firenze, *Ospedale di Santa Maria Nuova*, busta 193, fol. 13r (March 1560).

11. Salzberg and Rospocher, "Street Singers in Italian Renaissance Urban Culture," 12, referring to the text of Giovanni di Giorgio il Cieco, *Lamento di meloni, in barcelletta. Et un capitolo in lode della uva* (Venice: Matteo Pagan, 1557).

12. See Giorgio Caravale, "Censura e pauperismo tra Cinque e Seicento. Controriforma e cultura dei 'senza lettere,'" *Rivista di storia e letteratura religiosa* 38 (2002): 39–77. As Caravale explains, a high-level church official scribbled down a list of ten or so titles deemed to be subversive on the *protocolli* of the "Congregazione dell'Indice," a text preliminary to the Index, in which he noted the "Barzelleta di Vincenzo Citaredo sopra la carestia." Noting that there are no extant poems titled "Barzelleta" by Citaredo, Caravale hypothesizes that the authority might have been conflating the author Citaredo with another author, Faustino Perisauli da Terdocio, who wrote the *Barceleta de Messer Faustino da Terdocio, in laude de l'oro e de l'argento*—a work that we shall examine later in this chapter (see Caravale, "Censura e pauperismo," 41–42). But Citaredo must have been considered problematic enough to be linked with Perisauli's text.

13. Vincenzo Citaredo, *Speranza de' poveri opera nova di Vincenzo Citaredo da Urbino. Con licenza de' Superiori* (Urbino: Bartholomeo Ragusi, 1588); Biblioteca Universitaria Alessandrina di Roma, Misc. XIII.a.57.53.

14. Biblioteca Apostolica Vaticana, Misc. Capponi V.681.39.

15. Spelling and orthographical conventions in the popular texts of cheap print that I am discussing in this chapter are extremely irregular. For the most

part, except where the sense is unclear, I have transcribed the texts as they are, with all of their irregularities.

16. *Barzelletta de' falliti. Dove si contiene molti belli, et utili documenti*, Biblioteca Universitaria Alessandrina di Roma, Misc. XIII.a.57.5.

17. Monique Rouch, *Storie di vita popolare nelle canzoni di piazza di G. C. Croce. Fame, fatica, e mascherate nel' 500* (Bologna: Cleub, 1982), 11.

18. For a text of the autobiographical poem, titled *Descrittione della vita del Croce*, first published in Bologna in 1608, see ibid., 39–57.

19. These two poems are edited in ibid. under the titles "Lamento della povertà per l'estremo freddo" (135–42) and "Lamento de' poveretti i quali stanno a piggione" (151–58). Rouch's texts are based on, respectively, the *Lamento della povertà per l'estremo freddo del presente anno 1587* (Bologna: Fausto Bonardo, [probably written between 1588 and 1598]) and the *Lamento de' poveretti, i quali stanno a casa a piggione et la convegnono pagare* (Mantua: Benedetto Osanna, 1590).

20. Line numbers refer to the Rouch edition.

21. Carlo M. Cipolla, *Fighting the Plague in Seventeenth-Century Italy* (Madison: University of Wisconsin Press, 1981), 16.

22. Black, *Early Modern Italy*, 105.

23. *Banchetto de' Malcibati, comedia dell'Accademico Frusto, recitata dagli Affamati nella città calamitosa alli 15 del mese dell'estrema miseria, l'anno dell'aspra et insoportabile necessità, opera di Giulio Cesare Croce* (Ferrara: Vittorio Baldini, 1609).

24. Croce's major treatment of rural life can be found in his Bertoldo and Bertoldino collections: see *Le astuzie di Bertoldo e le semplicità di Bertoldino*, ed. Piero Camporesi (Milan: Garzanti, 1993).

25. Domenico Merlini, *Saggio di ricerca sulla satira contro il villano* (Turin: Ermanno Loescher, 1894).

26. Emilio Lovarini, "L'alfabeto dei villani in pavano, nuovamente edito ed illustrato," in *Studi sul Ruzzante e la letteratura pavana*, ed. Gianfranco Folena (Padua: Antenore, 1965), 413.

27. Biblioteca Nazionale Marciana, Venice, Misc. 1016.11.

28. Perugia: Angelo Righettini, 1614; Biblioteca Nazionale Marciana, Venice, Misc. 2183.9.

29. For a good edition of the text, accompanied by a translation into modern Italian, see Lovarini, "L'alfabeto dei villani"; line numbers refer to this edition. One of the earliest printed versions of the poem is available as *Lo alfabeto delli villani. Con il Pater nostro e il lamento, che loro fanno*, Biblioteca Nazionale Marciana, Venice, Misc. 2213.5.

30. Carlo M. Cipolla, *Before the Industrial Revolution: European Society and Economy, 1000–1700*, trans. Marcella and Alide Kooy, 2nd ed. (New York: Norton, 1976), 133.

31. Giovanni Liva, "Il controllo," 291–332.

32. Ibid., 308, referencing the Archivio Storico Civico, Milan, *Gride* 5, 12 June 1572.

33. *Viaggio di Zan Menes Tru. Opera nuua è non plu stampada composta per un Eccellent Dottur* . . . (Modena, n.d.); Biblioteca Apostolica Vaticana, Misc. Capponi V.681.55.

34. *Disgrazie del Zane, narrate in un sonetto di diciasete linguazi, come giungendo ad una hostaria certi banditi il volsero amazar* (The Disgrace of the *Zanni*, Told in Sixteen Languages, How When He Reached an Inn Certain Bandits Tried to Kill Him), Biblioteca Universitaria Alessandrina di Roma, Misc. XIII.a.57.13.

35. *Frottola a piè d'un colle adorno, con un viagio del Zane a Venetia, e narra la confusione de i venditori del Ponte del Rialto* (Venice: Iacomo Ghedini, 1579); Biblioteca Apostolica Vaticana, Misc. Capponi V.681.36.

36. The titles of the three works, all held by the Biblioteca Nazionale Marciana in Venice, are *Contrasto del Fortunato e del Zani in ottava rima. Con alcune stanze in lingua bergamascha del magnar del Zane* (*Contrasto* between Fortunato and Zanni in Ottava Rima, with a Few Stanzas in Bergamask on the Eating Feats of the Zanni), 1576, Misc. 2223.1; *Opera nuova di Stanze, Capitoli, Barzelette et altri nuovi suggetti composta per Zan Bagotto* (A New Work of *Stanze, Capitoli, Barzelette* and Other New Subjects Composed for Zan Bagotto), 1576, Misc. 2223.2; and *Opera nuova, nella quale si contiene uno insonio, che ha fatto il Zanni Bagotto, in lingua bergamascha* (*A New Work, Which Includes a Dream Vision, Done by Zanni Bagotto, in Bergamask*), 1576, Misc. 2223.3. Parenthetical citations refer to page numbers within each of these three different pamphlets.

37. For a discussion of the performative context of these pamphlets, see Robert Henke, *Performance and Literature in the Commedia dell'Arte* (Cambridge: Cambridge University Press, 2002), 117–20.

38. See note 36.

39. The second poem in Biblioteca Nazionale Marciana Misc. 2223.1, *Contrasto del Fortunato e del Zani.*

40. *Le allegre et ridiculose nozze di Zan Falopa da Bufeto. Con alcune stanze amorose, e una disperatione in sdrucciolo, e due Sonetti nella medesima lingua Bergamasa*. . . . Composte da Augustino Schiopi da Verona, Biblioteca Universitaria Alessandrina di Roma, Misc. XIIIl.a.58.47; and in Vito Pandolfi, *La Commedia dell'Arte. Storia e testi* (Florence: Sansoni, 1957), 1:231–39.

41. For the trope of the banishment of commerce, see *Il piacevole viaggio di Carnevale*, cited below.

42. See, for example, the extended list of delectable foods in the *Bando overo Decreto . . . contra . . . Carnevale . . . Publicato l'anno presente*, Biblioteca Universitaria Alessandrina di Roma, Misc. XIIIl.a.58.2, at 2v.

43. *Il piacevole viaggio di Cuccagna* (Rome: Per Giovanni Osmarino Giliotto); Biblioteca Apostolica Vaticana, Misc. Capponi V.681.18, IV.

CHAPTER 4

1. For an excellent study of Ruzante and acting, see Ronnie Ferguson, *Ruzante and the Evolution of Acting Practice in Renaissance Italy*, Goldsmith's Performance Research Pamphlets (London: Goldsmith's University of London, 2010). In general, this chapter has benefited enormously from the magisterial work of Ronnie Ferguson on Ruzante, particular his study *The Theatre of Angelo Beolco: Text, Context, Performance* (Ravenna: Longo, 2000).

2. Hannah Arendt, *On Revolution* (1963; London: Penguin, 1977), 50. My thanks to Paul Kottman for pointing out the relevance of Arendt's book to poverty and political theory.

3. Simone Weil, "The Iliad, or the Poem of Force," in *War and "The Iliad,"* trans. Mary McCarthy (New York: The New York Review of Books, 2005), 1–37.

4. Mario Baratto, *Tre studi sul teatro* (Venice: Neri Pozzo, 1964), 50.

5. All Ruzante citations are from the definitive edition of Ludovico Zorzi, *Ruzante. Teatro* (Turin: Einaudi, 1967), which includes a facing-page modern Italian translation of Ruzante's original that is mainly written in Paduan dialect. The number indicated after the scene number (or in the case of a full-length play, act and scene number) refers to Zorzi's line numeration.

6. Giorgio Padoan, *La commedia rinascimentale veneta (1433–1565)* (Vicenza: Neri Pozza, 1982), 66.

7. The term is taken from the will of Beolco's father, Giovanni Francesco Beolco. See E. Menegazzo and P. Sambin, "Nuove explorazioni archivistiche per Angelo Beolco e Alvise Cornaro," *Italia mediovale e umanistica* 7 (1964): 231–36.

8. For a discussion of the ambiguous positions of both Beolco and Cornaro, see Ferguson, *The Theatre of Angelo Beolco*, 111–15.

9. According to Emilio Lovarini, this is solidly based on a report in a 1601 Paduan manuscript. See his 1899 essay "Notizie sui parenti e sulla vita di Ruzante," collected in *Studi sul Ruzante e la letteratura pavana*, ed. Gianfranco Folena (Padua: Antenore, 1965), 43.

10. Francesco de' Nobili, in *arte Cherea* (the name is taken from a role in a play by Terence that he performed), was most noted for staging performances of Terence and Plautus, but also introduced in his *egloghe pastorali* dramatic versions of pastoral.

11. Ruzante's transformative use of these popular forms is discussed in Ferguson, *The Theatre of Angelo Beolco*.

12. Cited in Emilio Lovarini, *Studi sul Ruzante*, 45; from Bernardino Scarde-

one, *De antiquitate urbis Patavii et claris civibus Patavinis* (Basel: N. Episcopium, 1560), 255. The name "Ruzante" itself seems to have been taken from a particular village, Pernumia, frequented by Beolco (Lovarini, *Studi sul Ruzante*, 43–44).

13. Marin Sanudo, *Diarii*, ed. R. Fulin et al. (Venice: Visentini, 1879–1902), 27:253–56.

14. Cited by Padoan, *La commedia rinascimentale veneta*, 67.

15. Quoted in Zorzi, *Ruzante*, 1439, who draws upon the archival work of Menegazzo and Sambin in "Nuove esplorazioni archivistiche."

16. See Marzia Pieri, *La scena boschereccia nel Rinascimento italiano* (Padua: Liviana, 1983).

17. Zorzi, *Ruzante*, 1292 n.72.

18. Note Ferguson's astute catalogue of many genres and forms absorbed by the play (*The Theatre of Angelo Beolco*, 19).

19. Linda Carroll, *Angelo Beolco (Il Ruzante)* (Boston: Twayne, 1990).

20. Lovarini, "L'alfabeto dei villani," 298; Zorzi, *Ruzante*, 1344 n.261.

21. Ferguson, *The Theatre of Angelo Beolco*, 24.

22. Ibid., 36.

23. Ibid., 38.

Chapter 5

1. The best study of travel and the commedia dell'arte is Siro Ferrone, "L'invenzione viaggiante," in *Attori mercanti corsari*, 3–49.

2. The letter is from Martinelli to a ducal secretary in Mantua, 19 November 1609, and has been printed in Claudia Burattelli, D. Landolfi, and A. Zinani, eds., *Commedia dell'Arte. Corrispondenze* (Florence: Le Lettere, 1993), vol. 1, letter 12; hereafter "Burattelli et al., *Corrispondenze*."

3. From Domenico Bruni, *Le fatiche comiche* (Paris: Callemont, 1623); quoted in Marotti and Romei, *La Commedia dell'Arte*, 346. The statement is in the form of a fictional account by a commedia dell'arte player about the perils of travel.

4. Quoted in Ferrone, *Attori mercanti corsari*, 36 n.14.

5. In a 12 October 1601 letter to Don Pedro Enriquez, the governor of Milan, Isabella Andreini called for prohibitions against mountebanks performing in the piazzas of Milan. See Antonio Paglicci Brozzi, *Contribuito alla storia del teatro. Il teatro a Milano nel secolo XVII* (Milan: G. Ricordi, 1891), 12.

6. For an account of Rivani, see Henke, *Performance and Literature*, 214–15.

7. Brian Pullan, "Poveri, mendicanti, e vagabondi (secoli XIV–XVII)," in *Poverty and Charity*, 1009.

8. Andrea Zannini, "Flussi d'immigrazione e strutture sociali urbane. Il caso dei bergamaschi a Venezia," *Bollettino di demografia storica* 19 (1993): 207–15.

9. Stefano D'Amico, "Poveri e gruppi marginali nella società milanese cinque-seicentesca," in Zardin, *La città e i poveri*, 277.

10. The case for Martinelli as the first Arlecchino in a properly theatrical role (the *maschera* might have had a pre-stage life as a carnival persona or the like) has been made convincingly by Delia Gambelli in *Arlecchino a Parigi. Dall'inferno alla corte del Re Sole* (Rome: Bulzoni, 1993).

11. Burattelli et al., *Corrispondenze*, 390–92.

12. Ibid.

13. Ibid., 395 n.6.

14. Ibid., 394.

15. My thanks to Richard Andrews for this information.

16. The play was published in Milan in 1612. For a modern edition, see Laura Falavolti, ed., *Commedie dei comici dell'arte* (Turin: Unione Tipografico Editrice, 1982), 45–213.

17. See, however, Virginia Scott's meticulous article "Who Was Robert Triplupart L'Andouiller? Or, an Actors' Quarrel in Late Sixteenth-Century Paris," *Performing Arts Resources* 28 (2011): 25–31. Scott weighs the case alternatively for (1) Robert Guérin, (2) Agnan Sarat, and (3) an unidentified actor in Sarat's troupe who had copied Martinelli's Harlequin. My sincere thanks to the late Virginia Scott for her help with the French sources and the context of Martinelli's Paris performances.

18. All of the pamphlets are edited and printed in Delia Gambelli, *Arlecchino a Parigi. Dall'inferno alla corte del Re Sole* (Rome: Bulzoni, 1993), 389–416; hereafter "Gambelli, *Dall'inferno alla corte del Re Sole*."

19. See Henke, *Performance and Literature*, 56–60.

20. Gambelli, *Dall'inferno alla corte del Re Sole*, 394, ll. 177–78. All translations from French are my own.

21. See, for example, "Il zanni becco," from the manuscript scenario collection of Basilio Locatelli, collected in Anna Maria Testaverde, ed., *I canovacci della Commedia dell'Arte* (Turin: Einaudi, 2007), 231–37.

22. The reference to humiliation in a public square is in Gambelli, *Dall'inferno alla corte del Re Sole*, 397 ("accroché / Tu fus à un carcan, au milieu d'un marché" [ll. 19–20; you were strapped to a yoke in the middle of the market]). The allusion to the punishments of whipping and banishment may be found in ibid., 398 (ll. 39–41). Subsequent citations to this volume will be parenthetical in text.

23. Siro Ferrone, *Arlecchino. Vita e avventure di Tristano Martinelli attore* (Rome: Laterza, 2006), 136–37.

24. The only original imprint is found in the Bibliothèque Nationale; it is reproduced in Gambelli, *Dall'inferno alla corte del Re Sole*, 419–34.

25. Geremek, *Poverty: A History*, 23.

26. The play was published in Milan in 1612. For a modern edition, see Falavolti, *Commedie dei comici dell'arte,* 45–213.

27. Flaminio Scala, *Il teatro delle favole rappresentative,* ed. F. Marotti, 2 vols. (Milan: Il Polifilo, 1976). Citations to these volumes will be parenthetical, indicating volume and page number, unless the reference is to the scenario itself, in which case just the name and day of the scenario are given.

28. Carmelo Alberti, ed., *Gli scenari Correr. La commedia dell'arte a Venezia* (Rome: Bulzoni, 1996), 228–33.

29. See Francesco Cotticelli, Anne Goodrich Heck, and Thomas F. Heck, trans. and eds., *The Commedia dell'Arte in Naples: A Bilingual Edition of the 176 Casamarciano Scenarios,* 2 vols. (Lanham, MD: Scarecrow Press, 2001). For the English translation and the Italian original, respectively, of "Ricco epulone," see 1:481–83 and 2:479–82.

30. Ibid., 1:482 and 2:480. All Casamarciano translations are by Francesco Cotticelli.

31. Ibid., 2:481.

32. The textual question is magisterially discussed in the two-volume definitive edition of the *zibaldone,* Delia Gambelli, *Arlecchino a Parigi: Lo scenario di Domenico Biancolelli* (Rome: Bulzoni, 1997), 1:19–34, 69–83.

33. Citations here and below are to ibid. The original text, as well as Gambelli's edition, also has an Italian version of each scenario; I refer only to the French version.

34. Molière, *Oeuvres complètes,* vol. 1 (Paris: Gallimard, 1971).

35. See "Harlequin cru Prince" (Gambelli, *Lo scenario di Domenico Biancolelli,* 1:331).

36. See "Les quatre Harlequins" (ibid., 1:190); and "Les trois faux Turcs" (ibid., 1:229).

37. See "La cruauté du Docteur" (ibid., 1:339–40); and "Les maisons devalizées" (ibid., 1:285–88).

38. See "Harlequin cru Prince"; and "Harlequin laron, prevost, et juge" (ibid., 1:363–65).

39. "Le theatre sans comedie et les comediens juges et parties" (ibid., 2:439–52); "Le Pont-Neuf" (ibid., 2:469–70).

Chapter 6

1. For a discussion of this scene, see E. Pearlman, "The Duke and the Beggar in Shakespeare's 2 *Henry VI,*" *Criticism* 41 (1999): 309–21.

2. The original source for the story (not in Holinshed or Hall) is Sir Thomas More, *Dialogue . . . Wherein be treated divers matters . . . ,* 2nd ed. (London: William Rastell, 1530), bk. 1, ch. 14, leaf 25. John Foxe, in *Acts and Monuments* (ed.

Josiah Pratt, 4th ed. [London: Religious Tract Society, 1877]), includes the story (see Chapter 2, "King Henry VI"), as does Richard Grafton, *A Chronicle at Large and Mere History of the Affayres of Englande*, 2 vols. (London: Henry Denham, 1569), 1.630.

3. Ronald Knowles, "The Farce of History: Miracle, Combat, and Rebellion in *2 Henry VI*," *Yearbook of English Studies* 21 (1991): 168–86.

4. 18 Eliz. C.3: *The Statutes of the Realm*, 4.613. See William Shakespeare, *King Henry VI, Part 2*, Arden Shakespeare, 3rd ser., ed. Ronald Knowles (London: Thomson Learning, 2001), 207.

5. See Thomas Cartelli, "Jack Cade in the Garden: Class Consciousness and Class Conflict in *2 Henry VI*," in *Enclosure Acts: Sexuality, Property, and Culture in Early Modern England*, ed. Richard Burt and John Michael Archer (Ithaca, NY: Cornell University Press, 1994), 48–67.

6. For an excellent discussion of Sly as a tinker and beggar, see Carroll, *Fat King and Lean Beggar*, 163–67.

7. For a superb study of the working poor in early modern England, see Patricia Fumerton, *Unsettled: The Culture of Mobility and the Working Poor in Early Modern England* (Chicago: University of Chicago Press, 2006).

8. *King Henry VI, Part 2*, Arden Shakespeare, 3rd ser., ed. Ronald Knowles, 116–21.

9. The editors of the most recent Arden edition of *Timon of Athens* (3rd ser. [London: Cengage Learning, 2008]), Anthony B. Dawson and Gretchen E. Minton, hold that the play was co-written with Thomas Middleton. Susanne Gossett, in the most recent Arden edition of *Pericles* (3rd ser. [London: Thomson Learning, 2004]), supports the critical consensus that the play was co-written with George Wilkins. *Henry VIII* was co-written with John Fletcher.

10. Edward Bond, *Bingo and the Sea* (New York: Hill and Wang, 1975), xi–xii.

11. Ben Jonson, *The Alchemist*, ed. Elizabeth Cook (London: Norton, 1991).

12. Patterson, *Shakespeare and the Popular Voice*, 55.

13. William Shakespeare, *Hamlet: The Texts of 1603 and 1623*, Arden Shakespeare, 3rd ser., ed. Ann Thompson and Neil Taylor (London: Thomson Learning, 2006). All citations from the Hamlet Q1 version are from this edition.

14. Chris Fitter, "'The quarrel is between our masters and us their men': *Romeo and Juliet*, Dearth, and the London Riots," *English Literary Renaissance* 30 (2000): 154–83.

15. The price of oats nearly tripled in the mid-1590s on account of poor harvests. See chapters 4 and 5 in D. M. Palliser, *The Age of Elizabeth: England under the Late Tudors 1547–1603* (London: Longman, 1983).

16. For a fine study of the actor as beggar in Shakespeare, see Meredith Anne Skura, *Shakespeare the Actor and the Purposes of Playing* (Chicago: University of Chicago Press, 1993), 29–63, 85–148.

17. For a study of commedia dell'arte pastoral scenarios and *The Tempest*, see Robert Henke, "Transporting Tragicomedy: Shakespeare and the Magical Pastoral of the Commedia dell'Arte," in *Early Modern Tragicomedy*, ed. Subha Mukherji and Raphael Lyne (Cambridge: Boydell and Brewer, 2007), 43–58; and Richard Andrews, "*The Tempest* and Italian Improvised Theatre," in *Revisiting "The Tempest": The Capacity to Signify*, ed. Silvia Bigliazzi and Lisanna Calvi (New York: Palgrave Macmillan, 2014), 45–62.

18. For a study of Shakespeare's Athens as a site of both excessive feasting and Cynic austerity, see Robert S. Miola, "Timon in Shakespeare's Athens," *Shakespeare Quarterly* 31 (1980): 21–30.

19. For a discussion of this speech, see Skura, *Shakespeare the Actor*, 179–83.

20. Carroll, *Fat King Lean Beggar*, 8–10.

21. For an account of the social contexts informing Autolycus, see Barbara Mowat, "Rogues, Shepherds, and the Counterfeit Distressed: Texts and Infracontexts of *The Winter's Tale* 4.3," *Shakespeare Survey* 22 (1994): 58–76.

22. This phenomenon is analyzed by Annabel Patterson, *Shakespeare and the Popular Voice*, 41–51.

23. For the resonance of the Midlands Revolt and other popular disturbances in *Coriolanus*, see Peter Holland's introduction to William Shakespeare, *Coriolanus*, Arden Shakespeare, 3rd ser., ed. Peter Holland (London: Bloomsbury, 2013), 56–71; and John Walter, *Crowds and Popular Politics in Early Modern England* (Manchester, UK: Manchester University Press, 2006), 73–123.

24. Patterson, *Shakespeare and the Popular Voice*, 6–12.

25. *Woodstock: A Moral History*, ed. A. P. Rossiter (London: Chatto and Windus, 1946).

26. For a study of *As You Like It* in the context of English enclosure riots, together with a discussion of the forest as a liminal area, see Richard Wilson, "'Like the Old Robin Hood': *As You Like It* and the Enclosure Riots," *Shakespeare Quarterly* 43 (1992): 1–19.

27. Drayton's hermit appears in the thirteenth song of *Poly-Olbion*. The hermit is aligned with the Forest of Arden, which is given its own, female voice, crying out against landowners and enclosure. See Juliet Dusinberre's discussion on page 50 of her Arden edition of *As You Like It*.

Bibliography

Alberti, Carmelo, ed. *Gli scenari Correr. La commedia dell'arte a Venezia*. Rome: Bulzoni, 1996.

Lo alfabeto delli villani. Biblioteca Nazionale Marciana, Venice, Misc. 2213.5.

Le allegre et ridiculose nozze di Zan Falopa da Bufeto. Con alcune stanze amorose, e una Disperatione in sdrucciolo, e due Sonetti nella medesima lingua Bergamasa. . . . Composte da Augustino Schiopi da Verona. Biblioteca Universitaria Alessandrina di Roma, Misc. XIIIl.a.58.47.

Andreini, Giovan Battista. *Lo schiavetto*. Milan, 1612.

Andrews, Richard. "*The Tempest* and Italian Improvised Theatre." In *Revisiting "The Tempest": The Capacity to Signify*, ed. Silvia Bigliazzi and Lisanna Calvi, 45–62. New York: Palgrave Macmillan, 2014.

———, trans. and ed. *The Commedia dell'Arte of Flaminio Scala: A Translation and Analysis of 30 Scenarios*. Lanham, MD: Scarecrow Press, 2008.

Archer, Ian. *The Pursuit of Stability: Social Relations in Elizabethan London*. Cambridge: Cambridge University Press, 1991.

Arendt, Hannah. *On Revolution*. 1963. London: Penguin, 1977.

Astuzie de' villani. Perugia: Angelo Righettini, 1614. Biblioteca Nazionale Marciana, Venice, Misc. 2183.9.

Bando overo Decreto . . . contra . . . Carnevale . . . Publicato l'anno presente. Biblioteca Universitaria Alessandrina di Roma, Misc. XIIIl.a.58.2.

Baratto, Mario. *Tre studi sul teatro*. Venice: Neri Pozzo, 1964.

Barceleta de Messer Faustino da Terdocio, in laude de l'oro e de l'argento. No bibliographic information, probably late sixteenth century. Biblioteca Apostolica Vaticana. Misc. Capponi V.681.39.

Barzelletta de' falliti. Dove si contiene molti belli, et utili documenti. No bibliographic information. Biblioteca Universitaria Alessandrina di Roma, Misc. XIII.a.57.5.

Beier, A. L. *Masterless Men: The Vagrancy Problem in England, 1560–1640*. London: Methuen, 1985.

Ben-Amos, Ilana Krausman. *The Culture of Giving: Informal Support and Gift-Exchange in Early Modern England*. Cambridge: Cambridge University Press, 2008.

Black, Christopher. *Early Modern Italy: A Social History*. London: Routledge, 2001.

Bond, Edward. *Bingo and the Sea*. New York: Hill and Wang, 1975.

Bruni, Domenico. *Le fatiche comiche*. Paris: Callemont, 1623.

Burattelli, Claudia, D. Landolfi, and A. Zinani, eds. *Commedia dell'Arte. Corrispondenze*. 2 vols. Florence: Le Lettere, 1993.

Burford, E. J. *Bawds and Lodgings: A History of the London Bankside Brothels, c. 100–1675*. London: Peter Owen, 1976.

Camporesi, Piero. *Bread of Dreams: Food and Fantasy in Early Modern Europe*. 1980. Translated by David Gentilcore. Chicago: University of Chicago Press, 1989.

———. *Il libro dei vagabondi*. Turin: Einaudi, 1973.

Caravale, Giorgio. "Censura e pauperismo tra Cinque e Seicento. Controriforma e cultura dei 'senza lettere.'" *Rivista di storia e letteratura religiosa* 38 (2002): 39–77.

Carroll, Linda. *Angelo Beolco (Il Ruzante)*. Boston: Twayne, 1990.

Carroll, William C. *Fat King and Lean Beggar: Representations of Poverty in the Age of Shakespeare*. Ithaca, NY: Cornell University Press, 1996.

Cartelli, Thomas. "Jack Cade in the Garden: Class Consciousness and Class Conflict in 2 *Henry VI*." In *Enclosure Acts: Sexuality, Property, and Culture in Early Modern England*, ed. Richard Burt and John Michael Archer, 48–67. Ithaca, NY: Cornell University Press, 1994.

Cavell, Stanley, "The Avoidance of Love: A Reading of King Lear." In *Disowning Knowledge in Six Plays of Shakespeare*, 39–124. Cambridge: Cambridge University Press, 2003.

Chambers, David, and Brian Pullan with Jennifer Fletcher, eds. *Venice: A Documentary History, 1450–1630*. Oxford: Blackwell, 1992.

Chrysostom, St. John. *On Wealth and Poverty*. Translated by Catherine P. Roth. Crestwood, NY: St. Vladimir's Press, 1984.

———. *Opera omnia*. Basel, 1530.

Cicero. *Officia*. Augsburg, 1531.

Cipolla, Carlo M. *Before the Industrial Revolution: European Society and Economy, 1000–1700*. Translated by Marcella and Alide Kooy. 2nd ed. New York: Norton, 1976.

———. *Fighting the Plague in Seventeenth-Century Italy*. Madison: University of Wisconsin Press, 1981.

Citaredo, Vincenzo. *Speranza de' poveri opera nova di Vincenzo Citaredo da Urbino. Con licenza de' Superiori*. Urbino: Bartholomeo Ragusi, 1588. Biblioteca Universitaria Alessandrina di Roma, Misc. XIII.a.57.53.

Clay, C. G. A. *Economic Expansion and Social Change: England 1500–1700*. 2 vols. Cambridge: Cambridge University Press, 1984.

Cohen, Walter. *Drama of a Nation: Public Theater in Renaissance England and Spain*. Ithaca, NY: Cornell University Press, 1985.

Contrasto del cittadino el contadino. Late fifteenth or early sixteenth century. Biblioteca Nazionale Marciana, Venice, Misc. 1016.11.

Contrasto del Fortunato e del Zani in ottava rima. Con alcune stanze in lingua bergamascha del magnar del Zane. 1576. Biblioteca Nazionale Marciana, Venice, Misc. 2223.1.

Conway, Melissa. *The Diario of the Printing Press of San Jacopo di Ripoli 1476–1484: Commentary and Transcription*. Florence: Olschki, 1999.

Cotticelli, Francesco, Anne Goodrich Heck, and Thomas F. Heck, trans. and eds. *The Commedia dell'Arte in Naples: A Bilingual Edition of the 176 Casamarciano Scenarios*. 2 vols. Lanham, MD: Scarecrow Press, 2001.

Croce, Giulio Cesare. *Le astuzie di Bertoldo e le semplicità di Bertoldino*. Edited by Piero Camporesi. Milan: Garzanti, 1993.

———. *Banchetto de' Malcibati, comedia dell'Accademico Frusto, recitata dagli Affamati nella città calamitosa alli 15 del mese dell'estrema miseria, l'anno dell'aspra et insoportabile necessità, opera di Giulio Cesare Croce*. Ferrara: Vittorio Baldini, 1609.

———. *Lamento de' poveretti i quali stanno a piggione*. In Rouch, *Storie di vita popolare*, 151–58.

———. *Lamento della povertà per l'estremo freddo*. In Rouch, *Storie di vita popolare*, 135–42.

D'Amico, Stefano. "Poveri e gruppi marginali nella società milanese cinque-seicentesca." In Zardin, *La città e i poveri*, 273–90.

D'Andrea, David. "Charity and the Reformation in Italy: The Case of Treviso." In Safley, *The Reformation of Charity*, 30–46.

degli Arienti, Sabadino. *Le porretane*. Bari: Laterza, 1914.

di Giorgio, Giovanni (Il Cieco). *Lamento di meloni, in barcelletta. Et un capitolo in lode della uva*. Venice: Matteo Pagan, 1557.

Dionne, Craig, and Steve Mentz, eds. *Rogues and Early Modern Culture*. Ann Arbor: University of Michigan Press, 2004.

Disgrazie del Zane, narrate in un sonetto di diciasete linguazi, come giungendo ad una hostaria certi banditi il volsero amazar. No bibliographic information. Biblioteca Universitaria Alessandrina di Roma, Misc. XIII.a.57.13.

Dollimore, Jonathan. *Radical Tragedy: Religion, Ideology, and Power in the Drama of Shakespeare and His Contemporaries*. Brighton, UK: Harvester Wheatsheaf, 1989.

Eckstein, Nicholas. "'Con buona affetione': Confraternities, Charity, and the Poor in Early Cinquecento Florence." In Safley, *The Reformation of Charity*, 47–62.

Evangelista, Annamaria. "Le compagnie dei Comici dell'Arte nel teatrino di Baldracca a Firenze. Notizie dagli epistolary (1576–1653)." *Quaderni di teatro* 24 (1984): 50–72.

Falavolti, Laura, ed. *Commedie dei comici dell'arte*. Turin: Unione Tipografico Editrice, 1982.

Ferguson, Ronnie. *Ruzante and the Evolution of Acting Practice in Renaissance Italy*. Goldsmith's Performance Research Pamphlets. London: Goldsmith's University of London, 2010.

———. *The Theatre of Angelo Beolco: Text, Context, Performance*. Ravenna: Longo, 2000.

Ferrone, Siro. *Arlecchino. Vita e avventure di Tristano Martinelli attore*. Rome: Laterza, 2006.

———. *Attori mercanti corsari. La Commedia dell'Arte in Europa tra cinque e seicento*. Turin: Einaudi, 1993.

Fitter, Chris. "'The quarrel is between our masters and us their men': *Romeo and Juliet*, Dearth, and the London Riots." *English Literary Renaissance* 30 (2000): 154–83.

Foxe, John. *The Acts and Monuments of John Foxe*. Edited by Josiah Pratt. 4th ed. London: Religious Tract Society, 1877.

Frottola a piè d'un colle adorno, con un viagio del Zane a Venetia, e narra la confusione de i venditori del Ponte del Rialto. Venice: Iacomo Ghedini, 1579. Biblioteca Apostolica Vaticana, Misc. Capponi V.681.36.

Fumerton, Patricia. *Unsettled: The Culture of Mobility and the Working Poor in Early Modern England*. Chicago: University of Chicago Press, 2006.

Gambelli, Delia. *Arlecchino a Parigi. Dall'inferno alla corte del Re Sole*. Rome: Bulzoni, 1993.

———. *Arlecchino a Parigi. Lo scenario di Domenico Biancolelli*. 2 vols. Rome: Bulzoni, 1997.

García Lorenzo, Luciano, and J. E. Varey. *Teatros y vida teatral en el Siglo de Oro a través de las fuentes documentales*. London: Tamesis Books, 1991.

Garzoni, Tommaso. *La piazza universale di tutte le professioni del mondo*. Edited by Paolo Cerchi and Beatrice Collina. 2 vols. Turin: Einaudi, 1996.

Geremek, Bronislaw. *Les fils de Caïn. L'image des pauvres et des vagabonds dans la littérature européene du XVe au XVIIe siècle*. Translated by Joanna Arnold-Moricet et al. Paris: Flammarion, 1988.

———. *Poverty: A History*. Translated by Agnieszka Kolakowska. Oxford: Blackwell, 1994.

———. *Uomini senza padrone. Poveri e marginali tra Medioevo e età moderna*. Translated by Claudio Rosso. Turin: Einaudi, 1993.

Ginzburg, Carlo. *The Cheese and the Worms: The Cosmos of a Sixteenth-Century Miller*. 1976. Translated by John and Anne Tedeschi. Baltimore: Johns Hopkins University Press, 1980.

Grafton, Richard. *A Chronicle at Large and Mere History of the Affayres of Englande, Large of the History of the Affairs of England.* London: Henry Denham, 1569.

Greenblatt, Stephen. *Shakespearean Negotiations: The Circulation of Social Energy in Renaissance England.* Berkeley: University of California Press, 1988.

Harrington, Michael. *The Other America: Poverty in the United States.* New York: Macmillan, 1962.

Henke, Robert. *Performance and Literature in the Commedia dell'Arte.* Cambridge: Cambridge University Press, 2002.

———. "Transporting Tragicomedy: Shakespeare and the Magical Pastoral of the Commedia dell'Arte." In *Early Modern Tragicomedy*, ed. Subha Mukherji and Raphael Lyne, 43–58. Cambridge: Boydell and Brewer, 2007.

Hindle, Steve. "Dearth, Fasting, and Alms: The Campaign for General Hospitality in Late Elizabethan England." *Past and Present* 172 (2001): 44–88.

———. *On the Parish? The Micro-Politics of Poor Relief in Rural England c. 1550–1750.* Oxford: Clarendon Press, 2004.

Hobday, Charles. "Clouted Shoon and Leather Aprons: Shakespeare and the Egalitarian Tradition." *Renaissance and Modern Studies* 23 (1979): 63–78.

Joinville, Jean, sire de. *Histoire de Saint Louis.* Edited by N. de Wailly. Paris, 1868.

Jonson, Ben. *The Alchemist.* Edited by Elizabeth Cook. London: Norton, 1991.

Kinney, Arthur F., ed. *Rogues, Vagabonds, and Sturdy Beggars.* Barre, MA: Imprint Society, 1973.

Kluge, Friedrich. *Rotwelsch. Quellen und Wortschatz der Gaunersprache und der Verwandten Geheimsprachen.* Strassburg: Karl J. Trübner, 1901.

Knowles, Ronald. "The Farce of History: Miracle, Combat, and Rebellion in *2 Henry VI.*" *Yearbook of English Studies* 21 (1991): 168–86.

Liber vagatorum: Der Betler Orden. Nuremberg, ?1510.

Lis, Catharina, and Hugo Soly. *Poverty and Capitalism in Pre-Industrial Europe.* Translated by James Coonan. Atlantic Highlands, NJ: Humanities Press, 1979.

Liva, Giovanni. "Il controllo e la repressione degli 'oziosi e vagabondi.' La legislazione all'età spagnola." In Zardin, *La città e i poveri*, 291–332.

Lovarini, Emilio. "L'alfabeto dei villani in pavano, nuovamente edito ed illustrato." In *Studi sul Ruzzante e la letteratura pavana*, ed. Gianfranco Folena, 411–34. Padua: Antenore, 1965.

———. "Notizie sui parenti e sulla vita di Ruzante." In *Studi sul Ruzante e la letteratura pavana*, ed. Gianfranco Folena, 3–60. Padua: Antenore, 1965.

Manning, Roger B. *Village Revolts: Social Protest and Popular Disturbances in England, 1509–1640.* Oxford: Clarendon Press, 1988.

Marotti, Ferruccio, and Giovanna Romei, eds. *La Commedia dell'Arte e la società barocca. La professione del teatro.* Rome: Bulzoni, 1991.

Martinelli, Tristano. *Compositions de rhetorique*. Lyon, 1601.

Martz, Linda. *Poverty and Welfare in Habsburg Spain*. Cambridge: Cambridge University Press, 1983.

Marx, Karl. *Capital: A Critique of Political Economy*. Translated by Samuel Moore and Edward Aveling. 3 vols. New York: International Publishers, 1967.

———. *Das Kapital. Kritik der politischen Ökonomie*. 3 vols. Frankfurt: Europäische Verlaganstalt, 1967.

Menegazzo, E., and P. Sambin. "Nuove explorazioni archivistiche per Angelo Beolco e Alvise Cornaro." *Italia mediovale e umanistica* 7 (1964), 133–247.

Merlini, Domenico. *Saggio di ricerca sulla satira contro il villano*. Turin: Ermanno Loescher, 1894.

Miola, Robert S. "Timon in Shakespeare's Athens." *Shakespeare Quarterly* 31 (1980): 21–30.

Molière. *Oeuvres complètes*. Vol. 1. Paris: Gallimard, 1971.

Mollat, Michel. *The Poor in the Middle Ages: An Essay in Social History*. Translated by Arthur Goldhammer. 1978. New Haven, CT: Yale University Press, 1986.

More, Sir Thomas. *Dialogue . . . Wherein be treated divers matters . . . .* 2nd ed. London: William Rastell, 1530.

Mowat, Barbara. "Rogues, Shepherds, and the Counterfeit Distressed: Texts and Infracontexts of *The Winter's Tale* 4.3." *Shakespeare Survey* 22 (1994): 58–76.

Noakes, Susan. "The Development of the Book Trade in Quattrocento Italy: Printers' Failures and the Role of the Middleman." *Journal of Medieval and Renaissance Studies* 11 (1981): 23–55.

Nuovo modo de intendere la lingua zerga. Ferrara, 1545.

Opera nuova di Stanze, Capitoli, Barzelette, et altri nuovi suggetti composta per Zan Bagotto. 1576. Biblioteca Nazionale Marciana, Venice, Misc. 2223.2.

Opera nuova, nella quale si contiene uno insonio, che ha fatto il Zanni Bagotto, in lingua bergamascha. 1576. Biblioteca Nazionale Marciana, Venice, Misc. 2223.3.

Padoan, Giorgio. *La commedia rinascimentale veneta (1433–1565)*. Vicenza: Neri Pozza, 1982.

Paglicci Brozzi, Antonio. *Contribuito alla storia del teatro. Il teatro a Milano nel secolo XVII*. Milan: G. Ricordi, 1891.

Palliser, D. M. *The Age of Elizabeth: England under the Late Tudors 1547–1603*. London: Longman, 1983.

Pandolfi, Vito. *La Commedia dell'Arte. Storia e testi*. 6 vols. Florence: Sansoni, 1957.

Patterson, Annabel. *Shakespeare and the Popular Voice*. Oxford: Blackwell, 1989.

Pearlman, E. "The Duke and the Beggar in Shakespeare's 2 *Henry VI*." *Criticism* 41 (1999): 309–21.

Il piacevole viaggio di Carnevale. Rome: Per Giovanni Osmarino Giliotto. Biblioteca Apostolica Vaticana, Misc. Capponi V.681.18.

Pieri, Marzia. *La scena boschereccia nel Rinascimento italiano*. Padua: Liviana, 1983.

Pini, Teseo. *Speculum cerretanorum*. In Camporesi, *Libro dei vagabondi*, 5–77.

Pontano, Giovanni. *I dialoghi*. Edited by Carmelo Previtera. Florence: Sansoni, 1943.

Pugliatti, Paula. *Beggary and Theatre in Early Modern England*. Aldershot, UK: Ashgate, 2003.

Pullan, Brian. "Catholics and the Poor in Early Modern Europe." In *Poverty and Charity: Europe, Italy, Venice, 1400–1700*, 15–34. Aldershot, UK: Ashgate, 1994.

———. "Poveri, mendicanti, e vagabondi (secoli XIV–XVII)." In *Poverty and Charity: Europe, Italy, Venice, 1400–1700*, 981–1047. Aldershot, UK: Ashgate, 1994.

———. *Rich and Poor in Renaissance Venice: The Social Institutions of a Catholic State, to 1620*. Cambridge, MA: Harvard University Press, 1971.

Ribton-Turner, C. J. *A History of Vagrants and Vagrancy and Beggars and Begging*. London: Chapman and Hall, 1887.

Richards, Kenneth, and Laura Richards. *The Commedia dell'Arte: A Documentary History*. Oxford: Blackwell, 1990.

Rouch, Monique. *Storie di vita popolare nelle canzoni di piazza di G. C. Croce. Fame, fatica, e mascherate nel' 500*. Bologna: Cleub, 1982.

Safley, Thomas Max, ed. *The Reformation of Charity: The Secular and the Religious in Early Modern Poor Relief*. Boston: Brill, 2003.

Salzberg, Rosa. *Ephemeral Cities: Cheap Print and Urban Culture in Renaissance Venice*. Manchester, UK: Manchester University Press, 2014.

———. "Selling Stories and Many Other Things in and through the City: Peddling Print in Sixteenth-Century Florence and Venice." *Sixteenth-Century Journal* 42 (2011): 737–59.

Salzberg, Rosa, and Massimo Rospocher. "Street Singers in Italian Renaissance Urban Culture and Communication." *Culture and Social History* 9 (2012): 9–26.

Sanudo, Marin. *Diarii*. Edited by R. Fulin, F. Stefani, N. Barozzi, G. Berchet, and M. Allegri. 58 vols. Venice: Visentini, 1879–1902.

Scala, Flaminio. *Il teatro delle favole rappresentative*. Edited by F. Marotti. 2 vols. Milan: Il Polifilo, 1976.

Scardeone, Bernardino. *De antiquitate urbis Patavii et claris civibus Patavinis*. Basel: N. Episcopium, 1560.

Schoeck, R. J. "The Use of St. John Chrysostom in Sixteenth-Century Controversy: Christopher St. German and Sir Thomas More in 1533." *Harvard Theological Review* 54 (1961): 21–27.

Scott, Virginia. *The Commedia dell'Arte in Paris, 1644–1697*. Charlottesville: University Press of Virginia, 1990.

———. "Who Was Robert Triplupart L'Andouiller? Or, an Actors' Quarrel in Late Sixteenth-Century Paris," *Performing Arts Resources* 28 (2011): 25–31.

Shakespeare, William. *As You Like It*. Arden Shakespeare. 3rd ser. Edited by Juliet Dusinberre. London: Thomson Learning, 2006.

———. *Coriolanus*. Arden Shakespeare. 3rd ser. Edited by Peter Holland. London: Bloomsbury, 2013.

———. *Hamlet: The Texts of 1603 and 1623*. Arden Shakespeare. 3rd ser. Edited by Ann Thompson and Neil Taylor. London: Thomson Learning, 2006.

———. *King Henry VI, Part 2*. Arden Shakespeare. 3rd ser. Edited by Ronald Knowles. London: Thomson Learning, 2001.

———. *King Lear*. Arden Shakespeare. 3rd ser. Edited by R. A. Foakes. London: Thomson Learning, 1997.

———. *Pericles*. Arden Shakespeare. 3rd ser. Edited by Suzanne Gossett. London: Thomson Learning, 2004.

———. *The Riverside Shakespeare*. Edited by G. Blakemore Evans et al. 2nd ed. Boston: Houghton Mifflin, 1997.

———. *Timon of Athens*. Arden Shakespeare. 3rd ser. Edited by Anthony Dawson and Gretchen E. Minton. London: Cengage Learning, 2008.

Shuger, Debora K. "Subversive Fathers and Suffering Subjects: Shakespeare and Christianity." In *Religion, Literature, and Politics in Post-Reformation England, 1540–1688*, ed. Donna Hamilton and Richard Strier, 46–69. Cambridge: Cambridge University Press, 1996.

Skura, Meredith Anne. *Shakespeare the Actor and the Purposes of Playing*. Chicago: University of Chicago Press, 1993.

Slack, Paul. *The English Poor Law 1531–1782*. London: Macmillan, 1990.

———. *Poverty and Policy in Tudor and Stuart England*. London: Longman, 1988.

———, ed. *Rebellion, Popular Protest, and the Social Order in Early Modern England*. Cambridge: Cambridge University Press, 1984.

Sudermann, Daniel. *Centuria similitudinum . . . .* Strassburg, 1624.

Terpstra, Nicholas. *Lost Girls: Sex and Death in Renaissance Florence*. Baltimore: Johns Hopkins University Press, 2010.

Testaverde, Anna Maria, ed. *I canovacci della Commedia dell'Arte*. Turin: Einaudi, 2007.

Thomas, D. B., ed. *The Book of Vagabonds and Beggars*. London: Penguin, 1932.

Tierney, Brian. "The Decretists and the 'Deserving Poor.'" *Comparative Studies in Society and History* 1 (1959): 360–73.

Vecellio, Cesare. *Habiti antichi et moderni*. Venice, 1590.

Viaggio di Zan Menes Tru. Opera nuua e non plu stampada composta per un Eccellent Dottur. . . . Modena, n.d. Biblioteca Apostolica Vaticana, Misc. Capponi V.681.55.

La vida de Lazarillo de Tormes y de sus fortunas y adversidades. Edited by Alberto Blecua. Madrid: Castalia, 1972. Translated by W. S. Merwin as *The Life of Lazarillo de Tormes: His Fortunes and Adversities.* New York: The New York Review of Books, 2005.

Walter, John. *Crowds and Popular Politics in Early Modern England.* Manchester, UK: Manchester University Press, 2006.

Wandel, Lee Palmer. *Always Among Us: Images of the Poor in Zwingli's Zurich.* Cambridge: Cambridge University Press, 1990.

———. "The Poverty of Christ." In Safley, *The Reformation of Charity,* 15–29.

Weil, Simone. "The Iliad, or the Poem of Force." In *War and "The Iliad,"* trans. Mary McCarthy, 1–37. New York: The New York Review of Books, 2005.

Wiley, W. L. *The Early Public Theatre in France.* Cambridge, MA: Harvard University Press, 1960.

Wilson, Richard. "'Like the Old Robin Hood': *As You Like It* and the Enclosure Riots." *Shakespeare Quarterly* 43 (1992): 1–19.

Woodbridge, Linda. *Vagrancy, Homelessness, and English Renaissance Literature.* Urbana: University of Illinois Press, 2001.

Woodstock: A Moral History. Edited by A. P. Rossiter. London: Chatto and Windus, 1946.

Wrightson, Keith. *Earthly Necessities: Economic Lives in Early Modern Britain.* New Haven, CT: Yale University Press, 2000.

Zannini, Andrea. "Flussi d'immigrazione e strutture sociali urbane. Il caso dei bergamaschi a Venezia." *Bollettino di demografia storica* 19 (1993): 207–15.

Zardin, Danilo, ed. *La città e i poveri. Milano e le terre lombarde dal Rinascimento all'età spagnola.* Milan: Jaca, 1995.

Zorzi, Ludovico, ed. *Ruzante. Teatro.* Turin: Einaudi, 1967.

Index

STUDIES IN THEATRE HISTORY AND CULTURE

Actors and American Culture, 1880–1920
By Benjamin McArthur

The Age and Stage of George L. Fox, 1825–1877: An Expanded Edition
By Laurence Senelick

American Theater in the Culture of the Cold War: Producing and Contesting Containment
By Bruce McConachie

Athenian Tragedy in Performance: A Guide to Contemporary Studies and Historical Debates
By Melinda Powers

Classical Greek Theatre: New Views of an Old Subject
By Clifford Ashby

Czech Theatre Design in the Twentieth Century: Metaphor and Irony Revisited
Edited by Joseph Brandesky

Embodied Memory: The Theatre of George Tabori
By Anat Feinberg

Fangs of Malice: Hypocrisy, Sincerity, and Acting
By Matthew H. Wikander

Fantasies of Empire: The Empire Theatre of Varieties and the Licensing Controversy of 1894
By Joseph Donohue

French Theatre Today: The View from New York, Paris, and Avignon
By Edward Baron Turk

From Androboros to the First Amendment: A History of America's First Play
By Peter A. Davis

The Jewish Kulturbund Theatre Company in Nazi Berlin
By Rebecca Rovit

Jews and the Making of Modern German Theatre
Edited by Jeanette R. Malkin and Freddie Rokem

The Making of Theatrical Reputations: Studies from the Modern London Theatre
By Yael Zarhy-Levo

Marginal Sights: Staging the Chinese in America
By James S. Moy

Melodramatic Formations: American Theatre and Society, 1820–1870
By Bruce A. McConachie

Meyerhold: A Revolution in Theatre
By Edward Braun

Modern Czech Theatre: Reflector and Conscience of a Nation
By Jarka M. Burian

Modern Hamlets and Their Soliloquies: An Expanded Edition
By Mary Z. Maher

Molière, the French Revolution, and the Theatrical Afterlife
By Mechele Leon

The Most American Thing in America: Circuit Chautauqua as Performance
By Charlotte M. Canning

Music for the Melodramatic Theatre in Nineteenth-Century London and New York
By Michael V. Pisani

"Othello" and Interpretive Traditions
By Edward Pechter

Our Moonlight Revels: "A Midsummer Night's Dream" in the Theatre
By Gary Jay Williams

The Performance of Power: Theatrical Discourse and Politics
Edited by Sue-Ellen Case and Janelle Reinelt

Performing History: Theatrical Representations of the Past in Contemporary Theatre
By Freddie Rokem

The Recurrence of Fate: Theatre and Memory in Twentieth-Century Russia
By Spencer Golub

Reflecting the Audience: London Theatregoing, 1840–1880
By Jim Davis and Victor Emeljanow

Representing the Past: Essays in Performance Historiography
Edited by Charlotte M. Canning and Thomas Postlewait

The Roots of Theatre: Rethinking Ritual and Other Theories of Origin
By Eli Rozik

Sex for Sale: Six Progressive-Era Brothel Dramas
By Katie N. Johnson

Shakespeare and Chekhov in Production: Theatrical Events and Their Audiences
By John Tulloch

Shakespeare on the American Yiddish Stage
By Joel Berkowitz

The Show and the Gaze of Theatre: A European Perspective
By Erika Fischer-Lichte

Stagestruck Filmmaker: D. W. Griffith and the American Theatre
By David Mayer

Strange Duets: Impresarios and Actresses in the American Theatre, 1865–1914
By Kim Marra

Textual and Theatrical Shakespeare: Questions of Evidence
Edited by Edward Pechter

Theatre and Identity in Imperial Russia
By Catherine A. Schuler

Theatre, Community, and Civic Engagement in Jacobean London
By Mark Bayer

Theatre Is More Beautiful Than War: German Stage Directing in the Late Twentieth Century
By Marvin Carlson

Theatres of Independence: Drama, Theory, and Urban Performance in India since 1947
By Aparna Bhargava Dharwadker

The Theatrical Event: Dynamics of Performance and Perception
By Willmar Sauter

The Trick of Singularity: "Twelfth Night" and the Performance Editions
By Laurie E. Osborne

The Victorian Marionette Theatre
By John McCormick

Wandering Stars: Russian Emigré Theatre, 1905–1940
Edited by Laurence Senelick

Writing and Rewriting National Theatre Histories
Edited by S. E. Wilmer